The Taliesin Sourcebook

FRANK OLDING

GREEN MAGIC

The Taliesin Sourcebook © 2024 by Frank Olding.
All rights reserved. No part of this book may be used or reproduced in any form without written permission of the Author, except in the case of quotations in articles and reviews.

GREEN MAGIC
Seed Factory
Aller
Langport
Somerset
TA10 0QN
England
www.greenmagicpublishing.com

Designed and typeset by Carrigboy, Wells, UK.
www.carrigboy.co.uk

ISBN 978 1 915580 160

GREEN MAGIC

/|\

"Awen a ganaf, o ddwfn ys dygaf"

To
Philip, Elaine and Danu
for the inspiration.

Contents

Acknowledgements	8
Foreword	9
Introduction	10
The Power of Poetry	10
The Acquisition of Poetry	10
The Source and Use of Awen	11
Historia Brittonum	12
Earlier Historical Poems	13
Later Historical Poems	14
Legendary Poems	14
Ceridwen	16
Llywarch ap Llywelyn	18
Prophetic Poems	20
Ystoria Taliesin	21
Early Modern Oral Transmission	23
The Manuscripts	23

THE TEXTS

Historical Sources	28
1. Historia Brittonum ("The History of the Britons") (Harl. 3859)	28
Early Historical Poems	30
2. Trawsganu Kynan Garwyn ("Praise-Song to Cynan Garwyn") (BT 45)	30
3. Gweith Gwen Ystrat ("The Battle of Gwen Ystrad") (BT 56)	31
4. Uryen Yrechwyd ("Urien of Erechwydd") (BT 57)	33
5. Eg gorffowys can rychedwys ("With the Men of Rheged") (BT 58)	34
6. Ar vn blynedd ("For One Whole Year") (BT 59)	35
7. Gweith Argoet Llwyfein ("The Battle of Argoed Llwyfain") (BT 60)	36
8. Ardwyre Reget ("Let Rheged Arise") (BT 61)	37
9. Yspeil Taliessin ("The Spoils of Taliesin") (BT 62)	39
10. Dadolwch Vryen ("Reconciliation with Urien") (BT 65)	41
11. Marwnat Owein ("The Death-Song for Owain son of Urien") (BT 67)	42
12. Gwallawg 1 (BT 29)	43
13. Gwallawg 2 (BT 63)	45

Later Historical Poems — 48

14. Gwarchan Maeldderw ("The Song of Maeldderw") (BA 28) — 48
15. Etmic Dinbych ("In Praise of Tenby") (BT 42) — 50
16. Echrys Ynys ("Desolate the Island") (BT 68) — 53

Legendary Poems — 55

17. Ymddiddan Myrddin a Thaliesin ("The Dialogue of Myrddin and Taliesin") (BBC 1) — 55
18. Ymddiddan Taliesin ac Ugnach ("The Dialogue of Taliesin and Ugnach (BBC 101) — 57
19. Prif Gyuarch Geluyd ("The First Skilful Challenge") (BT 3) — 59
20. Buarth Beird ("The Meeting Place of Poets") (BT 7) — 62
21. Aduwyneu Taliessin ("The Fair Things of Taliesin") (BT 8) — 64
22. Angar Kyfundawt ("The Hostile Confederacy") (BT 19) — 66
23. Kat Godeu ("The Battle of the Trees") (BT 23) — 74
24. Mabgyfreu Taliessin ("The Juvenilia of Taliesin") (BT 27) — 85
25. Mydwyf Merweryd ("I am Uproar") (BT 31) — 87
26. Kadeir Taliessin/Golychaf-i Gulwyd ("The Chair of Taliesin"/ "I Entreat the Dear-Blessed One") (BT 33) — 90
27. Kadeir Teyrnon ("The Chair of Teyrnon") (BT 34) — 92
28. Kadeir Kerrituen ("The Chair of Ceridwen") (BT 35) — 95
29. Kanu y Gwynt ("The Song of the Wind") (BT 36) — 97
30. Kanu y Med ("The Song of the Mead") (BT 40) — 100
31. Kanu y Cwrwf ("The Song of Ale") (BT 40a) — 101
32. Teithi Etmygant ("They Admire Proper Qualities") (BT 41) — 103
33. Canu y Meirch ("The Song of the Horses") (BT 47) — 106
34. Y Gofeisswys Byt ("He Walked the World" – Alexander I) (BT 51) — 110
35. Anryuedodeu Allyxander ("The Marvels of Alexander") (BT 52) — 111
36. Preideu Annwfyn ("The Spoils of Annwfn") (BT 54) — 112
37. Marwnat Ercwl ("The Death-Song of Hercules") (BT 65) — 119
38. Madawc Drut ("Madog the Valiant") (BT 66) — 120
39. Marwnat Corroi m. Dayry ("The Death-Song of Cú Roí mac Dáiri") (BT 66a) — 120
40. Marwnat Dylan eil Ton ("The Death-Song of Dylan son of Wave") (BT 67) — 124
41. Mydwyf Taliessin/Cunedaf ("I am Taliesin/Cunedda") (BT 69) — 124
42. Marwnat Vthyr Pen[dragon] ("The Death-Song of Uthr Pendragon") (BT 71) — 126
43. Kanu y Byt Mawr ("The Greater Song of the World") (BT 79) — 128
44. Kanu y Byt Bychan ("The Lesser Song of the World") (BT 80) — 130

Prophetic Poems — 132
45. Arymes Prydein Vawr ("The Greater Prophecy of Britain") (BT 13) — 132
46. Daronwy (BT 28) — 138
47. Glaswawt Taliessin ("The Verdant Song of Taliesin") (BT 30) — 140
48. Kychwedyl a'm dodyw ("News has come to me") (BT 38) — 142
49. Dygogan Awen ("The Awen Foretells") (BT 70) — 144
50. Kein Gyfedwch ("A Fine Carousal") (BT 72) — 146
51. Rydyrchafwy Duw ("May God Raise") (BT 72a) — 147
52. Gwawd Lud y Mawr ("The Greater Song of Praise to Lludd") (BT 74) — 148
53. Yn wir dymbi Romani kar ("Truly shall the kinsman of the Romans come") (BT 76) — 152
54. Ymarwar Llud Bychan ("The Shorter Poem on the Discussion of Lludd") (BT 78) — 155
55. Darogan Kadwaladyr ("The Prophecy of Cadwaladr") (BT 80a) — 157

Medieval Prose Tales — 158
56. Culhwch ac Olwen ("Culhwch and Olwen") — 158
57. Branwen Uerch Lyr ("Second Branch of the Mabinogi") — 159

Early Modern Prose Tales — 162
58. Ystoria Taliesin ("The Story of Taliesin") – Elis Gruffydd — 162
59. Hanes Taliesin ("The History of Taliesin") – John Jones, Gellilyfdy — 180
60. A Fragment of Hanes Taliesin – Llywelyn Siôn, Llangewydd — 189
61. Triad 87: Tri Bardd Kaw ("Three Skilful Bards") — 192

Early Modern Oral Transmission — 194
62. William Aubrey – Siôn Dafydd Rhys — 194

Appendix I – Four Poems by Llywarch ap Llywelyn — 195
63. Mawl Gwenllïan ferch Hywel ab Iorwerth ("In Praise of Gwenllïan daughter of Hywel ab Iorwerth") — 195
64. Awdl yr Haearn Twym ("Ode to the Red-Hot Iron") — 196
65. Y Canu Bychan a gant Prydydd y Moch i Lywelyn fab Iorferth ("The Short Song that Prydydd y Moch sang to Llywelyn son of Iorwerth") — 197
66. Mawl Rhys Gryg o Ddeheubarth ("In Praise of Rhys Gryg of Deheubarth") — 200

Appendix II – References to Ceridwen by the Court Poets — 205

Bibliography — 209

Index — 217

Acknowledgements

Many of the translations included here were originally undertaken at the request of Philip Shallcrass of the British Druid Order. Many thanks to him for inspiration and encouragement and for many hours of fascinating "bardic enquiries".

Thanks are due also to Dr. John K. Bollard for supplying digital copies and a pagination concordance of his paper on "Myrddin in Early Welsh Tradition"; to Prof. Mary-Ann Constantine of the University of Wales Trinity-St Davids for a copy of her article on "The Battle for the Battle of the Trees" and to Prof. Ronald Hutton of Bristol University for his valuable assistance with the translation of Siôn Dafydd Rhys' Early Modern Cambro-Latin. Any remaining errors are entirely my own.

I owe an enormous debt of gratitude to Prof. Marged Haycock of the University of Aberystwyth without whose generosity of spirit and support this volume would never have appeared.

      FRANK OLDING
      Y Fenni

Foreword

The story of the ancient Welsh poet Taliesin and his transformation from the lowly pot-stirrer Gwion Bach to the radiant-browed, omniscient Chief Poet of the West by the power of Ceridwen's cauldron of *awen* plays a central role in the spiritual lives of many thousands of modern Pagans and Druids. Individual poems from the corpus such as *Preideu Annwfyn* ("The Spoils of Annwfn") and *Kat Godeu* ("The Battle of the Trees") have assumed an almost totemic significance in the discussion of the origins of the bards and their craft and feed into many people's sense of belonging in the Pagan tradition. It is a pity then that so much of this discussion depends on out-dated and woefully inaccurate translations of the original Welsh texts.

The main aim of this book, therefore, is to present modern, reliable translations of all the medieval poems assigned to or concerning Taliesin together with all three variant versions of the Early Modern prose tales known variously as *Ystoria Taliesin* ("The Story of Taliesin") or *Hanes Taliesin* ("The History of Taliesin"). Translations of medieval court poems with a bearing on the development of the Taliesin persona are also included in the appendices. An attempt has been made to return to the poems their unity as works of art, rather than regarding them as texts to be deciphered and dissected.

In undertaking this work, I am of course standing on the shoulders of giants. The veritable Bendigeidfran of modern Taliesin studies is Prof. Marged Haycock of the University of Aberystwyth. Her pioneering studies over forty years, together with her two major recent editions and translations of the legendary and prophetic poems of Taliesin are the bedrock upon which this book is built.[1] Even the most casual perusal of the footnotes and bibliography attached to this work will amply testify to the enormous debt it owes to the industry and generosity of Prof. Haycock over many years.

---

1 Haycock 2013 and 2015

Introduction

"The Book of Taliesin is the most valuable source we have for the dark underside of the early tradition, for the oracular, semi-learned facets of early poetic activity in Wales."[1]

This book deals mainly with poets and poetry. From the poems of the "historical" Taliesin traditionally assigned to the 6th or 7th centuries to the later fantastical, mystical, boasting poems of the legendary Taliesin persona, the over-riding concern is the status and importance of poets and poetic craft in medieval Welsh society. As such, the power of poetry and its acquisition seems a sensible place to begin our discussions.

THE POWER OF POETRY

In Wales and Ireland in the medieval period, the spoken utterances of poets still possessed magic power. The words of the poet could validate the standing and authority of a chieftain or a king; equally, their invective and satire could destroy it. Satire could even kill those against whom it was directed. Those who wielded such words were held in awe by the entire society.[2]

In early Irish society, the poet was still a member of a priestly or sacred class. In Wales, it could be argued that the bards retained the vestiges of a similar sacral authority. The poet was also a prophet and a seer, and it was their profound esoteric knowledge that could shape the words of power. Poetry could create reality and give birth to things. The poet possessed this power "by virtue of some external force that blew through him".[3] That external force was known in Ireland as *imbas* and in Wales as *awen*. To gain *awen*, the poet was required to go through authentic initiation and ritual transformation.

THE ACQUISITION OF POETRY

In early sources in both Irish and Welsh, poetry is seen as originating in and being contained in a cauldron. It is brewed from various herbs and elements and the cauldron is thought of as a womb which boils up poetic knowledge. In the Irish

---
1 Haycock 1983/4, 52
2 Ford 1992, 11
3 Ford 1992, 13–14

sources, there are three cauldrons involved in the process. The first, the cauldron of sustenance or warming, pours forth the oral language of poetry; the second, the cauldron of motion, boils the basis of all poetic knowledge and activates it, and the third, the cauldron of knowledge or wisdom, imparts knowledge or wisdom to the poetry.[4] In the case of *Ystoria Taliesin* (s. 58), the triple nature of the cauldrons is reflected in the three droplets that impart to Gwion Bach bardic knowledge and the powers of prophecy and shape-shifting. Taliesin is seen to emerge from three vessels – the cauldron that transforms Gwion into a prophet and a bard, the physical womb of Ceridwen as Gwion is reborn, and the symbolic womb of the leather bag, from which he emerges physically as well as spiritually transformed.[5]

By the power given to him by the three droplets, Gwion transforms himself into creatures of land, air and water. Finally, he becomes a seed and is ultimately reborn to the world in a salmon weir. In effect, Gwion becomes the seed or kernel of wisdom and is then transformed into a metaphorical salmon in the weir.[6] This calls to mind the Irish story of Finn mac Cumhaill's acquisition of poetic art by burning his thumb whilst cooking and then eating the salmon of wisdom. In this way, he learned "the three things that constitute a poet", namely *teinm láida* ("illumination of song"), *imbas forosna* ("knowledge which illumines") and *dichetul dichennaib* ("extempore incantation").[7] The wisdom embodied in the salmon originates, in turn, in the hazelnuts of knowledge swallowed by the fish in the well of Segais.[8]

In both traditions, the acquisition of poetic power also produces a physical transformation. In the Irish tale of Senchán Torpeist, an ugly youth is transformed into the spirit of poetry with the "most noble shape and whitest skin." The name Finn also means "white" or "radiant" and, of course, the name Taliesin is interpreted as meaning "lovely or radiant brow".[9] In their subtle symbolism, these tales express the liminal character of the poet in medieval Irish and Welsh society.

THE SOURCE AND USE OF AWEN

Medieval Welsh poets often debated the source and definition of *awen*. In the early 15th century, the preacher-poet from south-east Wales, Siôn Cent, argued that there were two kinds of *awen* – that which came from Christ and the Holy Spirit, and which should be used for the glory of God, and the lying *awen* possessed by the professional praise-poets. The primary bone of contention in these debates was

---

4 Breatnach 1981, 48–52; Henry 1979/80, 117–18
5 Ford 1992, 26–8
6 Ford 1992, 30
7 Meyer 1904, 186
8 Breatnach 1981, 67; Ford 1992, 17–20
9 Ford 1992, 22–5

whether *awen* should be used only for overtly Christian purposes as opposed to the praise poetry of the native bardic tradition. Was *awen* the gift of the Holy Spirit or a gift from the cauldron of Ceridwen? The Taliesin figure consistently represents the old native tradition, insisting on the magical origins of *awen* and its role as the source of traditional bardic knowledge. These debates are the ultimate reflection of the rivalry between clerics and poets that informs much of the legendary poetry of the Book of Taliesin.[10]

In *Ystoria Taliesin*, Taliesin's confrontation with Maelgwn Gwynedd's court poets is also concerned with the nature of *awen* and the proper function of poets and poetry. Taliesin again champions the esoteric and magical nature of *awen* as opposed to the sycophantic and insincere praise-poetry of Maelgwn's bards. To Taliesin, they have lost touch with the true nature of poetry, with authentic *awen*. Unless they too undergo a true initiation and transformation, they are merely empty vessels singing their "Blerwm, blerwm"![11]

HISTORIA BRITTONUM (s.1)

The earliest mention of Taliesin in any written source is found in the "Memorandum of the Five Poets" included in the Latin *Historia Brittonum* ("History of the Britons"). The work is conventionally attributed to Nennius and was originally composed in AD 829–30 in Gwynedd in north-west Wales.[12] The memorandum is found among material dealing with events in the Old North, that is those parts of northern England and southern Scotland that, prior to the incursions of the early English, were British (i.e., Welsh) kingdoms.

Of the five poets named, only works attributed to Aneirin and Taliesin have survived. The date of the careers of these poets is apparently fixed by the memorandum to AD 547 and this is the basis for dating the career of the historical Taliesin to the mid- to late-6th century.[13] Although a great deal of scholarly controversy has raged around the "historicity" of Aneirin and Taliesin and their work, recent assessments are more supportive of a 6th century date for their careers.[14] The memorandum is also the earliest source for the traditional connection between Taliesin and Maelgwn, king of Gwynedd.

---

10 Ford 1992, 35
11 Ford 1992, 32–33
12 Dumville 1986, 21–2; Fulton 2019, 27
13 Koch 2006, 751
14 See Fulton 2019 for a summary of the arguments

EARLIER HISTORICAL POEMS (ss. 2–13)

Aneirin and Taliesin are known in Welsh as the *Cynfeirdd* (the "First Poets" or "Earliest Poets"). John Koch has identified a corpus of works by the Cynfeirdd that celebrate military events of the mid-6th to mid-7th centuries. He has also identified the historical periods dealt with by the poems and thus potentially when the poems might have been composed.[15]

The standard mid-20th century view of the earliest Welsh poetry was that the poems of the Cynfeirdd corpus were composed as contemporary commemorations of major events, mostly in North Britain, which took place between the later 6th and mid-7th centuries. They were then preserved orally for several centuries before being first written down in Old Welsh orthography in the 9th or 10th centuries.[16]

Since then, however, Koch has concluded (based on the presence of archaic word-forms in the existing texts) that some of the surviving poetry goes back to written forms dating to before AD 750 and most likely to the mid-7th century. Most of these pre-Old Welsh word-forms occur in *Y Gododdin* attributed to Aneirin, but there are also examples in the poems of the "historical" Taliesin and this strengthens the case for the possibility that the poems were composed by an actual person called Taliesin in the mid- to late 6th century and recorded in writing in the mid-7th century.[17]

The nine poems dedicated to Urien Rheged and his son Owain (ss. 3–11) all deal with their military achievements against the Anglo-Saxons in the period AD 570–595. Some scholars have argued that they were first committed to writing in the period around AD 650.[18] Urien's kingdom Rheged extended from the area beyond the Solway Firth (in present-day Scotland) across Cumbria and Lancashire as possibly as far east as Catterick in Yorkshire.[19] The *Historia Brittonum* describes him as fighting with his sons against Theodric the Anglo-Saxon king of Bernicia (later part of the kingdom of Northumbria). Allied with other British kings, Gwallawg, Rhydderch Hen and Morgant, Urien besieged his enemies for three days and nights on the island of *Metcaud* (Lindisfarne) in about AD 575 but was then murdered by Morgant "from jealousy, because his military skill and generalship surpassed that of all the other kings".[20]

---

15 Koch 2013a, 22–23
16 Koch 2005, 3
17 Koch 2005, 5–6
18 Koch 2005, 6
19 Fulton 2019, 34
20 Morris 1980, 38, 79

LATER HISTORICAL POEMS (ss. 14–16)

There are also three later historical poems: *Gwarchan Maeldderw* (s. 14) a technically brilliant death-song preserved in the Book of Aneirin and dating to the 10th or 11th centuries. *Etmic Dinbych* (s. 15), a song in praise of the Dark Age fortress at Tenby and its lord Bleiddudd, dates to the 9th century. *Echrys Ynys* (s. 16) dates to the early 11th century and laments the death of Aeddon, lord of Anglesey. These poems were evidently not composed by the historical Taliesin but came later to be associated with his name. Were the court poets of the 9th–11th centuries also assuming the *persona* of Taliesin to add status and gravitas to their works?

LEGENDARY POEMS (ss. 17–44)

The Book of Taliesin is, in effect, an anthology which brings together poems reflecting different conceptions of Taliesin current at different periods. We have seen how the kernel of twelve historical poems may reflect military and political conditions of the 6th century and the career of an actual, human poet. The legendary poems deal with a very different conception of Taliesin – a being not born of human parents but created by magicians and seers; a being who has lived with the divine family of the children of Dôn and who has assumed many different forms and incarnations over many centuries.[21]

These legendary poems do not belong to the 6th century but must have been composed by different poets at different periods who assumed the *persona* of Taliesin for dramatic, poetic or possibly spiritual effect. In them, Taliesin is made to display his encyclopaedic knowledge of the poetic arts, science, medicine, astronomy and the natural world. He challenges other poets and also monks and clerics (his favourite adversaries) with a plethora of abstruse questions, to which only he knows the answers. He recounts with relish his past incarnations and transformations, his martial exploits and contacts with the characters of Welsh legend and mythology (especially those of the *Mabinogi*). Periodically, he breaks into prophecy and often mentions his patron Elffin and his court at Caer Seon (see ss. 16, 18, 29, 32).

In his legendary persona, Taliesin is mercurial and many-facetted. He knows the nature and origin of the *awen* and he has visited the Otherwordly sources of inspiration. He is "not bound by time or space".[22] He has met and befriended many historical and mythological personalities, especially the semi-divine children of the goddess Dôn and other characters from the Four Branches of the *Mabinogi*. In the

---

21 Haycock 2015, 9
22 Haycock 1983–4, 54

Second Branch, he is one of the seven survivors of the carnage caused by a war between Wales and Ireland (see s. 57).

Taliesin figures in early Welsh and Breton literature in various guises at various periods. We have what seems to be the bald historical record of the 9th century *Historia Brittonum* (s. 1) in stark contrast with the early 11th century Latin-Breton *Life of St. Iudic-hael* that claims that Taliesin is himself one of the semi-divine children of the mother-goddess Dôn.[23] Poems in the Black Book of Carmarthen dated between the 9th and 11th century cast him as a prophet, the equal and associate of Myrddin/Merlin (s. 17) who is also found in dialogue with Otherworld figures such as Ugnach, possibly an avatar of Gwyn ap Nudd (s. 18). By the mid-12th century, his association with Myrddin necessitated his inclusion in Geoffrey of Monmouth's *Vita Merlini* ("Life of Merlin") and, by 1155, Wace (the translator of Geoffrey of Monmouth from Latin into Norman-French) was claiming that Taliesin had foretold the birth of Christ.[24]

In *Echrys Ynys* (s. 16), Taliesin is associated with Caer Seon, the traditional seat of his patron Elffin. Even at this early stage, he is portrayed as the omniscient seer familiar from the legendary poems – important evidence that the legendary Taliesin was a well-developed figure as early as the beginning of the 11th century.[25] In fact, it has been suggested that the persona of the legendary Taliesin was invented as a bridge between monastic learning and vernacular court poetry as early as the 7th or 8th century. A developed Taliesin legend was already widely known in both Wales and Brittany by the year 1000.[26]

Other scholars have suggested that the elements of the Taliesin legend emerged in north-west Wales in the late 12th or early 13th centuries. In this area, traditionally "the land of Gwydion", Taliesin was associated with the semi-divine children of Dôn and seen, perhaps, as sharing their supernatural powers but with a specialised role in poetry and prophecy. It was in this milieu that the figure of Taliesin could be amplified and developed in order to modernise and enhance the standing of the professional court poets.[27]

And what of the professional court poets who may have composed and performed poetry "in character" as Taliesin? This may have had a dual purpose. Firstly, providing entertainment for a sophisticated and knowledgeable audience and secondly, enhancing their own standing and authority by adopting the persona of one of the founding fathers of their ancient bardic order.[28]

---

23 Koch 2013b, 180–81
24 Haycock 2015, 12
25 Charles-Edwards 2013, 668
26 Koch 2013b, 183, 193
27 Haycock 2015, 34
28 Haycock 1983–4, 58

Long ago, Ifor Williams claimed that the Taliesin of the legendary poems could not be fully understood without reference to the story of his transformation from Gwion Bach to Taliesin embodied in the late prose tales *Ystoria Taliesin* (s. 58) and *Hanes Taliesin* (ss. 59–60).[29] Some modern scholars are reluctant to acknowledge the primacy of the tale of Ceridwen and Gwion Bach in the formation of the Taliesin persona seen in the legendary poems.[30] Some of their arguments, however, seem (to me) overly cautious and potentially circular. As an example, Haycock suggests that the episode in the *Ystoria* where Ceridwen eats Gwion Bach as he lies disguised as a grain of wheat (only to give birth to him again as Taliesin) may derive from an over-literal interpretation of lines 249–52 of *Angar Kyfundawt* (s. 22):

> A hen conceived me –
> red of claw, a crested foe;
> I spent nine nights
> at peace in her womb.

The means of transmission by which an obscure reference in a riddling poem possibly composed by a court poet moving in the highest echelons of early 13th century Welsh society found its way into a folk-tale is far from clear. Some have suggested that the Book of Taliesin poems (or others similar to them) where used as a quarry for materials for *Ystoria Taliesin*.[31] Whilst this argument may hold good for the wording of some of the poems incorporated in the *Ystoria*, it seems to me equally possible that the references in *Angar Kyfundawt* and *Ystoria Taliesin* to Ceridwen as a hen are not dependent upon each other but draw instead on a common stock of traditional lore surrounding the transformation of Gwion Bach into Taliesin. However, this begs the question of how old the connection between Ceridwen and Taliesin really is.

CERIDWEN

Linguisitically, the earliest references to Ceridwen show that the correct form of the name is actually *Ceridfen*. However, as early as the 15th century, the form *Ceridwen* was gaining currency and by the 16th century was the widely accepted form of the name.[32] *Ceridwen* is now so widely known and accepted that it seems pointless to insist here on *Ceridfen*. Influenced perhaps by the portrayal of Ceridwen in *Ystoria Taliesin* (s. 58), Ifor Williams interpreted the name as meaning "the crooked,

---

29 Williams and Williams 1968, xviii
30 Haycock 2015, 19
31 Haycock 2003, 169
32 Haycock 2015, 312, 319

bent woman" – a suitable name for a crook-backed hag or witch.[33] However, more recent research has identified other possibilities – "the woman who causes fever or trembling", "the passionate woman", "the woman who inspires faith or belief".[34]

In the work of the court poets of the 12th and 13th centuries, there are five references to Ceridwen. In the anonymous poem in praise of Cuhelyn Fardd dating to c.1100–1130, the poet begins by asking God for poetic power like "the diginity of Ceridwen's song, of varied inspiration". In the 1160s, Cynddelw Brydydd Mawr claims familiarity with the "ways of Ceridwen's arts" and also mentions Taliesin, an indication perhaps that he knew of the association between them. In praising Gruffudd ap Cynan between 1194 and 1200, Prydydd y Moch asks for inspiration "as from Ceridwen's cauldron" – the first datable reference to Ceridwen's cauldron as the source of poetic inspiration.[35] Even more explicitly, in a poem dating to 1217, he asks for the "very words of Ceridwen, lady of poetry" coupled with power like Taliesin's in releasing Elffin. This is the earliest proof of the connection between Taliesin and Ceridwen and is also the first instance of the episode being set at Degannwy. In a poem dated to between c.1216 and 1222, Phylip Brydydd mentions Elffin's involvement in a poetic contest at the court of Maelgwn Gwynedd and also gives us the earliest reference to Gwion as a poet.[36] In about 1315, the Glamorgan poet, Casnodyn, asks for profound inspiration "like the cauldron of Ceridwen". It is not until the 14th century that the poets began to think of Ceridwen as a witch or hag. By that time, they seem reluctant to associate themselves with female control of the *awen*.[37]

In these earliest 12th to 13th century references, Ceridwen is certainly in charge of a cauldron of poetic inspiration and there is no suggestion that she was seen as a witch or hag. Her association with Taliesin seems well-established by 1217. In the Book of Taliesin itself, her character is clearly delineated. In *Mabgyfreu Taliessin* (s. 24), she is the primary source of *awen* from the beginning of the world:

I entreat my Lord
to allow me to consider awen:
what brought forth that needful thing
before Ceridwen,
in the beginning, in a world
that stood in need of it?

---

33 Williams 1957, 3–4
34 Haycock 2003, 152–3
35 Jones and Jones 1991, xxix
36 Haycock 2015, 128–2
37 Haycock 2015, 313–14; for detailed references and translations, see Appendix II

In *Golychaf-i Gulwyd/Kadeir Taliessin* (s. 26), she is, with God, the joint source of awen and Taliesin's song comes from her cauldron:

> I sang in a fine battle position in the morning before Urien
> until around our feet blood stained the grass.
> He defended my song that came from the cauldron of Ceridwen;
> unfettered is my tongue, a treasury of inspiration.
> The inspiration of poetry – my God created it
> together with milk and dew and acorns.

If *Kadeir Kerrituen* (s. 28) really did originate as a dialogue poem between Taliesin and Ceridwen, then she appears there as the mother of Afagddu and the owner of a cauldron (see below).

LLYWARCH AP LLYWELYN

In the light of detailed study of the phrasing and vocabulary of the legendary poems, Marged Haycock identified eleven poems that seem to bear the distinctive linguistic style of one particular court poet, Llywarch ap Llywelyn, also known as *Prydydd y Moch* ("The Poet of the Pigs").[38] For example, in *Kat Godeu* ("The Battle of the Trees", s. 23), there are over forty words and phrases that are matched in Llywarch's more formal court poetry. Comparison with other even more prolific court poets does not produce the same range of correspondences. It seems clear, therefore, that either *Kat Godeu* was entirely composed by Llywarch adopting the persona of Taliesin in order to entertain the royal court of Gwynedd or that he was reworking and expanding on earlier Taliesin material, possibly drawing on written sources now lost to us. Either way, in his Taliesin incarnation, Llywarch ap Llywelyn adopted a very different tone and style from his usual praise poems and death-songs.[39]

The poems bearing the strongest hallmarks of Llywarch ap Llywelyn's style are:

Aduwyneu Taliessin ("The Fair Things of Taliesin", s. 21)
Angar Kyfundawt ("The Hostile Confederacy", s. 22)
Kat Godeu ("The Battle of the Trees", s. 23)
Mabgyfreu Taliessin ("The Juvenilia of Taliesin", s. 24)
Mydwyf Merweryd ("I am Uproar", s. 25)
Golychaf-i Gulwyd/Kadeir Taliessin ("I Entreat the Dear-Blessed One", s. 26)
Kadeir Teyrnon ("The Chair of Teyrnon", s. 27)
Kadeir Kerrituen ("The Chair of Ceridwen", s. 28)

---
38 Haycock 2015, 27–36
39 For comparison see the translations in Appendix I

Kanu y Cwrwf ("The Song of Ale", s. 31)

Teithi Etmygant ("They Admire Proper Qualities", s. 32)

Marwnat Dylan eil Ton ("The Death-Song of Dylan son of Wave", s. 40)

It may be significant that eight of these eleven poems form a unified block in the manuscript. Less certain evidence of Llywarch ap Llywelyn's style is also found in:

Prif Gyuarch Geluyd ("The First Skilful Challenge, s. 19")

Kanu y Gwynt ("The Song of the Wind", s. 29)

Canu y Meirch ("The Song of the Horses", s. 33)

Preideu Annwfyn ("The Spoils of Annwfn", s. 36)

Marwnat Vthyr Pen[dragon] ("The Death-Song of Uthr Pendragon", s. 42)

Having identified Llywarch ap Llywelyn as the author or adaptor of some of the legendary poems, Marged Haycock applied the same methods to the prophetic poems and identified several that also bear his stylistic hallmark.[40] Of these, perhaps the most convincing are *Kychwedyl a'm dodyw* (s. 48), *Dygogan Awen* (s. 49), *Kein Gyfedwch* (s. 50) and *Gwawd Lud y Mawr* (s. 52). As *Dygogan Awen* and *Gwawd Lud y Mawr* also display possible 10th century linguistic features (see above), perhaps these represent adaptations by Llywarch of older material, rather than original compositions.

So, who was the man responsible for some of the most famous of the Taliesin poems? Llywarch ap Llywelyn was one of the greatest of the professional court poets known as the Poets of the Princes or the *Gogynfeirdd*. Llywarch was active in the royal courts of Gwynedd between c.1174/5 and c.1220. Many of his finest formal poems were sung to Llywelyn ab Iorwerth (also known as *Llywelyn Fawr* "the Great") after he became ruler over all of Gwynedd in 1199. Llywelyn's reign saw a cultural and political resurgence for the Welsh; he made huge territorial gains at the expense of the Normans and eventually much of Wales came under his influence. Such was his standing that Llywelyn Fawr granted the poet valuable lands and properties in north-west Wales.[41]

Llywarch ap Llywelyn was an exceptionally skilled and innovative poet who was able to draw on "a vast reserve of traditional and international learning".[42] The case for accepting him as the author or adaptor of many of the poems found in the Book of Taliesin is strengthened by the fact that his formal poetry (found in other manuscript sources) demonstrates Llywarch's familiarity with Ceridwen and her cauldron, the freeing of Elffin through the power of Taliesin's poetry at Degannwy, the semi-divine children of Dôn and their role in the Fourth Branch of the *Mabinogi*.[43]

---

40 Haycock 2013, 17, n. 82
41 Jones and Jones 1991, xxi–xxxiii
42 Haycock 2015, 32
43 Haycock 2015, 33; Jones and Jones 1991, 10.2, 25.2; 9.1; 25.3; 4.42 respectively

Perhaps one of the most intriguing aspects of Llywarch ap Llywelyn's career is the fact that there are no religious poems attributed to him.[44] Although it is obvious from references in Llywarch's formal poetry that he was brought up in a Christian milieu and was thoroughly familiar with scripture and Christian learning, he seems not to have been moved to compose overtly Christian poems. This is in stark contrast to other court poets of the period. He is also the only court poet ever to refer to Dôn in his poetry.[45] He also stands out among the court poets for turning to prophecy at the end of a poem in praise of Llywelyn the Great dating to 1217.[46] There, he claims that Llywelyn the Great fulfils the prophecy of Myrddin that a new royal line will emerge from the Welsh:

> *Darogan Myrddin dyfod breienin*
> *O Gymru werin o gamhwri;*
> *Dywawd derwyddon dadeni haelon*
> *O hil eryron o Eryri.*

"Myrddin foretells that a king shall come
from among the Welsh through heroism;
the druids foretold the rebirth of generous lords
from the lineage of the eagle-lords of Eryri."[47]

PROPHETIC POEMS (ss. 45–55)

There is considerable cross-over between the prophetic and legendary poems in the Book of Taliesin, with several of the latter containing a strong element of prophecy as well as Taliesin's demonstrations of his otherworldly knowledge and seership. However, in the prophetic poems proper, the Taliesin persona is less strident and the "voice" of the bard less personal.[48]

The main thrust of the prophecies concerns the promise of the political resurgence of the Welsh or Britons in the face of foreign enemies of various hues – Saxons, Vikings, and Normans. The promised deliverers include Cynan and Cadwaladr (as seen in *Armes Prydein*), Cadwallon and Hiriell, the last three associated particularly with the royal line of Gwynedd. Indeed, the poems may have acted down the centuries as a rallying call for the various claimants to power in Gwynedd who found themselves languishing in exile.[49] The Britons are regarded as the heirs of Rome, particularly in terms of their Christianity.

---

44 Jones and Jones 1991, xxxi
45 Jones and Jones 1991, poem 4.42; Haycock 2015, 196
46 Jones and Jones 1991, 247; Haycock 2003, 157
47 Jones and Jones 1991, poem 25.41–4, pp. 253–55
48 Haycock 2013, 6–10
49 Haycock 2013, 10

The prophetic poems in the Book of Taliesin can be dated very broadly to the period from the 10th to the 13th centuries. In some cases, the dating can be refined by linking the contents of the poems to historical events or personages.[50] Comparison with the language of *Armes Prydein*, dated to *c*.AD 939–42, shows some similarities between the language of that work and features present in *Daronwy* (s. 46), *Glaswawt Taliessin* (s. 47), *Kychwedyl a'm dodyw* (s. 48) and *Kein Gyfedwch* (s. 50); though the evidence is stronger in *Dygogan Awen* (s. 49), *Gwawd Lud y Mawr* (s. 52), *Yn wir dymbi Romani kar* (s. 53) and *Ymarwar Llud Bychan* (s. 54). However, it should also be borne in mind that the language of the prophecies is often couched in deliberately archaic terms.[51]

YSTORIA TALIESIN (ss. 58–60)

Ystoria Taliesin is the oldest surviving text of the Taliesin prose legend, a narrative described by its editor as "of central importance for the concept of poets and poetry in the Celtic tradition."[52] It reflects the concerns of contemporary poets and scholars with the ultimate source and nature of *awen* or poetic inspiration and with the traditional role of the poets and storytellers in the transmission of traditional lore and values.[53]

As we have seen, Ifor Williams maintained that the Taliesin of the legendary poems could not be fully understood without reference to the story of his transformation from Gwion Bach to Taliesin embodied in the late prose tales *Ystoria Taliesin* (s. 58) and *Hanes Taliesin* (s. 59). He also proposed that the legend of Taliesin as recorded in *Ystoria Taliesin* and *Hanes Taliesin* developed in three distinct stages:

STAGE I

At this point in the development of the story, there was no difference between Taliesin and the old Welsh gods. His legendary character sat easily alongside Lleu and Dylan, Gwydion and Math, Manawydan and Dôn and he was seen as partly the creation of Modron, the Celtic mother-goddess and thus a brother to Mabon/Maponos. At the same time, the legend also reflects his historical association with the kings and rulers of the 6th century.[54]

---

50 Haycock 2013, 5
51 Haycock 2013, 16
52 Ford 1992, vii
53 Ford 1992, 36
54 Williams 1957, 24

STAGE II

The second stage saw the gathering together of the poems ultimately preserved in the Book of Taliesin, but drawing on older material.[55] This is the period that sees the beginning of a process of Christianisation of many poems with any overtly "pagan" or "druidic" elements. The resulting mixture of Christian and pagan themes was evidence, he argued, that the old pagan religion still had a hold on the Welsh, in the guise of wizardry and also that "the Church fought against it, century after century, retaining the popular playfulness and entertainment, but transforming them [the poems] to her own purposes."[56]

For Williams, Stage II is exemplified by poems such as *Angar Kyfundawt* (s. 22) and *Kat Godeu* (s. 23). He sees the reference in *Angar Kyfundawt* (ll. 249–52) to Taliesin spending nine nights in the womb of the hen as a key element in the progression from Stage II to Stage III. Here, it is merely one of a series of Taliesin's transformations, appearing in the middle of a list. It is however "the seed that developed so brilliantly in Stage III of the tale".[57] On the basis of a date for *Glaswawt Taliesin* (s. 48) of AD 916–46, Ifor Williams dated Stage II to the second half of the 10th century.[58]

STAGE III

Stage III is represented by the 16th and 17th century prose tales, *Ystoria Taliesin* (s. 58) and *Hanes Taliesin* (s. 59) and their associated poems. At this stage, the episode of Taliesin being eaten by the crested black hen has become the climax of Taliesin's transformations.[59]

The poems *Pantion created* "which is today called one of the Four Pillars of Poetry", which appears in *Ystoria Taliesin* (s. 58.613) and *Bustl y Beirdd*, which appears in both tales (s. 58.553; s. 59.192) show clear signs of having been modernised in both language and content. Here, Williams argues, a priest or priests set about completely Christianising the "pagan and oracular elements" in the poems as they found them, eventually turning them "into sermons with almost no relationship at all to the old legend." On the basis of comparison with other medieval poems debating the nature of *awen*, Williams dated this process to the period c.1350–1400.[60]

---

55 Williams 1957, 18
56 Williams 1957, 22
57 Williams 1957, 19
58 Williams 1957, 23
59 Williams 1957, 19
60 Williams 1957, 19

In summary then, Ifor Williams offered the following dates for his scheme:

Stage I – between the 6th and 9th centuries,
Stage II – largely to the second half of the 10th century,
Stage III – the period *c.*1350–1400.

Few modern scholars would agree with his exact dating and the bulk of Stage II would now be assigned to the late 12th and early 13th centuries, but the general process of incremental Christianisation outlined above is a theory which still retains some merit. Indeed, references to Gwion in *Prif Gyuarch Geluyd* (s. 19) suggests that a Welsh audience would have been familiar with tales similar to *Ystoria Taliesin* (s. 58) at least as early as the late 12th century to early 13th century. A more developed version of the story of Gwion Bach and the cauldron may have been current by the end of the 15th century.[61]

EARLY MODERN ORAL TRANSMISSION (s. 62)

In his preamble to *Ystoria Taliesin* (s. 58), Elis Gruffydd tells us that the story of Taliesin was widespread in oral tradition throughout Wales in his own day.[62] This is certainly backed up by Siôn Dafydd Rhys's references to Taliesin material in his Latin grammar that show that the story and poems were still being transmitted orally in south Wales in the 1590s (s. 62). Further references to the tale of Taliesin in later 18th and 19th century sources support Elis Gruffydd's claim and show that it was "a living folklore and not static and dead".[63]

THE MANUSCRIPTS

All but three of the poems in this collection are preserved in the manuscript now kept in the National Library of Wales, Aberystwyth, and known variously as *Llyfr Taliesin,* the Book of Taliesin or Peniarth Manuscript 2. Together with the Book of Aneirin, the Black Book of Carmarthen and the Red Book of Hergest, it is one of the "Four Ancient Books of Wales" as named by William Forbes Skene in 1868.[64]

The title *Llyfr Taliesin* is not original and was probably coined by the Welsh antiquarian Robert Vaughan, who owned the manuscript in the second half of the 17th century.[65] The manuscript measures 178mm x 127mm – about the size

---

61 Haycock 2003, 170
62 Ford 1992, 58; Williams 1957, 10
63 Ford 1992, 45
64 Skene 1868
65 Haycock 1988, 357

of a modern paperback – and dates to the period c. 1300–1336.[66] The manuscript is incomplete, with several pages and quires missing. The very able scribe almost certainly came from mid- or south Wales and was probably working in a monastic scriptorium, possible at the Cistercian house of Llantarnam in south-east Wales or, more likely, Abbey Cwm Hir in the wilds of mid-Wales.[67]

The Book of Taliesin contains sixty-one poems. Eleven are purely religious (in a Christian sense) and scriptural and have been edited and rendered into modern Welsh elsewhere.[68] There are also eleven prophetic poems, ten of which have been edited by Haycock and the longer *Armes Prydein* (see ss. 45–55 below).[69] There are also twelve earlier historical poems which were edited by Ifor Williams who regarded them as the original 6th century work of the historical poet Taliesin whose career began in Wales and who then became active in the "Old North" (see below).[70] There are also two later historical poems *Etmic Dinbych* (s. 15) and *Echrys Ynys* (s. 16) which date to the 9th and 11th century respectively. All the other poems in the manuscript can be described as legendary and have been edited by Marged Haycock in her magisterial volume *Legendary Poems from the Book of Taliesin*.[71]

Of the three other poems included in this volume, *Ymddiddan Myrddin a Thaliesin* (s. 17) and *Ymddiddan Taliesin ac Ugnach* (s. 18) are found in the Black Book of Carmarthen, whilst *Gwarchan Maelderw* (s. 14) is preserved in the Book of Aneirin. *Llyfr Du Caerfyrddin* ("The Black Book of Carmarthen") also known as Peniarth Manuscript 1 is so called because of the colour of its binding and its reputed connection with Carmarthen Priory. The Black Book may have been compiled between 1204 and 1233 and is the earliest surviving collection of Welsh poetry. It is the work of a single scribe writing at different periods of his life and reflects the personal tastes and interests of the compiler. The earliest poems copied into the manuscript date to the 9th or 10th century.[72]

Llyfr Aneirin ("The Book of Aneirin") also known as Cardiff MS 2.81, is also a very small manuscript (160–170 x 127–129 mm) of only 38 pages. It contains a unique text of the long, elegaic 6th century poem called *Y Gododdin*, the oldest surviving Welsh literature. The manuscript dates to around 1250–1300 and may have been written at the Cistercian abbey of Aberconwy, in north Wales. Two different scribes contributed to the contents. One was copying an archaic text written between the late 8th and the late 11th centuries, and the second copied a later version, adding four additional poems, including *Gwarchan Maelderw*.

---

66 Haycock 1988, 362
67 Haycock 2015, 2
68 Haycock 1994
69 Haycock 2013
70 Williams 1960, Williams and Williams 1968
71 Haycock 2015
72 Jones 2019, 7

The extracts from the medieval prose tales *Culhwch ac Olwen* (s. 56) and the Second Branch of the *Mabinogi* (s. 57) are both preserved in *Llyfr Gwyn Rhydderch* ("The White Book of Rhydderch") also known as Peniarth Manuscript 4. It is one of the most important manuscripts in the National Library of Wales and is the earliest compendium of Welsh prose texts. The White Book dates to the mid-14th century and was probably produced at the Cistercian abbey of Strata Florida in Ceredigion on behalf of a local administrator and lawyer Rhydderch ab Ieuan Llwyd (c.1325–1400).

All of these manuscripts have been digitised and can be read at https://www.library.wales/discover-learn/digital-exhibitions/manuscripts/the-middle-ages.

The oldest copy of *Ystoria Taliesin* (s. 58) is found in National Library of Wales Manuscript 5276ii D in Elis Gruffydd's own hand and dates to the period between c.1529 and 1552. The Taliesin episode forms part of a larger work entitled *Cronicl o Wech Oesoedd* ("Chronicle of Six Ages"). John Jones' *Hanes Taliesin* (s. 59) is preserved in Peniarth Manuscript 111, again in the author's own hand and dating to 1607 to c.1610. The text of Llywelyn Siôn's fragment of *Hanes Taliesin* (s. 60) is preserved in his own hand in National Library of Wales Manuscript 13075B – an extensive collection of prose tales (formerly known as Llanofer MS B17) and dating to c.1590. The text of Triad 87 (s. 60) is found in Peniarth Manuscript 252 D, which dates to the 17th century. A fragment of the Triads occurs on pp. 169–70, but the manuscript is badly stained and difficult to read.[73]

National Library of Wales Manuscript 5276iiD and Peniarth Manuscript 252 D have been digitised and can be read at https://www.library.wales/discover-learn/digital-exhibitions/manuscripts/early-modern-period.

---

73 Bromwich 2014, xxxi

The Texts

HISTORICAL SOURCES

1. Historia Brittonum ("The History of the Britons")
Harleian MS 3859, f.188v (early 12th century)

This document contains the earliest mention of Taliesin in any written source and is known as the "Memorandum of the Five Poets". It is included in the Latin *Historia Brittonum* ("History of the Britons"), usually attributed to Nennius and dated to AD 829–30.[1] Despite academic controversy regarding the "historicity" of Aneirin and Taliesin, the memorandum clearly demonstrates that by the early 9th century, it was firmly believed that Aneirin and Taliesin had been famous Brythonic poets in the mid to late-6th century. The memorandum is also the earliest source for the traditional connection between Taliesin and Maelgwn, king of Gwynedd.

Maelgwn is also among the five 6th century rulers castigated by the monk Gildas in his *De Excidio et Conquestu Britanniae* ("On the Ruin and Conquest of Britain"). He is described as *insularis draco* ("the dragon of the island"), referring to Anglesey – the heart of the kingdom of Gwynedd. According to Gildas, Maelgwn gave up the throne to become a monk, changed his mind, and then murdered his own wife and nephew in order to marry his nephew's widow! Gildas also condemns him for his fondness for listening to his own praises sung by his poets.[2] This is probably the origin of Maelgwn's association with Taliesin.[3]

In the text, "at that time" refers to the reign of king Ida of Northumbria who ruled AD 547–579.[4] The Latin text is that of Morris and the translation is by John Koch.[5]

Ida, filius Eobba, tenuit regiones in sinistrali parte Brittanniae, id est Umbri maris, et regnauit annis duodecim, et iunxit Din-Guairoi guurth Berneich. Tunc [O]utigirn in illo tempore fortiter dimicabat contra gentem Anglorum. Tunc Talhaern Tat Aguen in poemate claruit, et Neirin, et Taliessin, et Bluchbard, et Cian qui vocatur Gue[ni]th Guaut, simul uno tempore in poemate Brittanico claruerunt. Mailcunus magnus rex apud Brittones regnabat, id est, in regione Guenedotae...

---

1 Dumville 1986, 21–2; Fulton 2019, 27
2 Winterbottom 1978, 32–36
3 Bromwich 2014, 429
4 Williams 1960, ix
5 Morris 1980, 37; Koch 2006, 751

"Ida son of Eobba held kingdoms in the northern part of Britain, that is the Humber Sea, and he ruled twelve years, and he joined Bamburgh to Brynaich. Then Eudeyrn at that time was bravely fighting against the English [or Anglian] people. Then Talhaearn Tad Awen, Father of poetic inspiration, was renowned in poetry, and Aneirin, and Taliesin, and Blwchfardd, and Cian who was called 'Wheat of Prophetic Verse', were at the same time famous in Brythonic poetry. Maelgwn the great king was ruling among the Britons, that is in the kingdom of Gwynedd …"

EARLY HISTORICAL POEMS

2. Trawsganu Kynan Garwyn ("Praise-Song to Cynan Garwyn")
(BT 45.9–46.4)

This is a praise-poem to Cynan Garwyn son of Brochfael, king of Powys in north-east Wales and describes events of the period c.AD 570–610. Though some scholars see it as a genuine 6th century poem first written down c.AD 650,[1] others have dated it to the 10th century.[2] More recent studies restore it to the corpus of 6th century poems,[3] though some have cast some doubt on the attribution to Taliesin.[4] However, the reference in ll. 7–8 of *Golychaf-i Gulwyd/Kadeir Taliessin* (s. 28) that Taliesin "sang before a praiseworthy lord on the meadows of the Severn, before Brochfael of Powys who loved my awen" shows that the attribution of this poem to Taliesin was an accepted part of tradition by the early 14th century.

Although the poem only lists Cynan's exploits against fellow Welshmen or Britons, his son Selyf died fighting the Saxons in the Battle of Chester around AD 615. Ifor Williams speculated that Cynan spent so much time fighting his Welsh neighbours that none were willing to come to Selyf's aid at Chester.[5] The reference to the men of *Cernyw* in l. 16 is probably to the descendants of the *Cornovii* of Shropshire rather than to Cornwall.[6]

This translation is based on the Welsh edition and notes by Ifor Williams with reference to the translation and notes by Isaac.[7]

> Cynan, protector of armies, gave me a gift.
> No lie is great praise to the harrier of farmsteads,
>   a hundred horses, each as swift as the other, silver their harness,
>   a hundred purple mantles, each has broad as the other,
>   a hundred arm-rings in my lap, fifty precious ornaments,   5
>   a sword with a jewelled scabbard, gold-hilted, best of all:
> acquired from Cynan – enemies detest the sight of it.
>
> Men sprung from the lineage of Cadell, a steadfast army,
>   they gave battle on the Wye with innumerable spears;
>   the men of Gwent cut down with bloody blades.   10

---

1 Koch 2005, 2
2 Isaac 1999, 178
3 Sims-Williams 2014, 39; Fulton 2019, 34
4 Koch 2013a, 31–32
5 Williams and Williams 1968, xxxi
6 Charles-Edwards 2013, 16
7 Williams 1960, 1, 17–25; Isaac 1999, 180–1

Battle in broad, lovely Môn, renowned in praise.
How easy, having crossed Menai, was the taking of her!
Battle on the hillock of Dyfed – Aergol in retreat:
his cattle were never seen being driven before another.
The land-hungry son of Brochfael, eager for spoil.   15
The men of the Cernyw were addressed, praise was not their fate.
He menaces them until they sue [for peace].

My protection is Cynan, famed lord of hosts.
With his flashing, far-flung flame he kindles conflagration.
Battle in the land of Brychan (his fortress is but a mole-hill!)   20
You wretched kings, tremble before Cynan!
A breastplate in battle, a true leviathan,
of the nature of Cyngen, the help of wide lands.

I have heard it said, all declare it –
throughout the whole world under the sun, they are slaves to Cynan.   25

3. Gweith Gwen Ystrat ("The Battle of Gwen Ystrad")
(BT 56.14–57.13)

A wonderfully dramatic poem, this time describing a battle in Cumbria between Urien and his unnamed enemies, possibly the Picts.[8] The *Idon* referred to in l. 21 is the river Eden and the "wine of Idon" of which his enemies have drunk their fill is the blood-stained water of the river! Neither *Gwen Ystrad* nor *Llech Wên* have been identified but they must be in the Vale of Eden, possibly along the stretch of the river between Appleby and Carlisle.[9] A recent attempt has been made to place the action of the poem in south-west Cumbria by amending *Gwen Ystrad* to *Gwensteri* and associating *Llech Wên* with Whitbarrow Hill in Winsterdale.[10] However, this seems an amendment too far to me!

The date of the poem is contested by scholars. It has been suggested that it dates to the 11th century or later,[11] but this has been fiercely challenged and recent studies place it firmly in the 6th century corpus.[12]

This translation is based on the Welsh edition and notes of Ifor Williams with reference to the edition and translation by Isaac.[13]

---

8   Williams 1960, 35
9   Williams and Williams 1968, xlix
10 Breeze 2015, 9 *et passim*
11 Isaac 1998, 68
12 Koch 2013a, 11–13, 23; Breeze 2015, 19
13 Williams 1960, 2, 26–39; Isaac 1998, 62–3

The men of Catraeth arise with the day
around the lord, the victorious cattle-raider:
it is Urien himself, the famed leader.
He curbs kings and cuts them down,
Warlike in his splendour, the vigorous lord of Christendom. 5
The men of Britain deal deaths in droves.
"At the battle-station of Gwen Ystrad, battle-whetter,
defender of your people, neither field nor forest shall shield
your enemy when he comes."
Like waves, harsh their noise, crashing over the land, 10
I saw gallant men in hosts;
and after morning battle, mangled flesh.
I saw a foreign army slaughtered.
A jubilant, fierce shout was heard.
In defence of Gwen Ystrad were seen 15
thinned ranks and dejected, exhausted warriors.
In the ford-gap I saw blood-stained men
throw down their weapons before the grey-haired warrior,
suing for peace in their weariness,
hands crossed, pale-faced, on the gravel of the ford. 20
They drank their fill of the wine of Idon.
The waves washed the manes of horses.
I saw despoiling men lose heart,
their clothing spattered with blood,
and a falling-in fast and tight for battle. 25
The shield of the army, he intended no retreat,
the lord of Rheged, I wonder that any should challenge him.
I saw a splendid host around Urien
when he clashed with his enemy at Llech Wên.
He, scatterer of his enemies, delighted in the fury of battle. 30
Warriors, take up your shields for battle.
May battle-lust be Urien's lot.

And until I grow weak with age,
in the dire need of death,
I shall have no joy 35
if I praise not Urien.

4. Uryen Yrechwyd ("Urien of Erechwydd")
(BT 57.14–58.12)

A fierce poem celebrating Urien's military prowess and ferocity. *Erechwydd* was identified by Ifor Williams as the old Welsh name for Swaledale in Yorkshire.[14] Archaeological fieldwork in Upper Swaledale has identified defensive dykes probably built by British polities against the Anglo-Saxon invaders in the 5th, 6th or early 7th centuries. Several episodes of dyke-building suggest a dynamic political situation coupled with effective local leadership.[15] Urien of Erechwydd may have left his mark on the Yorkshire landscape as well as on Welsh literature! A more recent study has argued that *Erechwydd* covered a wider area including York and the western part of North Yorkshire.[16]

> Urien of Erechwydd, the most generous man in Christendom,
> much you give to the men of this land:
> as you gather, so you scatter.
> The poets of Christendom shall be joyful as long as you live.
> Great is their delight in a warrior of fame: 5
> greater still their praise for Urien and his sons,
> for him as chieftain, the exalted lord,
> refuge of travellers, the first among his warriors.
> The men of England know him when they recount
> how they were dealt death and bitter disappointment, 10
> their lands ablaze, their chattels plundered,
> and many a loss and grievous suffering
> without relief from Urien of Rheged.
> Defender of Rheged, famous lord, the anchor of his country,
> I am pleased by all I hear of you. 15
> Hefty your spear-thrust when you hear battle:
> when you go to war, carnage follows;
> fire spreads through houses before daybreak before the lord of Erechwydd,
> fairest Erechwydd and her most generous men.
> The Angles lose their rights at the hand of the most heroic of kings 20
> with the finest of sons; you are the best there is,
> that was, that ever shall be: there is none to equal you.
> When he is looked upon, great is the terror.
> There is always joy in his presence, the genial king.
> In his presence, joy and abundant treasures, 25
> golden king of the North, the most exalted of kings.

---

14 Williams and Williams 1968, xliii
15 Fleming 1994, 27
16 Breeze 2010, 323

And until I grow weak with age,
in the dire need of death,
I shall have no joy
if I praise not Urien. 30

5. Eg gorffowys can rychedwys ("With the Men of Rheged")
(BT 58.13–59.6.)

This poem celebrates the other prime attribute of the idealized Dark Age Welsh king – prodigal generosity, especially to the bards! Urien causes such terror to his enemies that they groan with fear (l. 14) and he is constantly setting out to attack or returning from war surrounded by the stamping of horses and the revelry of his warriors (ll. 18). Urien is also lavish in his gifts to Taliesin – he prepares sumptuous feasts for his bard and his gifts include fine farmsteads, gold and silver, strong ale and splendid clothing (ll. 19–20). The land of "lovely Llwyfenydd" referred to in line 21 obviously formed part of Urien's kingdom and it has been suggested that the river Lyvennet between Carlisle and Catterick preserves the name.[17] *Eirch* has been identified with Arkendale and the river Ark near Swaledale in north Yorkshire.[18]

At my ease with the men of Rheged,
respect and warm welcome, mead and possessions,
possessions and mead and great rejoicing,
and fine lands [are given] to me in abundance.
Great abundance – silver and gold, 5
gold and gifts and great esteem,
no count is kept, such is the lust for gift-giving,
the lust for giving gifts to satisfy me!
He slaughters, hangs, prepares,
prepares, slaughters [beasts for the feast]. 10
Great respect he gives to the poets of the world.
The world, doubtless, submits to you,
bends to your will as God intended.
Lords groan for fear of your attack!
Battle-inciter, defender of your country, 15
your country's defender, inciter of battle,
always around you is the stamping of horses,
horses stamping and the quaffing of ale.

---

17 Williams 1960, 47
18 Williams and Williams 1968, 58

Ale to be drunk and fine farmsteads
and splendid clothing have all been given to me. 20
[The people of] lovely Llwyfenydd and all of Eirch,
great and small, sing with one voice
and Taliesin's song to you shall delight them also.
You are the best man I ever heard of
for inherent virtue. I praise your deeds. 25

And until I grow weak with age,
in the dire need of death,
I shall have no joy
if I praise not Urien.

6. Ar Vn Blynedd ("For One Whole Year")
(BT 59.7–60.7)

Another dramatic poem, this time describing Taliesin's state of mind with Urien away on another raiding expedition and the bard left behind to languish in the court. The poem opens with a stirring description of the war-band setting out for *Manaw Gododdin*, the southern shore of the Firth of Forth near Edinburgh (ll. 1–9). But then foreboding and fear set in: "I would have no joy, if Urien were killed". What if he is brought back on a bier, dead and blood-stained? What would become of his widow? (ll. 12–16). But then there is loud commotion outside. What is it? An earthquake, a tidal wave? No, it is Urien and his warriors returning, victorious and jubilant, from the fray!

For one whole year, he poured out freely
wine and malt liquor and mead, reward for valour.
Poets sang around the roasting spits
with their head-bands and their place of honour.
All set forth eagerly to battle, 5
[each with] his horse under him, to attack Manaw
for more wealth and booty a-plenty of all kinds besides:
eighty calves and cows of the same colour,
milch cows and oxen and other splendid things.
I would have no joy, if Urien were killed. 10
Dear was he [to me] before entering the spear-storm.
[What if] a bier is carried with is white hair washed [with blood],
and his bloody cheek, stained with blood?
And the great, ferocious man – his wife would be widowed

of her true sovereign, her sure hope, 15
her help, her fate and her lord [....]
Look, lad, through the door. What is that noise?
Does the earth quake? does the sea overflow?
The war-cries of his foot soldiers break like waves.
Foemen on a hill, Urien will route them; 20
Foemen in a hollow, Urien will stab them;
Foemen on a mountain, Urien will defeat them;
Foemen on a slope, Urien will wound them;
Foemen on a dyke, Urien will terrify them.
Foemen on a road, a crag, in every river's bend – 25
no parrying blow or two shall save them from death.
There shall be no hunger while cattle follow him.
Followed by a retinue, armoured in steel, glittering,
his spears are like Death itself, slaying his foemen.

And until I grow weak with age, 30
in the dire need of death,
I shall have no joy
if I praise not Urien.

7. Gweith Argoet Llwyfein ("The Battle of Argoed Llwyfain ")
(BT 60.7–26)

This is one of the most famous of Taliesin's historical poems and describes a dramatic scene where Urien and Owain meet their enemy Fflamddwyn ("the flame-bearer") who expects them to give up hostages. Having exchanged threats and insults, the Britons attack and defeat the Flame-Bearer. Fflamddwyn may be a nickname for one of the late-6th century Anglo-Saxon rulers, perhaps Theodric son of Ida, who reigned in Bernicia (part of Northumbria) between AD 572–9.[19] In the death-song for Owain (s.11), we learn that "When Owain killed Flame-bearer – he thought it no more than sleeping". *Goddau* is the old Welsh name for Galloway in southern Scotland.[20]

On Saturday morning, there was a great battle
from when the sun rose until it set.
Flame-bearer attacked in four war-bands,

---

19 Fulton 2019, 36
20 Haycock 2006, 14

with Goddau and Rheged mustering,
gathering from Argoed to Arfynydd –   5
they could not delay so much as a day.
Flame-bearer called out, the great swaggering oaf,
"Have the hostages been given up, are they ready?"
Owain answered, the scourge of the eastlands,
"They will not be given up. They were not, they are not ready.   10
And a whelp [descendant] of Coel would be hard pressed
indeed before he gave up any man as hostage."
Urien called out, the lord of Erechwydd,
"If they would parley now for our kinsfolk,
let us raise our rampart high on mountain   15
and carry our faces over shield-rim;
let us raise ours spears overhead, men,
and charge Flame-bearer amidst his army
and cut him down and all his following."

And before Argoed Llwyfain   20
there was many a corpse.
Ravens reddened with [the blood of] warriors
and the men charged with their chieftain.
For a whole year shall I sing of their triumph.

And until I grow weak with age,   25
in the dire need of death,
I shall have no joy
if I praise not Urien.

8. Ardwyre Reget ("Let Rheged Arise ")
(BT 61.1–62.16)

This poem presents several problems of interpretation and appears to include interpolations from at least two and, possibly, three different poems.[21] The first poem (ll. 1–29) gives a picture of decline and dishonour until the arrival of Urien and Wlff. They then fight a series of decisive battles until, finally, the English are thwarted by Wlff at the bloody battle at the ford (l. 29). The central part of this poem (ll. 9–17) with its references to Gwydion and, possibly, Lleu is very obscure. The next section (ll. 31–41) seems to be a poem to a certain Caw, describing his

---
21 Williams and Williams 1968, lii

splendid clothing and accoutrements and praising his defence of the borders of his country all summer long. The last section (ll. 41–56) returns to praising Urien.

Let Rheged of the glorious lords arise:
I have watched over you, though I am not of you.
They groan before spear-strife and blade-strife,
warriors moan beneath their round shields,
weaping dolefully like white gulls in Mathrau. 5
Not good, the fighting around a lord. Not good, lies.
But a true ruler prepares against misfortune!
He gives no gifts to those who seek them.
A splendid horseman of swift, generous praise is Gwydion.
Was the wise son of Dôn born of a bungling chieftain? 10
Until Wlff came to oppress his enemies,
until Urien came in his day to take Aeron,
there was no attack, no-one welcomed battle.
Noble-browed was Urien before [the men of] Powys.
Eager were the bold descendants of Gyrrwys, 15
of Hyfaidd of the Gododdin with Lleu [the fair one] to lead them.
Bravely they endured torture,
bore it without dishonour, [men] of the blood of Gwyddien.
This Llwyfenydd saw – lords contending
in hosts on ramparts of well-defended forts. 20
A battle for the crown at the ford of Dumbarton,
a battle at the cells of Brewyn, a battle that shall long be praised,
a battle in the thickets of Cadlew, a battle in Aber –
there was fighting with cruel steel.
Great was the battle at Cludfain, the battle at Pencoed – 25
where wolves fed on excess of blood.
Fierce warriors were broken,
the plans of the Angles were thwarted,
bloody from battle by Wlff at the ford.

[The next section is an interpolation from an unrelated poem:]

Better to praise a lord born, 30
the lord of Britain's kings, worthy of poetry.
No clothing, nor of blue nor grey,
nor red, nor purple was ever worn by a better champion.
No more ardent warrior ever set his thigh

on such princely, well-bred, brindled, eager steeds. 35
All summer long until winter with arms in hand,
he guarded ford and rampart,
sleeping under the dyke and stretching himself [at dawn].
To the world's ending, Caw shall be honoured
for sweeping aside armies ... 40

[The next section returns to praising Urien:]

I groaned in my breast within me before the noise [of battle],
spear on shoulder, shield in hand,
[with] Goddau and Rheged gathering for war.
I saw a man raiding cattle,
a dragon-lord brilliant of fame, an eminent trampler of enemies. 45
I know that war is foretold
and how much I shall miss shall be lost.
I will grow angry, intoxicated by mead,
following fierce, suffering Hyfaidd.
I have declared him [Urien] my shadow in battle. 50
My lord doled out gifts gladly,
worthless is any leader compared to Urien.

And until I grow weak with age,
in the dire need of death,
I shall have no joy 55
if I praise not Urien.

9. Yspeil Taliessin ("The Spoils of Taliesin")
(BT 62.16–63.24)

This poem stands at the root of the tradition of the boastful Taliesin of the later legendary poems. In it, Taliesin glories in his generous treatment at the hands of his patron Urien who can deny him nothing. Nudd the Generous (l. 47) was a historical figure who lived in the Old North in the period AD 550–600 and he also appears in the Triads as one of the "Three Generous Men of the Island of Britain".[22]

My valour asks in trouble
"May I proclaim truly whatever I see?"

---

22 Bromwich 2014, 464–6

I saw before the king (who saw not me)
every favoured man boldly delivering his message.
I saw at Easter many lights, much greenery,   5
I saw leaves bursting out brightly in right season,
I saw a branches of blossom, all equal in beauty,
I saw a lord of most generous custom,
I saw the leader of Catraeth beyond the plains.
May he long be by prince; his neighbouring kings have little love for him.   10
As payment for my song, great are his gifts;
the chieftain of men gives be large flocks.
My sacred awen is the ash shaft of a spear,
my shield against any lord is my winning smile.
The most generous of courageous princes is Urien,   15
but the turbulent cattle-raider,
surrounded by his retinue and clad in blue-grey armour,
the great one, the exalted one,
can refuse me nothing.
All trample the quaking coward in the court   20
of the swift lord who goes where he will.
Riches of yellow gold
in the wealthy, fortified hall of Aeron.
Great is his delight in poets and deer –
implacable is his anger towards his enemies.   25
He is great and mighty to his kinsmen, the Britons;
Like a wheel of fire across the lands,
like a wave is the rightful king of Llwyfenydd.
Like a song known by all or a prayer before battle,
like a vast, wealthy ocean is Urien.   30

[The next section is possibly an interpolation from another poem]

Pleasing are the flashing rays of daybreak spreading.
Pleasing is a lord, an ardent leader.
Pleasing to soldiers are swift, sturdy steeds.
At the beginning of May, armies rest.
Pleasing it is in Defwy when the eagle-chieftain   35
visits his people at the long ridge.
[or: "Pleasing it is in Defwy when the eagle
soars over river and ridge."]
I would join them on a spirited horse,

these fine people, plundering for Taliesin.
Pleasing is the charge of a champion on a steed. 40
Pleasing is the gift of a nobleman to a lord.
Pleasing is a herd of deer in a lonely place.
Pleasing is a wolf, ravenous among the broom.
Pleasing is the lord of Eginyr's son.
Just as pleasing is the sound of warriors clashing. 45
Just as pleasing is a fierce battle-cry
and a whelp [descendant] of Nudd the Generous ruling a fine country.
I delight in my life –
may he make the poets of the world joyful
before death comes to the sons of Gwyddien, 50
battle-leader of the army of Urien's blessed land.
[Or: "battle-leader of the army of the blessed land is Urien."]

10. Dadolwch Vryen ("Reconciliation with Urien")
(BT 65.5–24)

Here Taliesin is in disgrace! There has been a falling out between himself and Urien. He awaits his safe passage home from exile and sings a song of reconciliation to his patron. Ifor Williams speculated that the two poems to Gwallawg son of Lleënawg (s. 12 and 13) may have been the cause of this temporary rift between Taliesin and Urien.[23]

The most valiant chief, I shall never abandon him:
I will seek out Urien, to him shall I sing.
When my safe passage comes, I shall be made welcome
in the finest of regions ruled by the foremost of leaders.
I shall pay no heed to the princelings I see; 5
I shall not seek them out, I shall not keep their company.
I shall make my way to the North, to mighty kings.
And though I wager much,
I need not boast – Urien will not refuse me.
The lands of Llwyfenydd, mine is their wealth, 10
mine is their joy, mine their bounty,
mine their fine cloth and their luxuries.
Mead from horns and good things without asking
from the best of kings, the most generous I ever heard of.

---
23 Williams 1960, xxxvi–xxxix

The kings of all regions are slaves to you.   15
They rail against you but must avoid you!
Although I dared to jest at him, the aged man,
I loved none better before I came to know him.
Now I see how much I am given.
Except to God Almighty, I will not give him up.   20
Your kingly sons, the most generous of men,
sing their songs in the lands of their enemies.
[Or: "their splintered spears echo in the lands of their enemies."]

And until I grow weak with age,
in the dire need of death,
I shall have no joy   25
if I praise not Urien.

11. Marwnat Owein ("The Death-Song for Owain son of Urien")
(BT 67.18–68.4)

The death-song for Owain son of Urien is one of the most powerful and well-known of the poems of the historical Taliesin. It has always been highly thought of; indeed, written above the poem in the manuscript (p. 68) in a later hand is the note *goreu ynghymry o gerdd taliessin ben be[irdd]* – "the best in Wales of all of the poems of Taliessin chief of poets". In it, we learn that when Owain killed the Flame-bearer, "it was no more than sleeping" (ll. 11–12), which refers back to the dramatic incident in *Gweith Argoet Llwyfein* (s. 7). The poem also contains some of the most frequently quoted lines in the whole Taliesin corpus:

> *kyscit lloegyr llydan nifer*
> *a leuuer yn eu llygeit.*
> *A rei ni foynt haeach.*
> *a oedynt [hy]ach no reit.*

> The wide hosts of England sleep
> with daylight in their eyes
> and those that had not fled
> were braver than were wise!
>   (ll. 13–16)

The soul of Owain son of Urien,
may the Lord consider its need.

The prince of Rheged, the heavy green earth hides him:
no shallow thing was praising him in song!
In his grave is the warrior renowned in song, great his fame: 5
his whetted spears flashed like wings of dawn!
None is the equal
of the lord of resplendent Llwyfenydd;
reaper and seizer of enemies,
of the same undaunted spirit as his father and grandfather.   10
When Owain killed the Flame-bearer –
it was no more than sleeping.
The wide hosts of England sleep
with daylight in their eyes
and those that had not fled   15
were braver than were wise!
Owain punished them furiously
like a wolf-pack harrying sheep.
The splendid man, in his iridescent armour,
gave horses to supplicants.   20
Though he gathered wealth like a miser,
he shared it out freely for the sake of his soul,
the soul of Owain son of Urien.

12. Gwallawg 1
(BT 29.21–30.23)

The following two poems are to Gwallawg son of Lleënawg, the leader of Elfed, the modern Elmet in Yorkshire,[24] the first a praise-song listing his many battles and the second a death-song or lament. Gwallawg's kingdom lay to the east of Leeds, bounded to north and south by the rivers Wharfe and Don.[25] The *Historia Brittonum* names him, with Urien, as one of the four British kings who laid siege to Lindisfarne in about AD 575.[26] Elmet was conquered by Edwin of Northumbria at the beginning of his reign, perhaps in AD 617.[27] Ifor Williams speculated that these poems to Gwallawg may have been the cause of a temporary rift between Taliesin and Urien that had to be remedied by the poem of reconciliation called *Dadolwch Vryen* (s.10).

---

24 Fulton 2019, 34
25 Breeze 2010, 323; 2015, 9
26 Morris 1980, 38, 79
27 Breeze 2002, 159

The poems describe events of the AD 580s[28] and *Gwallawg 1* has archaic word-forms that help date the first written version of the poem to before AD 750 and probably to around AD 650.[29]

The geographical background to *Gwallawg 1* has been studied in detail by Andrew Breeze and the placenames in the translation are based on his identifications.[30] The *Gwensteri* referred to in l. 29 is probably Winsterdale, south-east of Windermere in Cumbria.[31] The "lovely church of Lleenawg" in l. 5 has been identified with "Staynlenok" near Millom, in south-west Cumbria.[32] *Arddunion* (l. 22), *Gwyddawl* (l. 26) and *Pen Coed* (l. 38) have not been identified.

These translations are based on Ifor Williams's edited text and notes with reference to the translations by Breeze.[33]

> In the name of the lord of heaven, the numerous host of saints
> shall protect the defender,
> sharp-pointed his lordly spear,
> the warlike, furious lord.
> He defended the lovely church of Lleënawg,   5
> the mighty host of watchful Unhwch.
> They recite to me from Pictland a tale
> from the region of Manaw and Edinburgh –
> united, the company of Clydwyn
> would brook no opposition.   10
> He made wood enough for a fleet
> by shattering spears in fierce battle;
> in his fury he makes coffins for all!
> Gwallawg unmanned armies –
> he preferred slaughter to trickery.   15
> Battle by the sea (the praise of poets encouraged him),
> he provoked the men of York.
> Battle in the region of High Rochester through great heat of fire,
> his fury is unrelenting.
> Battle near the fair fortresses,   20
> a hundred armies trembled at Ayr.
> Battle in the dominions of Arddunion and Ayr,
> great grief to sons.

---

28 Breeze 2002, 165
29 Koch 2005, 6
30 Breeze 2002, 168–170
31 Breeze 2015, 9 *et passim*
32 Rowland 1990, 100 n.102
33 Williams, 1960; Breeze, 2002, 166–68

Battle at Bathgate – food for spears all day long!
You set no store by your enemies! 25
Battle near Gwyddawl; of Mabon's achievements
no enemy shall live to tell the tale till Doomsday.
Battle at Gwensteri, subduing the English
spearmen, cruelly.
Battle at Rossington Moor at dawn, 30
Gwrangon was skilful in the fight.

As my poem began –
from kings, from ill-fated battles,
these men win byres full of cattle –
Haearddur and Hyfaidd and Gwallawg 35
and Owain of Anglesey of the line of Maelgwn, their custom
is to lay their enemies low.
At Pen Coed, there shall be short, stabbing swords –
doubtless – and rotting corpses
and crows scattering. 40
Among the Picts, around Edinburgh, he is famed;
in Gowrie, in the region of Brechin,
in Irvine; a man swift and well-armoured:
he never saw a hero who never saw Gwallawg.

13. Gwallawg 2

(BT 63.25–65.5)

Gwallawg 2 is a death-song perhaps declaimed in Elmet before Gwallawg's son, Ceredig.[34] The enemies named in l. 4 are Rhun prince of Galloway, Nudd Hael (the Generous), a North British prince of the late 6th century, and Nwython, a king of Strathclyde.[35] Lines 28–41 are regarded as an interpolation. The *Caer Caradoc* of l. 48 overlooks the Wye between Hereford and Ross.[36]

In the name of the Lord of Heaven, the host sing,
they lament their dragon-lord.
He drove back the attack of many foes,
Rhun and Nudd and Nwython.
I will praise with the song of the bards of the Britons – 5

---
34 Gruffydd 1994, 71
35 Breeze 2002, 170
36 Breeze 2002, 171

a generous band of wise, harmonious sages –
the singer of pitiful songs.
I will weave poems, I will sing to a lord
respected and feared in his own land.
He did not cause me, I will not cause him, grief. 10
Hard it is to lose riches – the wealth
of the lord who refuses none shall never fail.
To the onlooker, sad are kings
whilst they live because their wealth may not go with them to the grave.
They cannot boast of their way of life, 15
sharper for them are the pains of Hell, where they are headed.
A worldly host across Britain yields to despair.
The presumptuous shall be shamed, let them be shamed,
those who are feared shall be judged,
all condemned by the judicious man, 20
by him who was named law-giver in Elmet.
No tribute is paid to the unskilled man.
A fierce, arrogant youth will fall headlong underfoot.
Eager was Gwallawg in the fray;
unwilling and tardy in retreat. 25
Let no-one ask what the lord shall do:
he will not refuse me, he will not flee.

[Interpolation]

[Let the fattened stock be sold at summer's end.
He does not prosper except by fairness.
Sweet it is for you that this is praised 30
by a privileged poet, skilled in tales.
The ardour of kings in battle is fed by mead.
Like the splendid summer sun,
he is highly praised in loveliest fashion
by him of the wise song, the chieftain of the war-band. 35
May the druid of the army be like the face of summer,
like the ruddy face of the son of Lleënawg.
About the strong rampart, I know light,
I know heat, the haze of heat, the heat of haze;
whilst it shone, none escaped without shame the blow 40
of the lethal sword wielded by the slaughtering swordsman.]

He does not scatter the host by stealth:
not slow are his enemies to retreat!
They pierce shield-bosses before his horses,
in the great ferocity of the cavalry.   45
Your unyielding war-band love you,
wealthy are the hostages they take.
From Dumbarton to Caer Caradog,
and in the stronghold of Dumfries, O Gwallawg,
all the kings are subdued and silent before you!   50

LATER HISTORICAL POEMS

14. Gwarchan Maeldderw ("The Song of Maeldderw")
(BA 28.18–30.11)

Gwarchan Maeldderw is one of four *gwarchanau* ("songs" or "canticles") appended to the *Gododdin* in the *Book of Aneirin* and dates to the 10th to 11th century.[1] It defied all attempts at interpretation and translation until the pioneering work of Graham Isaac in 2002.[2] *Gwarchan Maeldderw* is a *marwnad* or death-song for the hero Maeldderw, contrasting his modesty in the court with his ferocity in battle. The poet displays extraordinary linguistic virtuosity, and the poem represents "a classic realization of the possibilities of the medieval Welsh poet's craftsmanship."[3]

In the *Book of Aneirin*, the poem is attributed to Taliesin and the rubric introducing it sets out the value attached to it in a bardic contest:

> "Here now begins the *Gwarchan* of Maeldderw. Taliesin sang it, and gave it high status, as much as all the *awdlau* of the *Gododdin* together with the three other *Gwarchanau* in a bardic contest."

This translation is based on Isaac's edition of the Middle Welsh text with reference to his translation and notes.[4]

> The doleful cry where two rivers meet around the fortress
> keeps me awake, crying for the lime-washed shield, the brilliant
> swift hero; two armies are bereft!
> Far flung his fame, he who seeks distress of battle;
> see the blood-stained clothes, the rough red cloak,   5
> the charge of the young auxiliaries
> who did not flee, who breached the enemy ranks.
> Though cowed by love, great his valour,
> swift his vengeance in arms!
> A house of straw we call   10
> the man who returns running from battle;
> like a bedfellow in a ramshackle hovel by a crooked hill,
> unlike those mourned with honour,

---

1 Isaac 2002a, 82n
2 Isaac 2002a
3 Isaac 2002a, 81
4 Isaac 2002a, 82–96

unlike your ferocity and ardour!
The ardent one was cut down, the fair nobleman,   15
beyond measure is his praise,
he cared nothing for his greatness!

May they demand fame's virtue for the great army!
The stronger champion would avert his eyes from a maiden,
the dazzling hero, claimant of payment due to lineage;   20
before the spoils of the red dragon of Ffaraon,
foster-brothers depart on the breeze.

Those who fell perished, those whose heads
came within reach of the hammerer, the horse-strider, and the blade of his axe.
His great retinue awaits the ashen spear-wall at sea.   25
He requires neither counsel nor retreat.
Foremost in attack, he devoted life and soul to the defence of borders;
no longer can he defend his fortress:
before the gate of Edinburgh,
handsome Cynan was the vanguard's wall.   30

He set sword
against the cowards' rampart,
was victorious for the Lord of lords;
a chief who gave no quarter,
a berserker.   35

The chief officers of Cynlas he summoned to the depths of battle;
the very sweet man does not cut down the very bitter – this he desired above all
     things;
may he desire a refuge on Enlli.
He who had his fill of fair portion at feast
piled up a fair portion of corpses for his people   40
on the border in the morning.

Like houses where the proudest play in pride,
once inhabited and – in the way of all wealth – lost,
so was he lost, but bliss [in heaven] was gained.
Rhun of the North, may the Lord defend him.   45
Around those returning, very thick
was the hedge of spears – thicker, they say, than honeysuckle –
around the generous lord, the battle-furious king.

Battle-furious, blades fall limp, the front-rank spearmen are distressed,
feasting-vessels for the chief, in full sight of the far-seeing one; 50
never was seen, by intention, such freedom,
never was seen, by intention, such faith;
ploughing through the sea, the blameless oak-like leader.

Canwelw is adjudged the swiftest steed;
fierce and wild was he who feasted on the couch, 55
before his burial beneath a pillar,
a great giver to the poor was Maeldderw:
the shapely one, I honour the earth where he lies.

O, ready guarantor of authority, High King,
may you wish a realm for me, wish for me, raise me up [to resurrection]. 60
The young champion attacked, a defence in turmoil,
no running shadow has he cast.
He attained the high realm [of heaven]:
he did not attain the slightest jot of shame.

15. Etmic Dinbych ("In Praise of Tenby")
(BT 42.16–44.16)

Edmyg Dinbych (to give it its modern Welsh form) is the oldest surviving court poem from south Wales and has been dated to AD 815 to *c.*AD 870 [5] or to the period around AD 895.[6] It is a *marwnad* or death-song to a lord by the name of Bleiddudd ("Wolf-Lord") and would have been declaimed or sung in his fortress at Tenby in Pembrokeshire, probably in the presence of his successor and his retinue. Bleiddudd's Dark Age fortress almost certainly occupied the headland where Tenby Castle now stands.

The "lineage of Erbin" (l. 14) were the descendants of the Irish kings who settled in west Wales in the 5th and 6th centuries. There is an interesting reference in ll. 45–7 to the "writings of Britain" being stored in a cell. This certainly refers to the preservation of either Welsh manuscripts or Latin manuscripts about Wales or Britain in the monastery of St. Teilo at Penally about a mile and a half from Tenby.[7] This implies that the 9th century Welsh bards were literate.

---

5 Charles-Edwards 2013, 662
6 Gruffydd 2002, 14
7 Gruffydd 2002, 25

This translation is based on the edited text by Ifor Williams and R. Geraint Gruffydd's rendering into modern Welsh.[8]

I entreat God – the saviour of his people –
the master of heaven and earth, his wisdom sublime in dignity.

A splendid fortress faces the ocean,
merry at New Year is that fair headland,
when the sea shows its mastery, 5
customary is the revelry of bards over mead-cups.
When the harsh waves wash it,
may they leave the green ocean to the tribe of the Picts
and may I obtain, oh God, for my prayers,
when I fulfil my pledge, reconciliation with you! 10

A splendid fortress stands on the broad ocean,
an impregnable, sea-girt stronghold.
Enquire, you men of Britain, for whom are these things fitting?
The head of the lineage of Erbin, may they belong to you!
There, in the hall, were retinue and war-band 15
and eagles above the clouds stalking a pale faced [enemy];
before the fine lord, before the harrier of foes,
the praiseworthy chief, they would form up for battle.

A splendid fortress stands on the ninth wave,
lovely are her warriors at their ease, 20
they derive no pleasure from shameful deeds,
it is not their custom to be niggardly.
I will tell no lie to the peril of my livelihood –
better a slave of Dyfed than the serfs of Deudraeth!
A throng of free men, sponsors of the feast, 25
includes, pair for pair, the best of men.

A splendid fortress stands where a host joins
in revelry and praise-poems with the melodious birds;
merry were their war-bands at New Year's Eve
around the mighty lord, the noble hero, 30
and before he was enclosed in oak
he gave me mead and wine from a glass quaffing-cup.

---

8 Williams 1980; Gruffydd 2002, 20–23

A splendid fortress stands on the headland,
splendidly everyone there is given his share;
Well do I know at Tenby – dazzling white is the gull – 35
the retinue of Bleiddudd, the lord of the small fortress.
My custom at New Year's Eve
was to stretch out at the king's side, the one mighty in battle,
in a purple mantle and enjoy the feast
until I became the tongue of the bards of Britain. 40

A splendid fortress overflows with gifts,
mine were any privileges I would choose,
I speak not of lawful right, I would respect due order,
he who knows not this deserves no New Year gift.
The writings of Britain were their most treasured thing, 45
where the waves storm in;
may it long endure, that cell I used to visit!

A splendid fortress rises,
wondrous her carousal, sublime her poetry of praise;
lovely nearby is the stronghold of warriors, 50
the long-winged cormorant frequents the place.
The raucous sea-birds flock to the summit of the rock.
May anger, ruled by fate, disappear over the hills
and may Bleiddudd enjoy the ultimate success, the most precious treasure
    [of all].
May the meaning of the laments for him be judged over beer. 55
The blessing of the Lord of harmonious Heaven shall carry the day.
Let him not make us cowherds for the great-grandson of Owain!

A splendid fortress stands on the sea-shore,
splendidly there everyone is granted his desire.
Ask Gwynedd … may they be yours! 60
They deserved rough, unyielding spears.
On Wednesday, I saw men locked in strife.
On Thursday, they suffered shame.
Blood on men's hair and keening on the strings [of harps].
Weary were the men of Gwynedd, the day they came, 65
and on the ridge of Llech Faelwy, they splinter shields.
With [my] nephew's son, a host of kinsmen fell.

16. Echrys Ynys ("Desolate the Island")
(BT 68.5–69.8)

This striking poem is also a *marwnad* or death-song, this time for Aeddon, a ruler of Anglesey, who met his death at "the stronghold of Seon" having come from "Gwydion's land", i.e. Arfon, the area of mainland Wales facing Anglesey.[9] Although dated by Gruffydd to sometime from the 9th to the 11th century, Charles-Edwards argues that the Aeddon of the poem is one and the same as Aeddan ap Blegywyryd, a ruler of Gwynedd killed with his four sons in 1017.[10]

Taliesin is portrayed in *Echrys Ynys* as "one of skilful utterance" (l. 10) conjured up by Math and Eufydd. Math also appears in *Prif Gyuarch Geluyd* (s. 19 ll. 78–9) and *Golychaf-i Gulwyd/Kadeir Taliessin* (s. 26 ll. 30). Here, Taliesin is the omniscient seer of the legendary poems – important evidence that the legendary Taliesin was a well-developed figure as early as the beginning of the 11th century.[11]

"The stronghold of Seon" is Caer Seion hillfort on Conwy Mountain facing Degannwy across the estuary of the river Conwy. It is traditionally the seat of Elffin, Taliesin's patron in *Ystoria Taliesin* (s. 58) and is also mentioned in *Ymddiddan Taliesin ac Ugnach* (s.18.13). Taliesin is called "the sage of Seon" in *Kanu y Gwynt* (s. 29 l. 91) and described as "the proud word-sower in Caer Seon" in *Teithi Etmygant* (s. 32, l. 33). In an interesting aside, Charles-Edwards interprets the "four bare-headed women" who appear in l. 8 as "supernatural creatures resembling Valkyries" rather than the arrogant slave-girls or daughters of Aeddon favoured by Ifor Williams.[12] Their "feasting" in l. 22 is taken to refer to the battle itself. Llywy in l. 26 is either a female personal name or "the fair, queenly one".

This translation is based on the editions by Ifor Williams and R. Geraint Gruffydd.[13]

> Desolate the island splendid in song, surrounded by strife.
> Fortunate Anglesey arose, splendid of valour, Menai its defensive door.
> I have drunk strong drink, wine and bragget, with a true brother.
> A handsome lord, his pomp at an end, has been destroyed.
> Full of sorrow are the nobles of the high lord since he fell.   5
> There never was, there never will be his equal in battle.
> When Aeddon came from Gwydion's land to the stronghold of Seon,
> bitter it was that four bare-headed women came at midnight.
> Warriors fell, forests gave no shelter, ferocious was the wind.

---

9 Charles-Edwards 2013, 665
10 Gruffydd 1999, 42–3; Charles-Edwards 2013, 666
11 Charles-Edwards 2013, 668
12 Charles-Edwards 2013, 667, n.79; Williams 1980, 179
13 Williams 1980; Gruffydd 1999

Math and Eufydd conjured one of skilful utterance; 10
while Gwydion and Amaethon lived, there was good counsel.
Pierced was the face of his shield; mighty and loath to flee, strong and resolute.
Mighty in the press of fierce fighting, he was no sea-raiding mercenary.
Mighty in carousal; in every gathering his will was done.
Before he died, he was beloved; whilst I live, he shall be praised. 15
May I receive from Christ, that I be not sad, an apostle's share.
The generous lord shall be welcomed by angels.

Desolate the island splendid in song, surrounded by fury of battle.
In the presence of a victorious youth, fortress of the Welsh, it was joyful to dwell.
Dragon-hero, rightful lord of Britain, 20
The lord has been destroyed, most high chieftain, earth covers him.
Four maidens after their feasting, cruel their presumption;
The cruel truth – on sea, on land, long-lived is their deceit
that for his faithful follower they will not do the slightest favour.
I would deserve reproach if I did not praise the one who has done me good. 25
After Llywy, who will forbid, who will impose order?
After Aeddon, who will safeguard Anglesey, abundant in wealth?
May I receive from Christ, that I be not sad, for good or ill,
a share of his mercy in the royal land – everlasting life!

LEGENDARY POEMS

Unless otherwise stated, the translations of the legendary poems from the Book of Taliesin (ss. 19–44 below) are based on the edition and translations by Marged Haycock (Haycock 2015).

17. Ymddiddan Myrddin a Thaliesin ("The Dialogue of Myrddin and Taliesin")
(Black Book of Carmarthen 1.1–7.2, mid-13th century)

This enigmatic dialogue poem is perhaps better known for its importance in the growth of the traditions and stories surrounding Myrddin/Merlin. Although the *Black Book of Carmarthen* dates to the mid-13th century, this poem has been dated to the period c.1000–1100.[1] It divides into two distinct sections. In the first half (ll. 1–22), Taliesin and Myrddin witness and lament the deaths of several heroes in a fierce battle between Maelgwn king of Gwynedd and the men of Dyfed (south-west Wales).[2] Maelgwn is mentioned in the *Historia Brittonum* (s. 1) as a contemporary of the historical Taliesin in the 6th century and is portrayed in *Ystoria Taliesin* (s. 58) and *Hanes Taliesin* (s. 59) as the poet's adversary in his efforts to free his patron Elffin from captivity. In the second half of the poem (ll. 23–38), Taliesin and Myrddin sing a joint prophecy regarding the battle of Arfderydd, at which Myrddin is destined to lose his mind before fleeing as Myrddin Wyllt (Myrddin the Wild) into the Caledonian Forest or Coed Celyddon.[3]

It has been argued that the dialogue between the two poets in this poem also inspired a similar discussion between them in Geoffrey of Monmouth's long poem *Vita Merlini* ("Life of Merlin") completed c.1148–51.[4]

This translation is based on the edition by Jarman with reference to the translation by Bollard.[5]

Myrddin:
How wretched am I, how wretched,
for the fate of Cedfyw and Cadfan.
Flashing, clamorous was the battle;
battle-stained shields rang out.

---
1 Bollard 1990, 16–19
2 Jarman 1967, 42
3 Bollard 1990, 16
4 Padel 2006, 46
5 Jarman 1967; Bollard 1990, 18–19

Taliesin:
I saw Maelgwn fighting; 5
his war-band is not silent before a great host.

Myrddin:
Against two warriors, they muster in Deuddwr.
Against Errith and Gwrrith on pale-grey horses;
slender, chestnut steeds, no doubt, they bring.
The war-band of Elgan will soon be seen, 10
alas for his death, a great way they came.

Taliesin:
Rhys Single-tooth – a hand-span wide his shield –
swiftly to you came the blessing of death [in battle].
Cyndur slain; they grieve beyond measure.
Men slain who were generous while they lived, 15
three men of distinction, great their fame with Elgan.

Myrddin:
Over and over, many and too many they came;
again and again terror came to me for Elgan.
They slew Dywel in his last battle,
son of Erbin, and his warriors. 20

Taliesin:
Maelgwn's army, with valour they came,
a war-band of shining warriors on the blood-soaked field.

For the Battle of Arfderydd (what was its cause?)
they prepare their whole lives long.

Myrddin:
Many bloody spear-thrusts on the blood-soaked field; 25
many mighty warriors will lie broken;
many when wounded, many when routed,
many in retreat from the fray.

Taliesin:
Seven sons of Eliffer, seven men when put to the test;
seven spears who will not flinch in their seven battle-stations. 30

Myrddin:
Seven blazing fires, seven opposing battalions;
one of the seven, Cynfelyn, always foremost in the charge.

Taliesin:
Seven stabbing spears, seven rivers
they fill with the blood of chieftains.

Myrddin:
Seven score generous ones lost their wits, 35
in the Forest of Celyddon they perished.
Since it is I, Myrddin, after Taliesin,
whose prophecy shall be correct.

18. Ymddiddan Taliesin ac Ugnach ("The Dialogue of Taliesin and Ugnach")
(Black Book of Carmarthen 101.10–102.14)

Here we have another dialogue poem, this time with the mysterious Ugnach son of Mydno. Taliesin is journeying from Caer Seon on Conwy Mountain, home of his patron Elffin, to the fortress of Lleu and Gwydion at Dinas Dinlle in north-west Wales, when he encounters Ugnach. Scholars are far from consensus on the age of the poem and possible dates range from the second half of the 9th century to the period around 1100 to the early to mid-13th century.[6]

Ugnach's name-ending -ach marks him out as alien and otherwordly and the name may mean something like "he from the lonely or remote place". Some scholars have identified Ugnach as an avatar of the Otherworld Hunter, Gwyn ap Nudd.[7] At any rate, Taliesin politely refuses to go with him to his court in Annwfn (l. 35). The reference to "large horns" in l. 2 is usually taken to refer to hunting horns but, as Isaac points out, if we accept Ugnach as the Otherworld Huntsman, it is not impossible that they actually grow out of his head.[8] If so, this is the earliest reference to Gwyn ap Nudd/Ugnach as a horned figure. Later folk tradition describes the leader of the cŵn annwn with horns on his head.[9] Another intriguing aspect is the reference in l. 25 to Ugnach's gorsedd. Whilst this is usually translated as "court" or "fortress", the word literally means a "mound" and may also be interpreted as an early reference to mounds and tumuli as entrances to the Otherworld.[10]

---

6 Respectively: Williams 1957, 24; Rowland 1990, 389; Isaac 2002b, 1
7 Isaac 2002b, 14
8 Isaac 2002b, 15
9 Rhŷs 1901, 215–16
10 Falileyev 2012, 114–15

This translation is based on the edited Middle Welsh text and modern Welsh version by G. R. Isaac with additions from Jenny Rowland.[11]

Tal. Horseman, making for his fortress
with his white hounds and large horns,
I do not know you, though I have just seen you.

Ugn. Horseman, heading for the estuary
on a sturdy steed, primed for battle,   5
come with me, do not refuse me.

Tal. I will not go there now,
the intention of battle brooks no delay:
the blessings of heaven and earth be upon you.

Ugn. Man, that I have not seen every day,   10
who has the look of a fortunate man,
where are you going, and whence do you come?

Tal. I come from Caer Seon,
from fighting with enemies:
I go to the fortress of Lleu and Gwydion.   15

Ugn. Come with me to the fortress
and you shall have mead from temperate Greece
and refined gold on your shield boss.

Tal. I do not know the bold man
who promises me fireside and bed;   20
though fine and sweet is your speech.

Ugn. Come with me to my homestead
and you shall have wine overflowing:
my name is Ugnach, son of Mydno.

Tal. Ugnach, a blessing on your court,   25
blessings and honour be upon you:
I myself am Taliesin, I will repay you for your feast.

---

11 Isaac 2002b, Rowland 1990

Ugn. Taliesin, foremost among men,
          challenger in bardic contention,
          remain here until Wednesday.   30

Tal. Ugnach, of wealth beyond measure,
          may you receive blessings in the highest land:
          I deserve no censure, but I will not stay.

19. Prif Gyuarch Geluyd ("The First Skilful Challenge")
(Red Book of Hergest cols. 1054.1–1055.14, BT 3.1–12)

This is the first poem in the Book of Taliesin and the first eighty lines are missing. Luckily, there is a complete copy of the poem in the Red Book of Hergest. Here, Taliesin demonstrates his rich esoteric knowledge by posing a series of challenging questions – "Which comes first, darkness or light?", "Why is an eagle grey?", "What is the measure of Hell?". Similar sequences of leading questions are also found in *Angar Kyfundawt* (s. 22), *Mabgyfreu Taliessin* (s. 24) and *Preideu Annwfyn* (s. 36).

The poem also contains prophetic material concerning the fortunes of the Saxons, Irish, Hiberno-Norse, the outcome of fierce battles between the Britons and sea-raiders and of other battles around the banks of the river Severn. The Welsh, says Taliesin, have lost God's favour and now must face the impending Day of Judgement. As in *Preideu Annwfyn*, Taliesin also attacks his opponents – firstly, the monks and clerics for their ignorance and immorality and, secondly, presumptuous poets who have the impudence to challenge Taliesin's pre-eminence. He is the wisest and best of poets and has enjoyed the company of the divine family of Dôn – Math, Gwydion and Lleu. Such is his poetic skill that he will always take the drink of honour in the mead-feast!

In its present form, the poem is unlikely to be earlier than the 12th century.[12] The only other references to Dôn in the court poetry are by Llywarch ap Llywelyn and so it is possible that this poem may have been composed or adapted by him and therefore dates roughly to the period 1175–1220.[13] In l. 84, Taliesin declares "I am old, I'm new, I'm Gwion." This is one of the earliest references to the transformation of the boy Gwion into the omniscient poet Taliesin and suggests that a Welsh audience would have been familiar with tales similar to *Ystoria Taliesin* (s. 58) at least as early as the late 12th century to early 13th century.

The first skilful challenge – where could it be read?
Which first, darkness or light?

---
12 Haycock 2015, 50
13 Haycock 2015, 196

Adam, whence came he? Which day saw his creation?
What are the foundations of the earth beneath our feet?

He who would be a monk has no taste for meditation;　　　　5
many are the sinners amongst them,
the people's priests shall forfeit the land of Heaven.
The son of the morning would come
if they sang three bells.
The Angles, the half-Irish Vikings　　　　10
shall make war.
Whence come day and night?
why is an eagle grey?
why is night dark?
why is a greenfinch green?　　　　15
why does the ocean seethe and foam?
Where it goes, you do not see.
There are three fountains
on Mount Sion;
a fortress full of gardens　　　　20
beneath the ocean wave.
You are asked:
what is the name of the gate-keeper?
Who was confessor
to Mary's courteous son?　　　　25
In whose perfect image
was Adam made?
What is the extent of Hell,
how thick its veil,
how wide its mouth,　　　　30
how deep its pits?
The tops of skeletal trees –
what bends them so low,
what wicked deeds
deform their trunks?　　　　35
Lleu and Gwydion,
were they skilful ones?
Do the bookworms know
whence come night and tide,
whence comes their annihilation,　　　　40
where night flees before day?
How is it that you do not see it?

"Our Father, I thunder out your Word
as give succour to the people
who ask me to whisper 45
the sign of the brave."

For fine reward
two skilful ones compete in song;
but God's rector preaches
the flames of hell for sin. 50
Their joy will be brief,
the Welsh will flock together in hell-fire,
in lamentation;
souls will be tried
before the legion of the damned. 55
The Welsh, the worst of foolish sinners –
a herd in utter perdition, beyond any blessing.
A long wailing and sighing
and open bloodshed.
Wooden horses [ships] will come 60
across the ocean, on the shameful sea,
Angles attacking.
Signs will be seen
of revenge on the Saxons;
our timorous whispers. 65
From the leaders
a master will emerge!
Against wild pirates
the sea-borne Britons will arise.
They shall sing prophecies 70
and reap their scattered foes
on both banks of Severn.
Theft by a flabby-skinned monk
……
I send up urgent prayer to the Trinity while I may,
Creator, Adonai [Lord], 75
deliver us from the heathens, let them disappear, far away.
I have been with the skilful ones,
with Math the Old, with Gofannon, 80
with Eufydd, with Elestron,
I have been companion to the mighty

for a year in the fortress of Gofannon.
I am old, I am new, I am Gwion;
I am complete, my skill wins the first drink. 85
The old Britons will face
Irishmen armed, pillaging,
… and the rule of revelling drunkards.
I am a poet, I set no store by serfs,
I am a leader, a seer in contest. 90
The mumbling monk in his monastery
would scatter far and wide his seed,
would not reap what he sowed.
Haughty poets, their learning a pretence,
will flock to the mead-vessels, 95
those who compose false poetry,
seeking a boon they shall not receive,
unlawful, lawless, of no proper standing.
And after that will come
chaos and a world turned upside down; 100
do not beg for peace, you shall have none!

20. Buarth Beird ("The Meeting Place of Poets")
(BT 7.12–8.20)

Here again, Taliesin vaunts his own knowledge and belittles that of his poetic rivals by comparing them to a long list of pointless or futile things (ll. 33–49).

Uproar – followed by pause for thought
for British poets of the futile songs.
My high standing, my exalted status,
cause disquiet among the poetic rabble,
I am the harsh scourge of poetry. 5
In the meeting place of poets who do not know their craft,
fifteen thousand seek qualification.
I'm a craftsman; I'm a singer fine and clear;
I am steel, I am a druid, seer, craftsman;
I'm a viper, I am lust, I gorge myself on learning; 10
I am no dumbfounded poet, I do not stammer:
when the singers sing their songs by rote,
they weave no wonder greater than myself.

With me to oppose them,
it is like accepting clothes without the hands to don them,
like sinking in a lake, unable to swim.
The tide-surge thunders in its fearless onslaught,
its noise is loud, it surges against homesteads.
A crag beyond the wave, set by providence –
bleak and terrifying is the refuge of enemies –
the crag of the chief ruler, the supreme judge,
where we shall be merry on the intoxication provided by the ruler.
I'm a cell, I am fragmented, I'm transformed;
I am a treasury of song, my condition ever-changing.
I love a wooded slope and cosy den
and a poet who composes and does not buy advancement.
I do not love a wrangler:
he who insults skilled poets will never prosper.
It is time to go to contend
in learning against learned men,
against false song, the custom of enemies!
Shepherd of the homelands, our refuge, our strength,
it is like marching to battle without feet,
like insisting on marching without feet;
gathering nuts where there are no trees,
like seeking wild boars in heather,
like ordering pillage without speaking,
like an army of war-bands with no leader,
like feeding lichen to the poor,
like a badger grubbing through ruined houses,
like grabbing air with a hook,
like stinting with the blood of thistles,
like showing a blind man light,
like doling out clothes for the naked,
like pouring buttermilk out on the beach,
like feeding milk to fishes,
like roofing halls with leaves,
like parrying at cudgels with twigs,
like the men of Dyfed mutating sounds before a word.
I am a poet of the hall, the up-and-coming poet in his chair;
I cause halting speech in other poets.
Before I am laid in my rough burial-enclosure,
may we gain sanctuary in your house, O son of Mary.

21. Aduwyneu Taliessin ("The Fair Things of Taliesin")
(BT 8.21–10.3)

Taliesin enumerates his "addfwynau", his most beloved things – the beauty and richness of nature in all its forms, heroism and bravery in battle, wheat ripening in the fields, eloquence in the Welsh language, the pure delight of a young girl at the gift of a ring. Skilfully and tightly constructed, the poem is full of the poet's dual joy in the beauty of creation and the raw power of well-crafted verse.

Aduwyneu Taliesin is almost certainly the work of Llywarch ap Llywelyn and may have been sung on a visit to south-west Wales to the court of Rhys Gryg, who was an ally of Llywarch's chief patron, Llywelyn the Great, from 1212 to 1234.[14] The poem therefore dates to 1220 when Llywelyn and Rhys renewed their alliance.[15] Llywarch also composed a splendid *awdl* in praise of Rhys on the same occasion.[16] Is this an occasion when the court poet sings "official" verse in his own voice but then assumes the *persona* of Taliesin to entertain the court? (For a translation of the poem to Rhys Gryg, see Appendix I.)

The reference in l. 19 to Einion ("a doctor to many") is to Einion ap Rhiwallon, one of the famous Physicians of Myddfai, reputed to have been the descendants of the Otherworld woman of the lake of Llyn y Fan Fach in Carmarthenshire.[17]

Fair is the virtue of great repentance for pride;
Another fair thing – that my salvation comes from God.

Fair is the feast untroubled by care;
Another fair thing – carousal around the mead horns.

Fair is Nudd, a leader, a wolf-lord;   5
Another fair thing – a generous, courteous man of standing.

Fair are berries at harvest time;
Another fair thing – wheat on the stalk.

Fair is the sun in the air, the cloudless sky;
Another fair thing – its fiery countenance at sunset.   10

Fair is a thick-maned stallion in a stud;
Another fair thing – the weave of a spider's web.

Fair is lust and a silver band;
Another fair thing – for a maiden a ring.

---
14 Haycock 2015, 92–3
15 Jones and Jones 1991, xxiv
16 Jones and Jones 1991, poem 26
17 Haycock 2015, loc. cit.

Fair is an eagle on the shore as the tide flows in;
Another fair thing – seagulls playing.

Fair is the stallion and the splendidly lime-washed round shield;
Another fair thing – a fine warrior in the breach.

Fair is Einion, a doctor to many;
Another fair thing – a generous, amiable musician.

Fair is May for cuckoos and the nightingale;
Another fair thing – when weather is more clement.

Fair is good order and a perfect wedding-feast;
Another fair thing – a beloved gift.

Fair it is to concentrate on the confessor's penance;
Another fair thing – bringing wine and water to the altar.

Fair is mead for the musician in the place of honour;
Another fair thing – around a brave warrior, a dense throng.

Fair is a sincere cleric in the church;
Another fair thing – a chieftain in his hall.

Fair are the staunch people and the God who leads them;
Another fair thing – being in the era of Paradise.

Fair is the moon that gleams on the world;
Another fair thing – when wealth comes my way.

Fair is summer and a long, languid day;
Another fair thing – visiting the one you love.

Fair is blossom in the tops of the pear-trees;
Another fair thing – with the Creator, reconciliation.

Fair are the lonely doe and hind;
Another fair thing – a foaming slender-waisted horse.

Fair is a vegetable garden when its leeks flourish;
Another fair thing – field mustard sprouting.

Fair is the horse in a leather halter;
Another fair thing – keeping company with a king.

Fair is a brave man who does not flinch from harm; 45
Another fair thing – eloquent Welsh.

Fair is heather in its purple bloom;
Another fair thing – a salt-marsh for cattle.

Fair is the time when a calf draws milk;
Another fair thing – riding a lathered horse. 50

And I have a fair thing no worse than that;
Fair is a drink from a horn as reward at mead-feast.

Fair is the fish in its splendid lake;
Another fair thing – the glinting surface of the water.

Fair is the word spoken by the Trinity; 55
Another fair thing – deep repentance for sin.

The fairest of all these fair things:
reconciliation with God on Judgement Day.

22. Angar Kyfundawt ("The Hostile Confederacy")
(Book of Taliesin 19.1–23.8)

At 266 lines, this is the longest poem in the Book of Taliesin and almost half the poem consists of Taliesin's riddling questions. It also features in lines 229–260 the first of the runs of Taliesin's famous transformations signalled by "Bûm ..." ("I have been ..."). Taliesin places himself in the front rank of the great Brythonic poets of the 6th century alongside Cian and Talhaearn who are named alongside him in the 9th century *Historia Brittonum* (s. 1). Here, the great bards are associated with otherworldly cauldrons burning without fire and producing poetic inspiration for ever and ever (ll. 19–22). The *awen* of the poets is immeasurable and it and its seven score constituent parts (*ogyrfen*) are created in Annwfn, the Welsh Otherworld (ll. 75–84). As Taliesin himself claims: "Awen I sing, from the deep I bring it" (ll. 179–80). References to the "profound one" who raises people from the dead "but still he is poor" are clearly to Christ. The mention of yews in ll. 42–3 is intriguing; does it refer to weapons of yew, or are those who come as ancient as the yews? Lladon (l. 46) may be derived from a Celtic name *Latona* "the goddess of strong drink".[18]

Taliesin mentions his second set of transformations (l. 239) and it has been suggested that his initial transformation may have been his creation anew as

---
18 Haycock 2015, 137

a poet by Math and Gwydion in *Kat Godeu* (s. 23, ll. 163–171). One of the most intriguing sections of the poem deals with the trials and tortures suffered by wheat in order to make bread or beer (ll. 241–60), which could be likened to the "Old John Barleycorn" folk-motif. This includes in l. 252 reference to Taliesin spending nine nights in the womb of the red-clawed hen. This immediately brings to mind the episode in *Ystoria Taliesin* (s. 58) where Ceridwen, in the guise of the tail-less black hen, swallows Gwion Bach as he hides as a grain of wheat, only to give birth to him as Taliesin. Haycock interprets this as a metaphor for a roasting kiln and wonders whether the *Ystoria* episode represents an over-literal understanding of our poem.[19] However, it seems to me equally possible that both *Angar Kyfundawt* and *Ystoria Taliesin* draw on a common stock of traditional lore surrounding the transformation of Gwion Bach into Taliesin.

> The poet – he is here!
> I sang whatever he may sing.
> May he sing when the learned man
> has finished, wherever he may be.
> A generous man who refuses me   5
> shall have nothing to give.
> Through the language of Taliesin
> comes the benefit of divine nourishment.
> Cian, before he died,
> numerous was his poetic retinue.   10
> Obscure until death
> shall be the poetic utterance of Afagddu:
> he brought forth with skill
> poetic speech in metre.
> Gwion it is who speaks,   15
> a profound one shall come;
> he would raise the dead to life
> but still he is poor.
> They created their cauldrons
> that would boil without fire;   20
> they would work their poetic materials
> for ever and ever.
> Song will be brought forth with passion
> by the world-renowned speaker.
> Hostile is the confederacy;   25
> what is its custom?

---

19 Haycock 2015, 108–9

As so many of a nation's poems
stuck to your tongues,
why will you not declaim
a blessing over sparkling drink? 30
When the poets are adjudged
I will bring a song
concerning the profound one who became flesh:
a conqueror has come,
the third of the judges, well-prepared. 35
Three score years
I endured solitude
in the encircling water,
in the lands of the world.
A hundred servants I had, 40
a hundred kingly splendours thereafter.
With the yews they went,
with the yews they came,
with a hundred songs
and he foretold it. 45
Lladon daughter of Lliant
(the goddess of strong drink, daughter of the sea)
had little desire
for gold and silver.
Who is yet alive who spilt
blood from the fair youth? 50
A rare one is spoken of,
a great one is praised.
I am Taliesin:
I compose song of true pedigree;
until the end of days 55
my praise of Elffin will endure.
It was rewarded
with valuable, well-earned gold.
When it was received, there was no love
for perjury and treachery; 60
but now there is no desire,
sadly, for our song.
He who may call me "brother",
compared to me knows nothing:
the wise man, the pre-eminent poet, 65

the learned one who teaches
biting satire and pursuit,
the turns of phrase of the profound poet,
about men of skilful song.
Let us approach God who is –
according to Talhaearn –
the judge of the world's worth,
who judged the qualities
of ardent poetry.
He, with his miraculous virtue, bestowed
awen without measure or limit:
seven score shades of inspiration
are there in *awen*;
eight score of every score …
… in every one.
In Annwfn he arranged them,
in Annwfn he made them,
in Annwfn below the earth,
in the air above the earth.
One there is who knows
which sadness is
better than joy.
I know the set grades
of awen and whence it flows;
the payments due to the skilled poet,
the propitious days,
a happy life;
the customs of the fortress,
the peers of kings,
how long their realms shall endure.
… equal
are they through the deliverance
of the honoured, learned seer-poet.
How did the wind of the high heavens
distribute itself?
Why is the mind lively?
why is it so lovely?
why is lineage fearless?
how was evening created?
or the sun set in place?

whence comes the roofing of the world?
the roofing of the world, what is its extent?
whence were drawn the streams?
whence were the streams drawn?
why is the earth green? 110
the earth, why is it green?
who composed poems?
poems, who composed them?
meaning, who considered it?
It was considered in books: 115
how many winds, how many waters,
how many waters, how many winds,
how many rivers in their courses;
how many rivers there are;
the earth, what is its width, 120
what is its thickness?
I know the ringing of blades
around a bloody warrior, around a champion.
I know what is arranged
between Heaven and earth; 125
why an empty place echoes,
why death attacks,
why silver gleams,
why a stream is dark;
why breath is black, 130
why liver is bloody;
why a buck is horned,
why a woman's horny,
why milk is white,
why holly is green, 135
why a kid is bearded
in many places;
why cow-parsley is hollow;
why a puppy is drunk; 140
why a sledgehammer's flat,
why a roebuck is dappled,
why salt is salty;
why beer is bitter,
why alder staves are reddened with blood, 145
why a greenfinch is green,

why rose-hips are red –
a woman has them;
whence falls night,
what transformation there is 150
in the golden sea;
no-one knows why
the sun's breast shines so red,
the colour so bright;
the death of a famous one; 155
what the harp string laments;
the cuckoo, what it grieves for, what it sings,
what its song defends;
who captures the stronghold
of Geraint at Wexford; 160
what engenders gems
from adamantine stones;
why meadowsweet smells sweet,
why ravens shimmer in the light.
Talhaearn is 165
the greatest poet-seer.
What outpouring of poetry
came from the Deluge on the appointed day?
I know good and evil,
where it goes … 170
where smoke disperses
in its great, moving mass.
The vessel, who fashioned it?
who extinguished the light of dawn?
What did they preach, 175
Elijah and Aeneas?
I know where summer cuckoos
go in winter.
Awen I sing,
from the deep I bring it. 180
The river that encircles the world:
I know its size and strength,
I know where it ebbs,
I know how it flows,
I know how it courses, 185
I know how it retreats.

I know what beasts
there are under the sea;
I know the nature
of each one in its shoal;   190
how each day is divided,
how many days in a year,
how many spear-shafts in a war-band,
how many droplets in a shower.
The poet unslighted in contention   195
will share his song in splendour.
I know about
the onslaught of Gwydion's trees,
how the river flooded
over Pharaoh's people;   200
who removes the fetters
of angry tumult;
the form of the ladder
by which people climbed to heaven;
who supported the covering layers of the sky   205
from the earth to air;
how many fingers He creates for me,
together with the palm of my hand;
I know the two words
that cannot fit into one cauldron;   210
whence comes the wild, drunken sea,
why fish are black –
seafood is their flesh;
why a stag is …
why fish are scaly,   215
why a white swan's foot is black,
a sharp spear mighty;
why the heavenly host never yields;
I know four sods of earth
whose limit is not known;   220
why pigs, why stags will wander.
I challenge you, poet of highest wisdom,
a man of your pre-eminence,
the bones of the mist, where are they?
and the two waterfalls of the wind?   225
My poetic utterance is declaimed

in Hebrew, in Hebraic,
in Hebraic, in Hebrew,
lauda tu, laudate Iessu ("praise thou, laudably, Jesus").
A second time was I transformed:
I was a blue salmon, 230
I was a dog, I was a stag,
I was roebuck on a mountain,
I was a block, I was a spade,
I was an axe in hand,
I was an auger in tongs 235
for a year and a half.
I was a white, speckled cock
covering the hens in Eidyn;
I was a stud stallion.
I was an ardent bull. 240
I was a sheaf milled,
the ground corn of farmers;
I was the single grain picked out,
it grew on a hill;
I'm reaped, I'm drilled, 245
I'm sent to the kiln,
I'm scattered by hand
to be roasted.
A hen conceived me –
red of claw, a crested foe; 250
I spent nine nights
at peace in her womb.
I was matured,
I was drink set before a ruler,
I was dead, I was alive, 255
a stick stirred me:
I was on the lees,
away from it, I was complete;
and the drinking cup gave me resolve,
the red-clawed one gave me passion. 260
A rare one is spoken of,
a great one is praised.
I am Taliesin:
I compose song of true pedigree;
my praise of Elffin 265
will endure until the end of days!

23. Kat Godeu ("The Battle of the Trees")
(BT 23.9–27.12)

At 249 lines, *Kat Godeu* is the second longest poem in the Book of Taliesin, running a close second to *Angar Kyfundawt* (s. 22). Without doubt, this is the most misunderstood, mis-quoted and mis-used poem in the whole Welsh bardic tradition. It has become enormously influential in modern Pagan traditions via Robert Graves' treatment of it in his "poetic history" *The White Goddess*; more of which anon. *Kat Godeu* is dense, allusive and complex. It is also rich, fascinating and inspiring with its short rhyming lines giving the poem enormous energy and drive. In rendering the poem into modern Welsh, Haycock has analysed the structure of the poem and identified nine distinct sections:

1, (ll. 1–23) Taliesin's transformations,
2, (ll. 24–40) Taliesin battles with monstrous creatures,
3, (ll. 41–74) The creation of an army of trees in Caer Nefenhyr,
4, (ll. 75–150) The great list of the trees and their feats in battle,
5, (ll. 151–177) Taliesin explains his essential nature and his creation by Math, Gwydion and others,
6, (ll. 178–206) Taliesin boasts of his poetic abilities, his weapons and his Otherworldly journeys,
7, (ll. 207–210) More of Taliesin's transformations,
8, (ll. 211–245) Taliesin boasts of his weapons, his horse, his journeys and his martial feats, the prophecy to (or about) Arthur,
9, (ll. 246–249) Taliesin's final boast claiming the prophetic powers of Virgil.[20]

In the first section, Taliesin sets great store by his past existences as liquids of various kinds, perhaps reflecting the flowing spirit of *awen*, ebbing and flowing.[21] However, in his battles with monstrous creatures, it is Taliesin's feats as a warrior that are pre-eminent. He fights and overcomes the great beast with a hundred heads, the black-forked toad and the speckled, crested serpent.

The main action of the poem takes place in sections 3 and 4. Gwydion, the powerful warrior-magician of the Fourth Branch of the *Mabinogi*, is commanded by God to conjure up trees to take part in a great battle. The identity of the enemy and the exact cause of the conflict are left rather vague in the poem. However, in Triad 84 of *Trioedd Ynys Prydain* ("The Triads of the Island of Britain"), it is listed as one of the "Three Futile Battles" of the Island of Britain:

> One of them was the Battle of Goddau: it was brought about because of the bitch, the roebuck and the plover;[22]

---
20 Haycock 2006, 7
21 Haycock 2006, 8
22 Bromwich 2014, 217

Later sources dating to the 17th century maintain that the battle was fought by Gwydion and his brother Amaethon against Arawn, king of Annwfn "because of a white roebuck and greyhound pup" that had been stolen from the Otherworld by Amaethon.[23]

The setting of the battle is *Yr Hen Ogledd*, the Old North, i.e., those parts of northern England and southern Scotland that were British kingdoms before the coming of the early English in the 5th and 6th centuries. In later centuries, the Old North became the semi-historical, semi-legendary landscape so beloved of the Welsh poets and story-tellers – the land of Urien and Myrddin, of terrifying witches and dog-headed warriors. The first line of section 3 tells us that the battle took place at *Caer Nefenhyr* ("The fortress of Nefenhyr"). Nefenhyr is a personal name derived from Brittonic *Novantorix* which means "king of the tribe of the Novantae". The Novantae were the Iron Age tribe that occupied Galloway in what is now south-west Scotland.[24] In the 6th century, the area was known as Goddau and appears in the "historical" Taliesin poems *Gweith Argoet Llwyfein* ("The Battle of Argoed Llwyfain", s. 7) and *Ardwyre Reget* ("Let Rheged Arise", s .8). The name *goddau* means "shrubs, scrubs" and it seems possible that an historical conflict may have become "mythologized" over time.

The real heart of the poem is the famous tree-list which enumerates the trees called to battle by Gwydion and describes their attributes and deeds. In the ancient law-books of Wales and Ireland, plants and trees were listed according to their value and usefulness and this may have influenced the poem, which also draws on international Classical learning.[25] In its use of language and imagery, the tree-list also echoes native lore and the old heroic poetry of the historical Taliesin and the *Gododdin*. Alder, for example, "in the vanguard, strikes first"; elm slashed "the centre, flank and rear of the enemy".

At this point (section 5) Taliesin explains how he was created by Math and Gwydion, who also create the maiden Blodeuwedd from flowers in the Fourth Branch of the *Mabinogi*. Here, though, they are joined by others – Eurwys and Euron, Modron the Celtic mother-goddess, and two hundred and fifty "learned ones". They conjure Taliesin from a unique combination of nine earthly elements, including the blossoms of trees and shrubs, primroses and flowers, and the water of the ninth wave. In *Kanu y Byt Mawr* (s. 43), he is made from seven elements – the familiar ones of earth, air, fire and water but also, wonderfully, from mist, flowers and the south wind.

In section 6, Taliesin again connects himself with the characters and actions of the Fourth Branch, this time with Dylan, the twin brother of Lleu Llaw Gyffes

---
23 Bromwich 2014, 218–19
24 Haycock 2006, 14
25 Haycock 2006, 18

(see also s. 40). In lines 87–90, we are also told of the dual source of his powerful poetic gift – it comes both from Heaven and from "the silver stream of Annwfn".[26] In section 7, one of Taliesin's previous incarnations is as a weapon wielded by "dog-headed warriors" who also appear fighting against Arthur and his warriors in the poem *Pa Ŵr Yw'r Porthor* ("What Man is the Gatekeeper") which dates to the period around 1100.[27]

In section 8, the wise men and druids are called upon to declaim their prophecies to or about Arthur (the meaning of the lines is ambiguous). On the basis of this reference, some scholars have argued that Arthur (in his mythological persona) is present as one of the main protagonists in the battle.[28] The evidence for this interpretation is tenuous to say the least and the lines in question could equally be understood as calling on the druids to foretell the return of Arthur. Lines 240–41 are equally difficult to unravel and have been seen as a reference to a 12th century tradition that Taliesin, like Virgil, had foretold the birth of Christ.[29]

The poem ends with Taliesin proclaiming "I am like a lovely jewel in a golden ornament" filled and exhilarated by the prophetic power of Fferyll i.e., the Roman poet Virgil. Taliesin is, as Haycock points out, the Virgil of the Welsh, a mediator between worlds and epochs, combining the wisdom of the ancient, pagan world with Christian learning. He was an inspiring figure for the creative poets and story-tellers of medieval Wales and still is for us today.[30]

So, what does all this mean? If, that is, it has to "mean" anything. The pioneering Welsh scholar, Ifor Williams saw the poem as a "pleasant phantasy" – entertainment for a courtly audience.[31] Marged Haycock goes so far as to regard *Kat Godeu* as a witty pastiche on the clichés of the old heroic poetry and argues further that some of the archaic language in the poem may have been chosen deliberately to strike an "antique note".[32] Other scholars have warned that tone and humour are the hardest things to judge in literature separated from us by many centuries and that the idea of "heroic pastiche" may be more a reflection our modern thinking than the medieval poet's original intention.[33]

There have been many other interpretations of the meaning of *Kat Godeu* since the 18th century, but perhaps the most influential is that of Robert Graves in his classic book *The White Goddess*. He argued that Kat Godeu is an acrophonic poem, i.e., that the names of the trees represent different letters of the alphabet and convey

---

26 Haycock 2015, 230
27 Sims-Williams 1991b, 39
28 Green 2007a, 62–7; Sims-Williams 1991, 51–2
29 Haycock 2015, 237–8
30 Haycock 2006, 21
31 Williams 1944, 57
32 Haycock 2006, 18
33 Constantine 2003, 46

a secret, coded message. This led him to connect the poem with runes, Ogham and a putative ancient Irish tree alphabet. Ever since, some Irish academics have been scathing about the idea, which they term "the arboreal fiction". This is due in part to their exclusive focus on establishing the original form, meanings and sounds of the Ogham alphabet by identifying "the oldest, least contaminated and therefore most trustworthy sources of information on the matter."[34] How later medieval Irish scholars and bards may have viewed and used Ogham seems of remarkably little concern to them.

Tree names do form a significant group in the original Ogham letter-names. Among the twenty original names, there are seven trees, one bush and one possible herb but in their original form the letters were not all named after trees.[35] Having said that, the various sets of 8th to 9th century Old Irish kennings on the Ogham letter-names include many references to trees, their uses and properties.[36] The idea that *all* the letters were originally named after trees developed among Irish bards and scholars sometime between the end of the Old Irish period (roughly the end of the 9th century) and the high Middle Ages. This process can be seen in the development of the *glosses* (i.e. marginal notes and explanations of words) on the manuscripts designed to instruct apprentice poets in Ogham and its uses.[37] By the time these glosses were being elaborated and fixed between the 10th and 13th centuries, the idea of the tree alphabet was fully formed. The *belief* in an Irish tree alphabet is absolutely *not* a modern fiction and has a venerable lineage in its own right.[38] A "fancy" it may be, but a 10th to 13th century fancy none the less.[39]

Whatever the merits of the Irish tree Ogham, there is no evidence that the ancient Welsh ever named their letters after trees. Many Welsh tree names begin with the same letter and, when set out according to Graves' theory, they make no sense in Welsh at all.[40] In addition, the work of Haycock and others in advancing our understanding of the medieval Welsh text has seriously undermined the translations offered by Graves' Victorian sources, mainly W.D. Nash.[41]

This is not to say that *The White Goddess* is a "bad book" and it has been stoutly defended (in its own terms) by Mary-Ann Constantine in an erudite and entertaining paper.[42] She also comments on the defensive attitude of Welsh academia towards Graves' more mystical interpretations. Earlier generations of Welsh scholars saw in *Kat Godeu* "an echo of old bardism" hinting at the old

---

34 McManus 1988, 129; 2004, 3
35 McManus 2004, 3
36 McManus 1988 137; 1991, 43
37 McManus 1988, 129, 167
38 Acken 2006, 1:3
39 McManus 1991, 150
40 Haycock 2006, 19
41 Nash 1858
42 Constantine 2003

druidic belief in the transmigration of souls. By the 20th century, Welsh scholars had become "increasingly uncomfortable in the presence of druids".[43] Back in the 1940s, Ifor Williams refuted the idea of "any mysticism, semi-mysticism or demi-semi mysticism" in *Kat Godeu* or any other poem in the Book of Taliesin.[44] Modern scholars in Wales seem more concerned with de-mystifying medieval Welsh literature; texts tend to be treated as problems to be solved and "only rarely does one sense delight or genuine engagement". The search for deeper or hidden meanings has been left to others:

> "The Battle for 'The Battle of the Trees' is fought by the cautious, ordered ranks of Welsh scholarship from behind a defensive lexicographical palisade against an attacking motley crew containing at least one mad vicar, an obstinate poet, and a shaman for the 1990s."[45]

Over the decades, there has been little consensus regarding the date of the poem. Green cites arguments that the poem had reached its written form by the mid- to late-8th century.[46] More recently, Haycock has argued convincingly that, as it stands, *Kat Godeu* is largely the work of Llywarch ap Llywelyn and probably dates to the period 1210–1220.[47]

1

I was in many forms
before I was freed of restraint.
I was a slender, mottled sword
forged by hand.
I was a droplet in air,   5
I was the stars' radiant starlight.
I was a word in script,
in my prime I was a book.
I was lantern light
for a year and a half together.   10
I was a bridge that spanned
sixty estuaries.
I was a path, I was an eagle,
I was a coracle at sea.
I was the fizz in drink,   15

---

43 Consantine 2003, 45
44 Williams 1944, 59
45 Constantine 2003, 47
46 Green 2007a, 66
47 Haycock 2015, 173

I was a drop of rain in a shower.
I was a sword in hand,
I was a shield in battle.
I was a harp-string,
under nine years' enchantment   20
and foam in water.
I was a fire's sparking tinder,
I was a tree in forest fire.

2

I am not one who does not sing:
I have sung since boyhood.   25
I sang in the battle of the branchy trees
before Britain's ruler;
I pierced the stall-fed horses
of those whose wealth is in fleets.
I pierced a great beast, horny-scaled: 30
on him were a hundred heads
and a fierce war-band
beneath the root of his tongue.
Another war-band is found
in each of his napes.   35
A black-forked toad:
with a hundred talons.
A serpent, speckled, crested,
a hundred souls for their sins
are tormented in his flesh.   40

3

I was in the fort of Nefenhyr Nine-teeth
when trees and vegetation attacked.
Poets were singing,
soldiers attacking.
The resurgence of the Britons   45
was brought about by Gwydion.
On the Lord he called,
on Christ all-powerfull,
that He might deliver them,
their Lord who made them.   50
The Lord answered him:

"By means of earth and word,
conjure magestic trees,
a hundred war-bands into one host,
and impede the vigorous one,   55
the wealthy battle-giver."
When the trees were conjured up –
an unexpected source of hope –
the trees then hewed the enemy
with their mighty tendrils.   60
Around the armies they attacked,
for thirty days of battle.
Bitterly a woman groaned
and lamentation broke out.
A woman in the van of the fight,   65
the spoil – the buck of Anhun.
No disaster befell us
from blood of men up to our thighs.
The greatest cataclysm of the three
that in the world have come to pass: 70
and one came about
from the Deluge and its tale.
Christ's passion was the second,
the third is Judgement yet to come.

4

Alder inthe vanguard   75
struck first;
Willow and Rowan
were late to the army.
Spiky blackthorn
Eager for slaughter.   80
The skilful Medlar
anticipator of battle.
Rose advanced
against an angry host.
Raspberry took action: 85
he built no defensive palisade
to protect his life.
Privet and Honeysuckle
and Ivy, despite the look of him,

how fiercely they went into the fray! 90
Cherry taunted.
Birch, despite best intentions,
was slow to don armour,
not from cowardice,
but rather because of his largeness. 95
Golden Rod kept his resolve –
foreigners over foreign torrents.
Pine, in the place of honour,
contended for the chair.
Ash performed fine deeds 100
before princes.
Elm, despite his wealth,
did not veer by so much as a foot:
he slashed the centre,
flank and rear of the enemy. 105
Hazel adjudged
the weapons for the conflict.
Dogwood, of blessed life,
the bull of battle, lord of the fray.
A great host brings salvation. 110
Beech flourished,
Holly grew green;
he was in the valorous combat.
Skilfull, splendid, renowned Whitethorn:
his hand dealt pestilence. 115
Vine the destroyer
hewed in battle.
Bracken, the despoiler;
Broom in the van of the war-band
was wounded in the rucked-up ground. 120
Gorse was not fortunate:
despite that, he marshalled forces.
Heather, renowned pillager,
was conjured into the army.
Black Cherry the harrier. 125
Oak of the swift battle-cry:
before him Heaven and Earth trembled.
Woad, a valiant warrior,
his name is worthy of record on wax tablets.

The sickly tree's onslaught [elm?]   130
caused terror:
he would, he did repulse
others and stabbed them.
Pear caused oppression
on the field of battle.   135
A terrifying array
was surging Clover.
Shy Chestnut,
a fierce adversary among the mighty trees.
Jet is black,   140
Mountain rounded,
the trees are armed,
the great oceans are swifter
since I heard the battle-cry.
The crown of the Birch grows leaves for us,   145
its vigour strengthened us;
The crown of the Oak ensnared us
with Maeldderw's Song.
The laughing sea-wave that covers the rock,
a lord who disdains the shoal.   150

5

Not from mother and father
was I made,
and my creation was created for me
from nine forms of element:
from fruit, from fruits,   155
from God's fruit in the beginning;
from primroses and flowers,
from blossom of trees and shrubs,
from earth, from sod,
was I made;   160
from nettle blossom,
from the water of the ninth wave.
Math conjured me
before I was completed.
Gwydion conjured me –   165
great enchantment made by a magic staff;
by Eurwys, by Euron,

by Euron, by Modron;
by five skilled enchanters –
similar to godparents – 170
was I reared.
A ruler conjured me
when a great area was burned.
The wisdom of sages conjured me
before the creation of the world, 175
when I had being,
when the world was still small.

6

A lovely poet of unusual gifts,
I possess in song
whatever the tongue utters. 180
I played in light,
I slept in purple.
I was in the citadel
with Dylan son of Sea,
my bed in the centre of the fort 185
between the knees of kings.
The two keen spears of my poetic gift:
from Heaven they come;
in the silver stream of Annwfn
arrayed for battle they come. 190
Four score hundred men
I pierced despite their greed.
They are no older, they are no younger
than me in their wrath.
Everyone had the passion of a hundred men 195
and I had nine hundred.
My blood-stained sword
wins me honour by bloodshed.
[….] from his burial place
by a meek one was the boar slain. 200
My sword made and re-made,
made languages and peoples.
His name is Llachar ("Radiant"), strong of hand,
like a flashing blade he led the host;
they scattered like sparks 205
from a drop on high.

7

I was speckled snake on hill,
I was viper in lake,
I was a bill-hook wielded by dog-headed warriors,
I was a stout hunting spear. 210

8

My chasuble and my thurible
I prepared not ill.
Four score clouds of smoke
it brings to all;
five times fifty bondwomen 215
is its value, with my knife.
Six yellow horses:
a hundred times better
is my stallion, Melyngan ["Pale-yellow"],
as swift as a seagull! 220
I myself am not tardy
between sea and shore:
I caused a massacre
of nine hundred of the foremost warriors.
Of ruby is my round shield, 225
of gold is my shield-ring.
None was born in the breach …
none visit me now
except Goronwy
from the Water-meadows of Edrywy. 230
Long and pale are my fingers,
it is long since I was a herdsman.
I shape-shifted into a champion
before I was a man of letters.
I shape-shifted, I circulated, 235
on a hundred islands I slept;
I stayed in a hundred forts.
Druids, wise men,
prophesy of Arthur!
There is that which has been before 240
and it is of that which has been that they sing:
[or "There is one who is swifter still
and it was of him they sang:"]

and one came to pass
because of the tale of the Flood,
and Christ's crucifixion
and Judgement Day to come. 250

Like a splendid jewel in a golden ornament,
I am resplendent
and I am exhilarated
by the prophecy of Virgil.

24. Mabgyfreu Taliessin ("The Juvenilia of Taliesin")
(BT 27.13–28.21)

Another series of probing questions, this time regarding more theological topics such as the relationship between body and soul (ll. 31–4), what it is that sustains the world (ll. 43–4) and the brevity of human life (l. 77). These ruminations are coupled with further attacks on monks and pompous poets (ll. 7–34; 35–54). The opening six lines of the poem also speculate on the nature and origin of *awen* (poetic inspiration). At the beginning of the world, Taliesin asks, before Ceridwen, who created *awen*? This is the first reference in the Book of Taliesin to Ceridwen who features so strikingly in *Ystoria Taliesin*. For further discussion, see s. 28 (*Kadeir Kerriduen*) below.

I entreat my Lord
to allow me to consider awen:
what brought forth that needful thing
before Ceridwen,
in the beginning, in a world 5
that stood in need of it?
You monks who read,
why won't you tell me,
why won't you challenge me
now that you don't persecute me? 10
Why did smoke rise?
What created evil?
What fountain shines in beauty
above the cloak of darkness?
From where do white stalks come, 15
from where does a moonlit night come
and another so dark you cannot even see

your shield outside?
Why is it loud,
the crash of waves against the shore?   20
Avenging Dylan,
it grasps at us.
Why is a stone so heavy?
Why is hawthorn so sharp?
Do you know which is better –   25
its trunk or its crown?
What set a wall
between man and the cold?
Whose death is better,
young or old?   30
Do you know what you are
when you sleep:
a body, a soul
or a radiant mystery?
You, skilful in song,   35
why won't you tell me?
Do you know where
night waits for day?
Do you know how many leaves
there are on trees?   40
what lifted the mountain
before the world was destroyed?
what supports the wall
of the earth as a home for humanity?
The soul, by whom is it lamented?   45
who saw it, who knows it?
I marvel that in books
they do not know for certain
where the soul's resting place is,
how its limbs look;   50
from which region flows
the great wind, the great stream
in bitter warfare
that endangers the sinner.
I marvel in song: 55
whence came their lees,

Legendary Poems

what made drunkenness
from mead and bragget;
what set their destiny
but God the Trinity?   60
Why should I declaim a declamation
of anything but You?
Who struck a penny
from rounded silver?
Where does the galloping sea   65
of eager sin come from?
Death has sure foundations,
it is shared out in every land:
death above us –
wide its veil;   70
higher than Heaven and the sky;
a man is oldest when he is born
and grows ever younger with time.
There is anxiety
concerning the world's just desserts;   75
after all our riches,
why does He give us so brief a life?
Sadness will come
of our lodging in the grave.
And the Man who made us   80
(from the exalted realm)
let it be He, our God,
who gathers us to Him at the end.

25. Mydwyf Merweryd ("I am Uproar")
(BT 31.21–32.25)

Although in the manuscript this poem is given the title *Kadeir Taliessin* ("The Chair of Taliesin"), Haycock argues that this is a scribal error and that the name actually belongs to the next poem in the collection, *Golychaf-i Gulwyd/Kadeir Taliessin* (s. 26).[48]

In *Mydwyf Merweryd*, Taliesin explores the connections between seemingly incompatible things and phenomena, e.g. "What connects moisture … with the burden drawn by the moon?" (ll. 36–8); "What connects poets with flowers and

---
48 Haycock 2015, 258

pleached hedges?" (ll. 5203). There is also learned discussion of medicinal herbs and various sorts of liquids, including "Gwion's river" (l. 66) – a possible reference to flowing inspiration.[49]

> I am Uproar
> who will praise Lord God
> like a harmonious song in contest,
> like the words of the poet-sage.
> Lovely is the wise man's breast   5
> when he responds.
> Awen – where does it flow
> at midnight and noon?
> Gabbling, flashy poets –
> their song does not impress me.   10
> On the wide valley floor, at the border,
> great guile arises.
> I am not mute in song:
> I challenge the region's poets.
> I hurry the foolish along,   15
> I delay the rash,
> I awake the silent one,
> O fierce, eager lord.
> I am not shallow in song:
> I challenge the poets of tumultuous contention   20
> with their Judas-coin reward,
> fit only for the depths of ocean.
> Who embraced the despised
> and the deformed in all their nakedness?
> Whence comes dew on grass,   25
> and wheat ale,
> and the strong drink of the bees,
> and gum and resin
> and exotic salves,
> and the yellow colour of orpine,   30
> and a fine silver mantle,
> and rubies and red berries
> and sea-foam?
> What makes a spring flow fast

---
[49] Haycock 2015, 259

where peppery watercress grows?　　　　　　　　　　35
What connects the moisture
of malt – the "starter" of ale –
with the watery burden drawn by the moon,
with a lifeless, stagnant, brackish pool?
and the seers of good sense　　　　　　　　　　　　40
with the sage and his many moons?
and the lovely trees bending
with the wind from the sky?
and ale and an inlet of ocean
with luxuries from over the sea?　　　　　　　　　　45
and a vessel of glass
in a pilgrim's hand
with pepper and pitch?
and the venerated eucharist
with a doctor's herbs　　　　　　　　　　　　　　　50
and his beneficial texts?
And what connects poets with flowers?
and pleached hedges
with primroses and mashed leaves
and the crowns of trees in the wood?　　　　　　　55
And what connects malt and wealth
with many hoarded riches,
and bowls of wine from Rome
with the wild moorlands of Wales,
with deep, sweet, flowing water,　　　　　　　　　60
a blessing of God's providence?
The staff of the bard shall be
fruitful in its pre-eminence;
it will boil up riches fiercely
above the five-legged cauldron.　　　　　　　　　　65
Together with Gwion's river,
and the beauty of fine weather,
and honey and clover,
and the mead-horns of revellers –
pleasing to the dragon-lord　　　　　　　　　　　　70
is the talent of his druids.

26. Kadeir Taliessin/Golychaf-i Gulwyd ("The Chair of Taliesin"/"I entreat the Dear-Blessed One [God]")
(BT 33.1–34.14)

As we have seen, the title *Kadeir Taliessin* almost certainly refers to this poem, not number 25. As such, this is the first of a series of three poems with the word *kadeir* (Modern Welsh "cadair") in the title. The primary meaning of *kadeir/cadair* is "chair", but it also developed secondary meanings such as "fortress" or "stronghold" and "song or "metre". It is with this latter meaning that it is generally (though not always) used in the Book of Taliesin.[50]

It is in this poem that we see perhaps one of the clearest delineations of the "legendary" (as opposed to the "historical") figure of Taliesin. We are told of his dealings with a host of Welsh legendary and mythical characters. He sings before the sons of Llŷr at Ebyr Henfelyn (ll. 3–4) and accompanies Brân the Blessed on his bloody expedition to Ireland (ll. 31–4), both of which tie in with the narrative in the Second Branch of the *Mabinogi* (s. 57 below). The reference in ll. 22–26 to Taliesin coming to Degannwy to contend with the all-powerful Maelgwn Gwynedd and free his lord Elffin "in the presence of noblemen" foreshadows the narrative of *Ystoria Taliesin* (s.58). In ll. 29–30, Taliesin is with Lleu and Gwydion in the Battle of the Trees and his *awen*, his poetic inspiration, comes from the cauldron of Ceridwen (ll. 11–14). In addition, lines 45–51 offer an enchanting description of *Kaer Sidi*, one of the names of the Welsh Otherworld, adding to the picture offered by *Preideu Annwfyn* (s. 36)

Despite the reservations of some scholars,[51] references to Brochfael of Powys and Urien Rheged echo the earlier poems of the "historical" Taliesin (s. 2, 3–11). The poem also embodies prophecies regarding sea-raiders around Bardsey Island and "ravaging English hosts" (ll. 15–22).

> I entreat the Dear-Blessed One [God] – lord of every lineage,
> lord of hosts, publicly for a covenant.
> I sang in a feast over mournful drink,
> I sang before the sons of Llŷr at Aber Henfelen.
> I saw the violence of combat and sadness and distress; 5
> blades glinted on fearless heads.
> I sang before a praiseworthy lord on the meadows of the Severn,
> before Brochfael of Powys who loved my awen.
> I sang in a fine battle position in the morning before Urien
> until around our feet blood stained the grass. 10

---

50 Haycock 2015, 263
51 Haycock 2015, 273

He defended my song that came from the cauldron of Ceridwen;
unfettered is my tongue, a treasury of inspiration.
The inspiration of poetry – my God created it
together with milk and dew and acorns.
Let us consider deeply before confession to a priest,   15
that death, without doubt, draws nearer and nearer.
And around the lands of Bardsey misfortune will come:
Ships will speed across the surface of the ocean,
let us call on the Man [God] who made us:
may he protect us from the wrath of the merciless host.   20
When Anglesey is called a lovely, open plain
blessed are the leaders of the English in battle-tumult.
I came to Degannwy to contend
with Maelgwn, the all-powerful.
I freed my lord in the presence of noblemen,   25
Elffin, ruler of splendid men.
I have three songs of consistent harmony
and until Judgement they shall be preserved by poets.
I was in the Battle of the Trees with Lleu and Gwydion:
Eufydd and Elestron, they conjured trees.   30
I was with Brân in Ireland:
I saw when the mighty-thighed warriors were slain;
I heard the clash of ferocious men
with Irish devils, wily plunderers.
From the headland of Penwith to Loch Ryan: 35
Welshmen of one mind, with the courage of Gwrion.
A salvation to the Welsh in the battle-tumult
will be three ferocious nations of true qualities:
Irishmen and Britons and Romans
will make war and chaos.   40
And around the borders of Britain – fair her settlements –
I sang before kings over mead-vessels.
The first drink, noblemen served it to me,
for I am the chief sage with gifts in a flood.
Well-prepared is my chair in Caer Siddi,   45
Sickness and old age do not strike those in it,
as Manawyd and Pryderi know.
Three musical instruments around the fire play before it,
and around its corner-turrets streams the sea;
and the fruitful fountain above it –   50

sweeter than white wine is the drink in it.
And after I entreat You, King Most High,
before burial in earth, may I be reconciled to You.

27. Kadeir Teyrnon ("The Song of Teyrnon")
(BT 34.15–35.21)

The Teyrnon of the title is a personal name and probably refers to Teyrnon Twrf Liant, lord of Gwent, who appears in the First Branch of the *Mabinogi*. The son of Rhiannon, queen of Dyfed, is born on May Eve but is abducted. Rhiannon is accused of his murder and suffers seven years of punishment. She has to wait at the horse-block outside the gate of the court and offer a ride on her back to any visitor who wishes. The same May Eve, Teyrnon Twrf Liant, lord of Gwent, is determined to solve the mystery of why his fine foals (also born each May Eve) disappear. He waits up all night with his new-born foal until a gigantic claw appears through the window of the stable and clutches at the animal. Teyrnon draws his sword, cuts the claw off and runs outside to see what creature has been stealing the foals. He sees nothing but, on his return, finds a fine baby boy alongside the foal. Teyrnon and his wife name the boy Gwri and raise him for seven years until they realise that Gwri is actually Rhiannon's long-lost son and return him to his parents, who rename him Pryderi.[52] Llanfihangel Nant Teyrnon (the Welsh name for Llantarnam near Cwmbrân in south-east Wales) is probably the scene of this episode. The court poets of the late 12th and early-13th centuries cite Teyrnon as an exemplar of valour and sound common sense – which is certainly in accordance with his character in the First Branch.[53]

However, despite the poem's title, Teyrnon is not the main subject of the poem. In fact, the first twenty-two lines appear to be in praise of Arthur, described here as being "blessed" and of "the lineage of Aladur".[54] The Welsh name *Aladur* is derived from a Romano-British god *Mars Alator*, commemorated on two inscriptions.[55] The association with Mars implies that *Alator* was some kind of war-god and *Aladur* may be being used here to emphasise the war-like character of Arthur.[56] Interpretations of the name itself vary – "the Huntsman", "the Wild One" or, perhaps less likely, "The Nourisher".[57] The idea of the wild warrior-huntsman certainly fits with Arthur's role in stories such as *Culhwch ac Olwen* where he battles supernatural

---

52 Davies 2007, 16–21; Williams 1930, 20–27
53 Haycock 2015, 299
54 Green 2007b, 239–40
55 RIB 218, 1055; Ellis Evans 1970, 510
56 Green 2007a, 197
57 RIB 218; Ellis Evans, *loc. cit.*; Ross 1967, 174, 201

enemies and hunts the giant magical boar, Twrch Trwyth, from Ireland and across Wales to Cornwall (s. 56). This connection with *Mars Alator* has led some scholars to speculate that Arthur was originally a protective and benevolent pagan god, rather than a historical battle-leader.[58] Arthur's raid on the giant Cawrnur is also referred to in *Marwnat Uthyr Pen[dragon]* (s. 42). Cawrnur means "giant-lord" and the reference may be an allusion to a lost tale in which Arthur and his warriors make off with the possibly Otherwordly horses of Cawrnur and his sons.[59] *Rheon* (l. 6) may be a reference to Loch Ryan near Stranraer.

The second half of the poem is clearly spoken by Taliesin.[60] The three stewards referred to in ll. 23–4 are named in Triad 13 as Caradog son of Brân, Cawrdaf son of Caradog and Owain son of Macsen.[61] We then have another list of "splendid things" in lines 29–35, ending with the truth that emanates from the cauldron. This leads to another demonstration of Taliesin's poetic pre-eminence and omniscience together with prophecies regarding the coming of fleets and a devastating wind (ll. 52–8). Finally, the poem foretells the arrival of a future ruler of outstanding power and generosity and calls for the release of Taliesin's patron Elffin.

> Here is declaimed a clear-toned song,
> full of awen beyond measure
> regarding a man, a courageous man of authority,
> of the lineage of Aladur.
> Is he renowned, is he wise   5
> or the steward of Rheon?
> Or a royal ruler
> with his reverence for scripture,
> and his red spear-shower,
> and his attack over the rampart,   10
> and his well-made praise-song
> amidst a lordly hero's war-band?
> He carried away from Cawrnur
> pale, saddled horses.
> Teyrnon, the veteran,   15
> Heilyn, the fattener,
> the third profound song of the wise one
> is to bless Arthur.
> Arthur has been blessed

---

58 Green 2007a, 229
59 Jones 2019, 130; Sims-Williams 1991, 53
60 Jones 2019, 127
61 Bromwich 2104, 25

in harmonious song – 20
a defence in battle,
trampling nine in a single charge.
Who were the three high officials
who guarded the country?
Who were the three learned ones 25
who guarded the sign,
who will come as wished for
to meet their lord?
Splendid is the virtue of the fort,
splendid is the lively company of a fine man, 30
splendid a mead-horn circulating freely,
splendid cattle at mid-day,
splendid is truth when it shines,
more splendid when it speaks out,
splendid it is when there comes from the cauldron 35
the ogyrwen of the three-fold awen.
I have been a torqued nobleman
with my horn in my hand.
He who does not cherish my words,
the brilliant contest-song 40
of eloquent, confident awen,
deserves no chair.
What are the names of the three fortresses
between high-tide and low water?
He who is not ardent 45
does not know the nature of their stewards.
Four fortresses are there
in the lands of Britain;
uproar of lords –
since it may not be, it shall not be; 50
it shall not be since it may not be,
but fleets there shall be.
A wave covers the shingle,
the sea-realm, surely the land of Dylan;
there will be neither wooded slopes nor shelter, 55
nor hill nor hollow,
nor shelter from the blast
of the furious wind.
The song of Teyrnon –

may the skilful poet perpetuate it. 60
A famous one in battle will be sought,
Cedig will be sought –
soldiers are gone astray.
I am grieved and angered
at the destruction of the lord 65
of fiery nature,
with the armour of Lleon.
A ruler will arise
for the sake of the fiery, numerous warriors.
He will shatter the van 70
of the feeble war-band –
a sharp outbreak of wounding
on the border where the fighting is most intense.
The foreign peoples
are a flash-flood 75
of sea-voyagers.
From the spawn of the Saracens,
the evil hosts of the depths of Hell,
let us release Elffin!

28. Kadeir Kerrituen ("The Song of Ceridwen")
(BT 35.22–36.22)

Again, despite the title, Ceridwen does not appear to be either the main subject or the speaker of the poem. The title may have been suggested to the 14th century scribe of the manuscript by the reference in l. 24 to "my song and my cauldron and my rules". The dominant voice in the poem is that of Taliesin himself, demonstrating his poetic skill, his familiarity with the natural world and his knowledge of the contents of learned books (ll. 34–37). He also recounts his interactions with characters from the Fourth Branch of the *Mabinogi*, Gwydion, Lleu and Arianrhod (ll. 5–8; 13–27, 32). Some scholars have raised the possibility, albeit tentatively, that the poem may once have originated as a dialogue between Taliesin and Ceridwen.[62] In which case, it is perhaps Ceridwen's own voice we hear in ll. 9–12 and 22–25:

> *Afagddu, my own son –*
> *blessed God made him –*
> *in poetic contention*
> *his sense excelled my own.*

---

62 Haycock 2015, 312

> *When the chairs are judged,*
> *the best of them shall be mine:*
> *my song and my cauldron and my rules,*
> *and my well-crafted declamation, worthy of a chair.*

This translation is based on Haycock's text, translation and notes and her earlier rendering into modern Welsh.[63] In the Middle Ages, "cadair" ("chair") also had the meanings "poem", "song" or "fortress" and there is punning word-play throughout the poem. Miniog son of Lleu does not appear in any other source and his story and background are lost to us. Euronwy and Euron are female personal names and the latter also appears in *Kat Godeu* (s. 26, ll. 167–8) together with the Celtic mother-goddess Modron as one of the creators of Taliesin.

Lord, may you grant me	
forgiveness for my sins.	
At midnight and at dawn prayers,	
my lights burn brightly.	
Noble the life of Miniog son of Lleu	5
when I'd see him here not long ago;	
his ending was the slab-grave of Dinlleu,	
fierce his thrust in battle.	
Afagddu, my own son –	
blessed God made him –	10
in poetic contention	
his sense excelled my own.	
The most skilful man I ever heard of	
was Gwydion son of Dôn who made splendid things,	
who conjured a woman from flowers,	15
who stole pigs from the South –	
since his learning excelled all others,	
bold in battle, a woven interlace of cunning –	
who conjured horses	
to appease the court,	20
and wondrous saddles.	
When the chairs are judged,	
the best of them shall be mine:	
my song and my cauldron and my rules,	
and my well-crafted declamation, worthy of a chair.	25
I am called deep of knowledge in the court of Dôn,	
myself and Euronwy and Euron.	

---

63 Haycock 2015, 316–27; Haycock 2003, 158–60

I saw fierce fighting in Nant Ffrancon
at dawn on Sunday between birds of prey and Gwydion.
On Thursday, sure enough, they went to Anglesey 30
in search of a wily one and enchanters.
Arianrhod, praised for her beauty, more radiant than lovely weather,
her deepest shame came from stepping over the magic staff;
a raging river surges around her court,
a river that beats savagely, wildly against the land: 35
it is dangerous, poisonous as it flows around the world
(they tell no lies, the books of Bede).
Here am I, the guardian of song,
and until Doomsday it shall endure in Europe.
May the Trinity grant us 40
forgiveness on the Day of Judgement,
the true charity of noble men.

29. Kanu y Gwynt ("The Song of the Wind")
(BT 36.23–38.10)

This wonderfully lively and exuberant poem stands at the head of a long tradition of riddling poems in the Welsh poetic tradition. According to the rubric in the original manuscript, it was worth a massive three hundred points in bardic competitions, perhaps reflecting its complexity and ingenuity.[64]

The riddling format is another opportunity for Taliesin to demonstrate his knowledge of the natural world and in the second half of the poem, from l. 69 on, he describes the movements of the planets, the seven elements or "consistencies" that make up the world, and the ten-fold structure of the Christian heaven. In line 91, Taliesin describes himself as "Seon sywedyd" ("the sage of Seon"), namely Caer Seon on Conwy Mountain, home of his patron Elffin. There are other references to Seon in *Echrys Ynys, Ymddiddan Taliesin ac Ugnach* and *Teithi Edmygant* (ss. 16, 18, 32. See the introductions to those poems for more details).

Ifor Williams dated this poem to the 9th century, but Haycock has drawn attention to similarities with the language of the court poets Cynddelw Brydydd Mawr, active in the late mid to late 12th century and Llywarch ap Llywelyn whose career spanned the period from c.1175–1220.[65]

---

64 Haycock 2015, 328
65 Haycock 2015, 331

Guess who:
created before the Deluge,
a mighty creature,
without flesh, without bone,
without veins, without blood, 5
without head, without feet.
He shall grow no older, no younger,
than at the beginning.
He shall falter in his quest
for neither fear nor death. 10
He does not have the needs
that creatures have.
Great God, how lively he is
when at first he comes.
Great are the miracles 15
of the Man who made him.
He is in open ground, he is in woods,
without hand, without foot,
without old age, without illness,
untroubled by affliction. 20
And he is as old
as the Five Ages of the World,
and is also older,
by how many half-centuries?
And he is as broad 25
as the face of the earth.
And he was not born
and he has not been seen.
He is at sea, he is on land;
he sees not, neither is he seen. 30
He is not to be depended on:
he does not come when he is wanted.
He is on land, he is at sea,
he is indispensable.
He is invincible, 35
he is without peer.
He comes from the four corners of the World,
he will not be counselled.
He drags the anchor
above the marble stone. 40

He speaks out, he is mute,
he is uncouth.
He is daring, he is fearless
when he passes over a country.
He is mute, he speaks out,   45
he is all commotion,
his is the loudest noise
on the face of the earth.
He is good, he is bad,
he is difficult to see;   50
he is not obvious,
for he cannot be seen for looking.
He is bad, he is good,
his here, he is there.
He causes disorder   55
and makes no amends for what he does.
He makes no amends for what he does
since he is not to blame.
He is wet, he is dry;
he comes often   60
from the heat of the sun
and the coldness of the moon.
The moon is barren
because it has less heat.
The one Man who made them,   65
all the creatures,
to him belongs the beginning
and the inevitable ending.

No skilful poet is he
who does not praise the Lord;   70
no proper singer is he
who does not praise the Father.
Unheard of is a plough
without irons, without seed.
There was no light cast   75
before the first matter was created.
No priest is he
who does not bless the Host.
The contentious one does not know

his own seven constituent elements. 80
Ten realms were set out
in the angelic land.
The tenth, unloved,
was rejected by the Father.
A reviled host 85
was utterly destroyed –
Lucifer, the corrupter,
of accursed nature.
Seven planets have existence
due to the seven blessings of God; 90
the sage of Seon [Taliesin]
knows their properties:
Mars, decrepit,
the Sun, like a wheel,
the labouring Moon, 95
Jupiter, Venus.
From the sun, from the flowing waters,
the Moon brings light.
The remembrance is not vain,
the crucifixion is not doubted. 100
Our Father and *Pater*,
our Friend, shall receive us.
Our Lord, let us not be put asunder
by the host of Lucifer.

30. Kanu y Med ("The Song of the Mead")
(BT 40.3–20)

"The Song of the Mead" forms a natural partner to the next poem in the Book of Taliesin, *Kanu y Cwrwf* ("The Song of Ale", s. 31) and reflects. The scene is a feast, probably at the court of Maelgwn Gwynedd at Degannwy, with copious amounts of mead, where Taliesin beseeches God to release Elffin from his captivity. The poem contains many similarities in terms of its language and diction with the work of the court poets of the late 12th and early-13th century.[66]

I praise the lord, the ruler of every place,
He who supports Heaven, lord of every thing.

---

66 Haycock 2015, 352–56

He who made water good for all,
He who made every drink and makes them ferment:
let him rule over Maelgwn of Anglesey and he will make us drunk   5
and the foam of his mead-horn shall adorn the strong drink.
The bees collect it, yet they don't enjoy it –
the famous filtered mead, its praise is sung in every place.
Earth nurtures many creatures
that God made for man, to endow him: 10
some loud, some mute – man has use of them;
some wild, some tame – it is God who makes them
liberally for them, as clothes, as chattels,
as food, as drink – so it shall continue until Judgment Day.

I entreat the Lord, ruler of the land of peace,   15
to release Elffin from his exile:
the man who gave me wine, and beer, and mead,
and large, princely horses of splendid appearance.
May he give to me again as, in the end,
by God's will, he will give with honour   20
five times fifty calends feasts in a peaceful gathering –
Elffin the horseman, may you possess the Old North.

31. Kanu y Cwrwf ("The Song of Ale")
(BT 40.20–41.15)

This poem is in part a song of praise to God for the perfection and bounty of creation, the source of all human comfort and joy. Interestingly, it also includes a very detailed description of the process of making ale – from the initial steeping of the grain in water to the point where the beautifully clarified beverage is brought from the cellar to be served to the king in his "fine feasts" (ll. 24–35). This whole section is interpreted by Haycock as an extended metaphor on the Christian doctrine of the resurrection of the body and she sees the whole poem as a meditation on sin.[67]

To return to less theological matters, line 37 tells us that honey is an essential ingredient in the ale. Adding honey to the ale caused a second fermentation that produced a more potent brew that kept much longer. Adding even more honey produced *bragawt* ("bragget"), a strong, sweet ale for which medieval Wales was famous and which was exported to Ireland and England.[68]

---
[67] Haycock 2015, 359–60
[68] Haycock 2015, 368

Oh, that they had honoured the inherent qualities
of the One who guards the wind!
When His glory comes,
the earth shall be full of wailing
but also joy eternal.   5
It is You who orders
the pattern of midnight and day:
by day, armour is donned,
by night, there is rest
and praise for happiness   10
engendered by the great Lord.
Great God made
the sun of summer and its fierce heat,
and He it was who made
the fruits of woodland and field.   15
The tide shall be summoned,
sparkling, spirited, boundless;
every ebb-tide shall be summoned –
God help me!
And before the host of the world   20
comes to the special hill of Judgment,
they could not achieve the smallest thing
without the power of the great Lord.
He soaks it in water
until it germinates;   25
He soaks it a second time
until it becomes malt:
what the earth nurtures
becomes rank.
Its vessels shall be cleaned   30
and its wort shall be made pure.
And when it has clarified,
it shall be brought forth from the cellar,
it shall be set before kings
in their fine feasts.   35
No couple shall reject it,
honey made it.
Miraculous God, bitter
shall be its nature.

Most generous is the Trinity: 40
it makes drinkers as drunk
as fish –
their little homesteads
as numerous as grains of the salt sea
at neap tide and spring tide, 45
the grains of the salt sea
beneath the sand.
The rightful Lord said,
"I myself have ransomed myself."
Nothing is achieved 50
without the power of the Trinity.

32. Teithi Etmygant ("They Admire Proper Qualities")
(BT 41.16–42.15)

This fascinating poem seems to alternate between Taliesin's trademark self-aggrandisement (ll. 1–14) and boasting of his former existences and past glories (ll. 32–42) and two sections that deal largely with the heroic past of the kingdoms of Gwent and Ergyng in south-east Wales (ll. 21–31, 43–58). Gwrfoddw, king of Ergyng, and his sons appear as worthy candidates for the drink of honour in the feast and special attention is given to the "long-haired men of Gwent" and their victories against the Saxons led by their generous king, Ynyr.

Both Gwrfoddw and Ynyr were actual historical figures active in south-east Wales in the late 6th and early 7th century. Gwrfoddw ruled over Ergyng, a small Welsh kingdom now forming part of south-west Herefordshire and is recorded as fighting the Saxons c.AD 615. Ynyr ruled over Gwent (now largely corresponding to the modern county of Monmouthshire) and his son, Iddon, is also recorded fighting the Saxons in the period c.AD 595–600. This would place the reign of Ynyr possibly in the 570s to 580s.[69] In legendary terms, Iddon son of Ynyr of Gwent also figures in Triad 42 as the rider of *Cethin Carnawlaw* ("Roan Cloven-Hoof").[70]

It is almost certain that *Teithi Etmygant* is the work of Llywarch ap Llywelyn and, in a brilliant piece of historical detective work, Marged Haycock has established that the poem probably dates to shortly after 1218 when the Treaty of Worcester recognised the claim of Llywelyn the Great (Llywarch's patron) to be regarded as *de facto* Prince of Wales. At the time, Llywelyn was also keen to foster and strengthen

---
69 Howell 2004, 262
70 Bromwich 2014, 111

alliances in south-east Wales.[71] This may account for the emphasis on Gwent in the poem and we can perhaps speculate that it was performed by Llywarch (in the persona of the legendary Taliesin) at a gathering or feast for Llywelyn's allies.

Fascinatingly, the editors of Llywarch's "official" court poetry also assign the same context to "Y Canu Bychan a gant Prydydd y Moch i Lywelyn fab Iorwerth" ("The Short Poem that Prydydd y Moch sang to Llywelyn fab Iorwerth").[72] Therefore, we have here an example where we can see an official court poem and one of the legendary Taliesin poems that appear to have been composed at the same time and in the same political context. (For a translation of "The Short Poem", see Appendix I below.)

Teithi Etmygant is not the only poem by Llywarch ap Llywelyn with strong connections with Gwent. As a young man in the 1190s, he was sent by Rhodri ab Owain Gwynedd to Gwent with a string of horses as a wedding gift for Gwenllïan the daughter of Hywel ab Iorwerth, lord of Caerleon, and his poem in praise of her beauty has survived. It is also possible that whilst in Gwent Llywarch fell foul of the law, was accused of murder and underwent trial by ordeal to prove his innocence, an experience recorded in his poem *Awdl yr Haearn Twym* ("Ode to the Red-Hot Iron").[73] (See Appendix I)

Dygen is the old name for the hills to the east of Welshpool in mid-Wales. The reference to Hardenhuish, near Chippenham in Wiltshire, is, frankly, baffling. Attempts to construct a Gwentian placename from the *Hardnenwys* of the manuscript are unconvincing.[74]

> They admire proper qualities,
> being Tryffin's kinsmen,
> eager for a fierce warrior,
> swirling like a whirlpool
> as the poet strikes string. 5
> The night, where will it come?
> where does it hide from day?
> Does the skilled poet know
> what hearts conceal?
> Let him give me that which warms me 10
> from the land of dawn [i.e. the sun].
> What took away the colour of winter?
> What congress was there in the place of beginnings?

---

71 Haycock 2015, 371
72 Jones and Jones 1991, 247
73 Jones and Jones 1991, poem 15; Jones 1992, 72
74 Haycock 2015, 385

Our generous God,
the wise, renowned, auspicious one: 15
He awakes the sleeper,
He deserves a torrent of song
from the Welsh, the possessors of strongholds,
to their beloved Father.
Loud is the lamentation of the hosts, 20
loud is the lamentation of the ruler of Anglesey,
because of great, appalling perjury.
The long-haired men of Gwent
surround Worcester.
Who deserves the drink of honour? 25
Maelgwn of Anglesey?
or Dyfydd of Aeron?
or Coel and his hounds?
or Gwrfoddw and his sons?
Because Ynyr has taken hostages, 30
his enemies do not laugh.
Poets hasten to
the proud word-sower in Caer Seon [Taliesin].
I have quaffed wine
in the great hall of Uffin, 35
in oceans of drink of Gododdin;
I was powerful in scattered form,
the early morning magician of Brân.
I am an ancient wayfarer,
my words are merry; 40
and beyond Dygen,
it is for me to praise Urien.
One radiant in integrity,
a fitting, eager leader of a host:
red reaper of the men of Wessex – 45
those who defiled him became reddened with blood;
in battle in Harddnenwys,
Ynyr wounded them.
He gives welcome at a hundred calends feasts,
with a hundred kinsmen at his table. 50
I saw great men
hastening to battle.
I saw blood on the ground

before the onslaught of swords;
the wings of dawn grew blue 55
with the volley of spears.
For three hundred calends feasts – a praiseworthy gathering –
Ynyr's ploughlands shall be reddened with blood.

33. Canu y Meirch ("The Song of the Horses")
(BT 47.19–48.27)

This difficult poem has been described as "untitled, incomplete and in places unintelligible".[75] The modern title was coined by Ifor Williams, the pioneer of Taliesin studies and almost half of this poem is indeed given over to a list of famous horses and their equally renowned riders.[76] However, it opens with a section in praise of the sun its all its varies moods and manifestations (ll. 1–15). It has been suggested that the "wild horse" referred to in the opening couplet may once have been thought of as drawing the sun across the firmament.[77] The horse-list is followed by a fascinating description of some of Taliesin's previous existences (ll. 59–68). Here, yet again, Taliesin is demonstrating his knowledge of the lore of the heroic past gleaned during his multiple incarnations.

Canu y Meirch has understandably been compared with *Trioedd y Meirch* ("The Triads of the Horses") which also list heroes and their steeds.[78] However, there seems to be little consensus regarding the relationship between the two texts. Rachel Bromwich, the editor of the Triads, saw a close connection between them, with any divergences the result of corruption during the process of oral or written transmission. She also saw a triad lurking in lines 43–49: "the three geldings/who will never go out to stud".[79] However, as Haycock points out, the poem is likely to date to the 12th or 13th century and is certainly not based on the content of the Triads. Even where the same horses are named in both texts, their owners do not always correspond.[80] The likelihood is that each text draws on independent sources.

The subject of ll. 15–21 "the mighty one, terrible in onslaught" is far from clear – the poet may be praising the Christian God sitting in judgement, the all-powerful sea, or some un-named hero.[81] The last six lines of the poem are also difficult to interpret as the manuscript breaks off where its final quire is missing.

---

75 Jones 2019, 133
76 Williams and Williams 1968, xxiii–iv
77 Haycock 2015, 387
78 Bromwich 2014, lxxx–lxxxvii; 103–28
79 Bromwich 2014, lxxxiv
80 Haycock 2015, 388
81 Haycock 2015, 287

Canu y Meirch gives us a veritable role-call of historical and legendary Welsh heroes, including Arthur and Lleu Llaw Gyffes. *Nwython* (l. 15) was a historical 6th century ruler of the British kingdom of Strathclyde.[82] *Caradog Freichfras* ("Caradog of the Mighty Arm")(l. 29) is a legendary figure from whom the medieval rulers of Glamorgan in south Wales claimed descent. In Triad 38, his horse is named as *Lluagor* ("Host-Splitter").[83] *Gwythur son of Greidawl* (l. 31) appears in *Culhwch ac Olwen*, where he must fight Gwyn ap Nudd for the hand of the summer maiden, Creiddylad, every May Eve until the ending of the world.[84] *Gwawrddur* (l. 31) is one of the 6th century warriors commemorated in the *Gododdin* – "He fed black ravens on the rampart of a fortress/Though he was no Arthur".[85] *Cunin Cof* ("Lord of Excellent Memory") (l. 38) was regarded as the grandson of Brychan Brycheiniog, legendary founder of the kingdom of Brycheiniog (modern Breconshire in mid-Wales).[86] *Ceidio* (l. 45) appears in the Triads as the father of Gwenddolau, one of the combatants in the battle of Arfderydd where Myrddin/Merlin went mad with grief (see s. 18).[87] *Rhydderch Hael* ("the Generous")(l. 49) was a real 6th century ruler of the British kingdom of Strathclyde and is recorded in the *Historia Brittonum* (s. 1) fighting alongside Urien of Rheged against the early English (ss. 3–11). In legendary terms, he was Gwenddolau's adversary at Arfderydd.[88] *Sadyrnin* (l. 53) is a saint's name; there are churches dedicated to him on Anglesey and in west Wales.[89] *Custennin* (l. 54) is the Welsh version of the name Constantine and the name appears in Welsh sources from at least the 10th century. It could refer to Constantine the Great, the first Christian Roman emperor (AD 306–337), the British usurper who had himself proclaimed emperor by his troops in AD 407, or an early ruler of Cornwall.[90] The other heroes named in the poem remain obscure, though the name *Maeog* (l. 27) means "the plainsman".[91]

This translation is based on Haycock's edition with reference to Bromwich's text and translation of ll. 25–58 and Jones' notes and discussion.[92] Both Haycock and Jones interpret line 26 as referring to "the plough-teams of the days of yore", but this seems to me to be an over-reading of the text.

---

82 Haycock 2015, 397
83 Bromwich 2014, 304–5
84 Bromwich and Evans 1997, 35; Davies 2007, 207
85 Williams 1938, l. 359; Jarman 1988, 64
86 Bromwich 2014, 318
87 Bromwich 2014, 311
88 Bromwich 2014, 494
89 Haycock 2015, 401
90 Bromwich 2014, 318–9
91 Isaac 1994, 230
92 Haycock 2015, 387–403; Bromwich 2014, lxxxi–lxxxiv; Jones 2019, 133–35

A wild horse has been broken in,
with his fine gait beneath a warrior.
Praise the one who rises above the earth,
the flaming fire of dawn,
higher than the sky-wind, 5
higher than every cloud,
great in its ferocious heat.
It will not stay hidden
for longer than its wedding-feast with the sea,
the sea's flowing path 10
to the angry waters of the estuaries.
The bright radiance of evening
contrasts with dawn, with the sea's ferocity,
with every comparable thing.
To Nwython's peers, 15
to Afaon, the foot-soldier,
I exalt him who will judge,
the mighty one, terrible in onslaught,
his enmity deep in battle.
I am not a grey-haired cowardly man 20
like the scum at the gate.
My two friends are thus –
two listless ones without desire,
from my hand to your hand they give something.
May the protection of the nine 25
be on a return to ancient days,
for the horse of Maeog,
and the horse of Genethog,
and the horse of Caradog,
a lively thoroughbred, 30
and the horse of Gwythur,
and the horse of Gwawrddur,
and the horse of Arthur –
fearless in inflicting pain –
and the horse of Taliesin, 35
and the horse of Lleu, hand-reared,
and Pebyrllei ("lively-grey") the stud,
and Grei ("grey") the horse of Cunin;
Cornan ("the horned horse"), the supportive one,

Awydd ("eagerness"), the eager one, 40
famous Du Moroedd ("black of the seas")
the horse of Brwyn of the Wily Breast,
and the three geldings
who will never go out to stud.
Kethin ("roan") the horse of Ceidio, 45
hard the hoof of him,
skittish Ysgwyddfrith ("dappled shoulder") –
a leaping steed,
the horse of Rhydderch the magnanimous;
Llwyd ("grey") the colour of stags, 50
and Llamrei ("grey leaper") with his fine leap
and powerful Ffroenfoll ("flaring nostril")
the horse of Sadyrnin
and the horse of Custennin
and others in battle 55
before the afflicted land;
Henwyn ("old white") who happily carried
the good news from Hiraddug.

I have been a sow, I have been a buck,
I have been a sage, I have been a ploughshare, 60
I have been a piglet, I have been a boar,
I have been the roar of a winter storm,
I have been a far-reaching flood,
I have been a wave in storms,
I have been a vessel sent out on the Flood, 65
I have been a speckle-headed cat on three trees,
I have been a godwit on an elder tree,
I have been a crane eyeing his next meal.
The great ardour of the war-band of Morial,
a fine lineage in battle. 70
Of all those under the sky
in the wake of enemies
not alive ...
of the great many who know me.
Sustainer ... [MS breaks off]

34. Y Gofeisswys Byt ("He Walked the World" – Alexander I)
(BT 51.1–52.5)

This is the first of three poems in the Book of Taliesin dealing with the classical heroes Alexander (s. 34, 35) and Hercules (s. 37) and demonstrates that the Welsh poets of the late-12th and early-13th century were at least familiar with their stories and the traditions surrounding them.[93] The beginning of the poem is lost due to a gap in the original manuscript. The use of the word-form *ystlynet* ("kin, lineage") in l. 38 may point to the influence of Llywarch ap Llywelyn as it appears also in his poem in praise of Rhys Gryg, prince of west Wales, of 1220.[94]

> ... he walked the world and subdued it;
> he ruled over twelve neighbouring lands,
> he was the most generous and splendid man ever born,
> a bitter, ferocious killer was he, woe to his foes.
> He overcame Darius three times in battle,   5
> scarce a shrub was left in his land.
> Darius, on powerful wings, fled far;
> Alexander overtook him with great fury.
> Woe to him imprisoned in golden fetters;
> not for long was he imprisoned – death came for him: 10
> with a cry he was assaulted by a host.
> Before him, no-one attacked ...
> the riches of the world, fair in splendour.
> Generous Alexander took them then:
> the land of Syr and Siryoel and the land of Syria,   15
> and the land of Dinifdra and the land of Dinitra,
> the lands of Persia and Mesopotamia and Canaan,
> and the islands of Pleth a Pletheppa,
> and the peoples of Babylon and Asia,
> and the land of Galldarus, of little wealth,   20
> until he went to a country, a land
> where they [the Amazons] content themselves with wrongful hunting:
> they yoke together hostages in Europe
> and pillage lands in the wild places of the Earth.
> Fiercely they [Alexander's men] raped these proud women,   25
> the burnt-breasted ones, the immodest ones.
> Of the battles against Porus it is told

---

93 Haycock 2015, 404
94 Jones and Jones 1991, poem 26.90, pp. 260–78; Haycock 2015, 422

that warriors took action, wrought great affliction.
Of the soldiers of Macedon it is told
that the promised land of Your servants was robbed of its faith. 30
For Your enemy, there shall be no relief from fatigue,
from confinement in fetters and harshness.
A hundred thousand retinue-warriors died of thirst,
with their unwieldy helmets and beasts of burden.
His servant poisoned him before he could return home; 35
it would have been better had it been done the sooner.
To my prosperous ruler of the Land of Glory [Heaven],
the pleasant land of the Lord, the country perfect in harmony,
let me make amends, may my refuge be with You.
All who hear me, may my wish be theirs also: 40
may they do God's will before the oppressive weight of earth lies upon them.

35. Anryuedodeu Allyxander ("The Marvels of Alexander")
(BT 52.18–53.2)

The second of the Alexandrian poems, this deals with the two most celebrated episodes in the legends that grew up in the medieval period around the historical figure of Alexander the Great – his celestial flight drawn by griffins and his visit to the bottom of the ocean. Such stories about Alexander were at their most popular in the 12th and 13th centuries.[95]

I marvel that the Heavenly Abode
does not fall to earth
with the death of the war-leader,
Alexander the Great.
Alexander of Macedon 5
sowed a hail of iron spears.
He of the powerful sword-thrust
went under the sea;
under the sea he went
to seek learning and art. 10
He who would seek learning,
let him be daring of mind.
He went above the wind
flying between two griffins

---
95 Haycock 2015, 426

to see a vision. 15
A vision he saw:
the full extent of the world.
He saw a wonder:
the tyranny of the fish.
What he desired in his thoughts and heart, 20
he gained from the world;
and also, by his death,
mercy from God.

36. Preideu Annwfyn ("The Spoils of Annwfn")
(BT 54.16–56.13)

One of the earliest pieces of Arthurian literature, *Preideu Annwfyn* is an important source for lost tales of Arthur's adventures in the Welsh Otherworld.[96] It is also the work of a master poet. The long line he adopts, often with internal rhyme and alliteration, not only demonstrates his technical skill to best advantage but also enhances the narrative drive and emotional effect of the poem. The form of *Preideu Annwfyn*, divided into *awdlau* – single-rhyme stanzas – was well-established by the 10th century and is also used in *Etmic Dinbych* ("In Praise of Tenby", s. 15) which dates to the 9th century.[97]

The "unifying personality" in the poem is not Arthur but Taliesin himself who tells us of his adventures with Arthur in Annwfn, the Welsh Otherworld.[98] The fact that the poem sets out to tell a story, albeit in an oblique and allusive way, is unusual in Welsh poetry of the period. It is likely that the audience was already familiar with the stories themselves.[99] The basic narrative elements are:

1, Arthur and his men sail in his ship Prydwen to steal the magic cauldron of the Lord of Annwfn,
2, Two warriors called Lleog and Lleminog have an active role in securing the cauldron,
3, Only seven men (including Taliesin) return from the raid.
4, Arthur may also be responsible for releasing a character called Gwair from his imprisonment in the Otherworld (which somehow forms part of the story of Pwyll and Pryderi).

---

96 Jones 2019, 143
97 Haycock 1983/4, 53
98 Sims-Williams 1991, 54
99 Haycock 1983/4, 55

The poem also gives us the most detailed description of Annwfn in early Welsh poetry and this is supplemented by the enchanting description of *Kaer Sidi* (one of the many names of the Welsh Otherworld) in ll. 45–51 of *Golychaf-i Gulwyd/Kadeir Taliessin* (s. 26):

> *Well-prepared is my chair in Caer Siddi,*
> *Sickness and old age do not strike those in it,*
> *as Manawyd and Pryderi know.*
> *Three musical instruments around the fire play before it,*
> *and around its corner-turrets streams the sea;*
> *and the fruitful fountain above it –*
> *sweeter than white wine is the drink in it.*

Between them, *Preideu Annwfyn* and *Golychaf-i Gulwyd/Kadeir Taliessin* allow us to form a fairly clear impression of the Otherworld as understood in the Welsh bardic tradition:

1, It has many names,
2, It is found in or under the sea, beyond the Fortress of Glass,
3, It abounds in poetry – both sad and joyous – and the sound of musical instruments,
4, There is an abundance of alcohol, especially wine,
5, Those who live there suffer neither sickness nor old age,
6, It is home to magical objects and treasures,
7, Its fortress is square rather than round and can revolve,
8, It is ruled by *Penn Annwfyn* "the Chief of the Otherworld",
9, It can be reached by mortals bent on carrying off its treasures.

As can be seen, the poem alludes to several other sources and stories. In the Triads, Gwair, together with Llŷr and Mabon son of Modron, is one of the "Three Exhalted Prisoners" of the Island of Britain.[100] In *Culhwch ac Olwen*, Arthur and his warriors free Mabon who has been imprisoned since the world began. Like Gwair, Mabon is also heard singing sadly in his captivity.[101] In the poem, the imprisonment is said to form part of the story of Pwyll and Pryderi, an unusual conflation of Arthurian material and the action of the Four Branches of the *Mabinogi*. There are also similarities between Arthur's attack on Annwfn and the expedition of Brân the Blessed to Ireland in the Second Branch. In both tales, a cauldron plays a central role in the action and Taliesin is among only seven survivors (see s. 57 below).

---
100 Bromwich 2014, 373–4
101 Bromwich and Evans 1997, ll. 910–12

In *Preideu Annwfyn*, the cauldron that "will not boil a coward's food" (l. 17) is reminiscent of the cauldron of Dyrnwch the Giant, one of the Thirteen Treasures of the Island of Britain.[102] Lleog and his "sword of lightning" (l. 18) can also be compared with Llenlleog in *Culhwch ac Olwen* who slays Diwrnach the Irishman in order to steal *his* cauldron on another raid led by Arthur, this time to Ireland.[103] There, Diwrnach is killed with Arthur's own sword, Caledfwlch, and it is possible that *Lleminog* ("the Leaper", l. 19) is an epithet for Arthur himself.[104]

The Nine Maidens are a fascinating feature of the poem and there are several analogues and parallels in other early sources. In Geoffrey of Monmouth's long poem *Vita Merlini* ("Life of Merlin") completed c.1148–51,[105] Telgesinus (i.e., Taliesin) describes nine enchantresses who live on the *Insula Pomorum* ("The Island of Apples") i.e. Avalon:

> "That is the place where nine sisters exercise a kindly rule over those who come to them from our land. The one who is first among them has greater skill in healing, as her beauty surpasses that of her sisters. Her name is Morgen, and she has learned the uses of all plants in curing the ills of the body … They say she had taught astrology to her sisters – Moronoe, Mazoe, Gliten, Glitonea, Gliton, Tyronoe, and Thiten, – Thiten, famous for her lyre."[106]

The Nine Witches of *Caerloyw* (Gloucester) appear in *Historia Peredur vab Efrawc* ("The Story of Peredur son of Efrawg") which also dates to the 12th century.[107] Having been defeated by Peredur, one of the witches gives him a horse and weapons and he stays at their court for three weeks. There, the nine witches teach him to ride his horse and use his weapons.[108] At the end of the tale, Peredur returns with Arthur and his warriors and all nine witches are slain, albeit unwillingly on Peredur's part.[109] The theme of the training of the hero by Otherwordly women is paralleled in Irish sources such as *Tochmarc Emere* ("The Wooing of Emer") where Cú Chulainn is trained to fight in the house of the fearsome *Scáthach*.[110]

Nine witches also appear in the Latin-Breton *Vita Samsonis* ("Life of St Samson of Dol"), which probably dates to the period AD 735–772.[111] St Samson and his companion are attacked as they travel through a wood by a "very old woman with

---

102 Bromwich 2014, 258
103 Bromwich and Evans 1997, ll. 1036–56
104 Jones 2019, 142
105 Padel 2006, 46
106 Clarke 1973, 101–103
107 Goetinck 1976, xxiii
108 Goetinck 1976, 29–30
109 Goetinck 1976, 70
110 Cross and Slover 1996, 162–8; Kinsella 1970, 29–37
111 Koch 2006, 1558

shaggy hair and that already, grey, with her garments of red, holding in her hand a bloody trident". Having been rendered immobile by the saint, she explains that she is a sorceress (as are all the women of her race) and that although she now lives in the wood alone, her eight sisters and her mother still live in an even more remote wood further away. By the power of St Samson's prayers, the defiantly unrepentant sorceress dies on the spot.[112] In another version found in the *Book of Llandaff* – a compilation of Dark Age and medieval saints' lives and charters from south-east Wales dating to *c.*1119–1134 – the sorceress is called Theomaca ("she who fights against God").[113]

Both of these episodes are set in south-east Wales or the borders and that is also the setting for the Arthurian poem *Pa Gur yv y Porthaur* ("What Man is the Gate-keeper?") which is found in the Black Book of Carmarthen and dates to between 900 and 1100.[114] Here, we see Arthur's companion Cai also fighting nine witches:

Yguarthaw Ystawingun
Kei gwant nav guiton;

"In the uplands of Ystawingun
Cai pierced nine witches;"[115]

It has been suggested that *Ystawingun* is a partially garbled form of the Old Welsh version of *Porth Ysgewin*, the medieval Welsh name for Portskewett in Monmouthshire. The place envisaged as the site of this skirmish may be the Neolithic long barrow called Heston Brake, just outside the village.[116]

All of these sources may draw on the same tradition that gave rise to the Nine Maidens of *Preideu Annwfyn*. However, they may all have their ultimate source in the ancient Gallic priestesses reported as living on the island of Sein off the coast of Brittany by the Roman geographer Pomponius Mela *c.*AD 43:

"In the Britannic Sea, opposite the coast of the Ossismi, the isle of Sena [Sein] belongs to a Gallic divinity and is famous for its oracle, whose priestesses, sanctified by their perpetual virginity, are reportedly nine in number. They call the priestesses Gallizenae and think that because they have been endowed with unique powers, they stir up the seas and the winds by their magic charms, that they turn into whatever animals they want, that they cure what is incurable among other peoples, that they know and predict the future, but

---

112 Taylor 1925, 1:26–7
113 Coe 2004, 1; Evans and Rhŷs 1893, 13–14; de Gray Bich 1912, 12–13
114 Jones 2019, 30; Sims-Williams 1991, 39
115 Jones 2019, 51
116 Sims-Williams 1991, 44

that it is not revealed except to sea-voyagers and then only to those traveling to consult them."[117]

The "Fort of Glass" in lines 30–32 echoes a story in the early 9th century *Historia Britonnum* where thirty shiploads of exiles from Spain "saw a glass tower in the midst of the sea, and saw men upon the tower, and sought to speak with them, but they never replied." The exiles attack the tower "and when they all disembarked on the shore that was around the tower, the sea overwhelmed them and they were drowned". Only one of the ships survives with thirty men and thirty women, who eventually settle and people Ireland.[118] The original source of the story was probably a lost Latin text about the legendary origins of the peoples of Ireland.[119] There are other similarities between *Preideu Annwfyn* and early Irish literature, for example Cú Roí's expedition with Cú Chulainn to the Isle of Man to carry off a cauldron, a woman and magic cattle (see s. 39 below). However, the only direct borrowing from Irish tradition is "Caer Siddi" (l. 3) which is derived from *sídhe* the Irish name for the fairy mounds and their inhabitants.[120]

The "Meadows of Defwy" (l. 38) are a mystery, though the name *Defwy* may mean something like "the black river" and it has been compared to the river Styx of Greek myth.[121] Perhaps one crosses it to reach the Otherworld?[122] In which case, "the one who did not go to the Meadows of Defwy" is someone who has not died and passed over into the Otherworld. "The "Brindled Ox" (l. 39) is a legendary creature that figures in several medieval Welsh sources.[123] In Triad 45, it is one of the "Three Principal Oxen of the Island of Britain" and in *Culhwch ac Olwen* it is specified by Ysbaddaden Chief of Giants among the oxen needed to plough a field to provide food and drink for the wedding-feast of the hero and heroine (l. 563).[124] The "fort of Manddwy"(l. 42) also appears in the poem *Ymddiddan Rhwng Gwyddneu Garanhir a Gwyn ap Nudd* ("The Discourse between Gwyddno Garanhir and Gwyn ap Nudd") in the Black Book of Carmarthen as the site of an Otherworldly battle witnessed by Gwyn ap Nudd himself.[125] Possible dates for the poem range from the second half of the 9th century to the period around 1100.[126]

In the second half of *Preideu Annwfyn*, Taliesin sets about taunting and berating monks and churchmen for their ignorance and feebleness. Some have doubted

---

117 Romer 1998, 115
118 Morris 1980, 20
119 Sims-Williams 1991, 55
120 Sims-Williams 1991, 57
121 Jones 2019, 155
122 Haycock 2015, 447
123 Jones 2019, 155
124 Bromwich 2014, 124–5; Bromwich and Evans 1997, 22
125 Jarman 1982, 72; Rowland 1990, 461
126 Roberts 1978, 285; Rowland 1990, 389

whether this reflects any real, historical enmity between the bardic profession and the Church whilst others have seen it as a defining factor in the development of the persona of the legendary Taliesin.[127] The poet may be using the persona of Taliesin to strike a "playful blow for the secular poets or *cyfarwyddiaid* [story-tellers] against the vain pretensions of the Welsh clerical orders".[128] At any rate, it gives Taliesin an opportunity to boast of his own encyclopaedic knowledge of the art of poetry, native lore, the nature of Annwfn, the heroes and stories of the mythic past and the wonders of the natural world, about all of which the monks (he says) are woefully ignorant.

Whilst Haycock has dated the poem to sometime between the 9th and the 12th centuries, others argue for a date in the 8th or 9th century.[129] Haycock has also speculated that it may have been composed by a professional court poet "wearing a different hat". In other words, the court poets may have composed poems like *Preideu Annwfyn* "by setting aside their ceremonial *gravitas* and assuming the persona of a poet who was regarded by them as one of their founding fathers".[130] Perhaps others would argue that they may have been possessed by the spirit of Taliesin himself?

> I praise the lord, the ruler of the kingly land,
> who extended his dominion over the shores of the world.
> Well-prepared was Gwair's prison in Caer Siddi,
> throughout the tale of Pwyll and Pryderi.
> Before him, none went into it, 5
> into the heavy grey chain that guards the faithful youth.
> And before the Spoils of Annwfn, sadly he sang,
> and our poetic prayer shall last until Judgement Day.
> Three shiploads of Prydwen we went into it:
> save seven, none returned from Caer Siddi. 10
>
> I am fair in fame – my song was heard
> in the four-cornered fortress, revolving to the four quarters.
> My first word, of the cauldron it was spoken,
> by the breath of nine maidens it was kindled.
> The cauldron of the Chief of Annwfn, what is its nature 15
> with its dark rim and pearls?
> It will not boil a coward's food – it is not destined –

---

[127] Haycock 1983–4, 57; Koch 2013b, 185
[128] Sims-Williams 1991, 54
[129] Haycock 1983–4, 57; Koch 2003, 310
[130] Haycock 1983–4, 57–8

Lleog's sword of lightning was thrust into it,
and in the hand of the leaper (Arthur) it was left.
And before the door of Hell's gate, lanterns burned   20
and when we went with Arthur, famed in adversity,
save seven, none returned from the Mead-Feast Fort.

I am fair in fame – songs are heard
in the four-cornered fortress, strong door of the island.
Fresh water and jet are blended;   25
sparkling wine is their drink set before their war-bands.
Three shiploads of Prydwen we went on the sea,
save seven, none returned from the Fort of Rigidity.

I set no value on paltry men and their Christian writings,
who never saw Arthur's valour beyond the Fort of Glass;   30
three score hundred men would stand guard on the wall,
it was difficult to speak to their watchmen.
Three shiploads of Prydwen went with Arthur:
save seven, none returned from the Fort of Impediment.

I set no value on paltry men, their shields trailing,   35
who do not know who is created on which day,
what hour at noon God was born,
who made the one who did not go to the Meadows of Defwy;
who know nothing of the Brindled Ox with his stout collar,
seven score links in its chain.   40
And when we went with Arthur, grim journey,
save seven, none returned from the fort of Manddwy.

I set no value on paltry men, of weak resolve,
who do not know on what day the Lord was created,
what hour at noon the Ruler was born,   45
what creature they guard with its silver head.
When we went with Arthur, sad conflict,
save seven, none returned from the Angular Fort.

Monks crowd together like a pack of hounds
because of the contention of lords of learning who know   50
whether all winds are one, all the waters one sea,
whether all fire, irresistible force, comes from one spark.

Monks pack together like wolves
because of the contention of lords of learning.
They do not know how darkness and dawn divide,   55
nor the wind's path, nor its onslaught,
what place it destroys, what land it strikes,
how many saints and altars are in the void.
I praise the Lord, the great Ruler:
may I not be sad: Christ will reward me.   60

37. Marwnat Ercwl ("The Death-Song of Hercules")
(BT 65.24–66.8)

Although the figure of Hercules was known to medieval Welsh poets, other references to him in the Welsh tradition are fairly rare and brief.[131] He appears in Triad 47, with Samson and Hector, as one of the three heroes endowed with the strength of Adam.[132] Llywarch ap Llywelyn also cites the three together in his poem of *c.*1175–90 in praise of Rhodri son of Owain Gwynedd:

> *Ercwlff a Samswn, seirff galon,*
> *Ac Echdor gadarn, gad wyllon.*

> "Hercules and Samson, stabbers of enemies,
> And mighty Hector, warriors fierce in battle."[133]

Other Poets of the Princes cite Hercules as an exemplar of courage showing that they were familiar with some of the Latin texts containing his story and the poem probably dates to the late-12th or early-13th century.[134]

The earth turned
as when night falls in daytime,
because of the death of the renowned one,
Hercules, lord of the world.
Hercules would say   5
that he set no store by death.
Shields in halls
would break on him.
Hercules could set in place

---

131 Haycock 2015, 453
132 Bromwich 2014, 129
133 Jones and Jones 1991, 39, poem 4.9–10
134 Haycock 2015, 458

> the whole, golden moon.   10
> Four pillars equal in height
> with red gold along them,
> the Pillars of Hercules,
> no coward will challenge them.
> No coward would dare to challenge them;   15
> the sun's heat would not allow him.
> No-one under heaven
> went as far as he went.
> Hercules, the battle-rampart,
> the sand covers him.   20
> May the Trinity grant him
> mercy on the Day of Judgment
> in unity, without need.

38. Madawc Drut ("Madog the Valiant")
(BT 66.9–11)

The Madog who is the subject of this poem is probably the son of Uthr Pendragon and therefore the brother of Arthur. The relationship is confirmed by the possibly 12th century poem *Ymddiddan Arthur a'r Eryr* ("The Dialogue of Arthur and the Eagle"), where Arthur refers to Eliwlod son of Madog (who has been transformed into an eagle) as "my nephew".[135]

> Madog, defender of joy,
> Madog, before he went to his grave,
> was a fortress of splendour,
> through heroic feats and merriment.
> The son of Uthr, before he was slain,   5
> swore an oath by his hand.

39. Marwnat Corroi m. Dayry ("The Death-Song of Cú Roí mac Dáiri")
(BT 66.18–67.8)

This fascinating poem commemorates the legendary Irish hero Cú Roí mac Dáiri, king of Munster, and seems to shed a little light on the exchange of stories between the Irish and the Welsh in the 12th and 13th centuries. However, serious doubts have been expressed about how much the Welsh poet actually knew about

---
[135] Sims-Williams 1991b, 57–8

Cú Roí's exploits and whether his name even meant anything to contemporary audiences in Wales.[136]

Having said that, several references in the poem imply a certain level of familiarity with the character and his adventures. The main Irish sources in which Cú Roí appears are the prose tales *Fled Bricrend* ("Bricriu's Feast"),[137] *Táin Bó Cúailnge* ("The Cattle-Raid of Cooley"),[138] *Mesca Ulad* ("The Intoxication of the Ulstermen")[139] and *Aided Chon Roí* ("The Death of Cú Roí") of which there are two versions, *Aided I* dating to the 9th century and *Aided II* dating to the 12th century.[140] He also appears in several poems attributed to his court poet Ferchertne including *Amra Con Roí* ("The Elegy of Cu Roí") dating to the first half of the 8th century,[141] the 10th century *Brinna Ferchertne* ("The Dream-Vision of Ferchterne")[142] and the 11th century *Atbér Mór do Mathib*.[143] The latter has never been fully translated and references here are based on secondary sources.[144]

In l.4 of our poem, Cú Roí is described as "a man fierce by nature" and in *Fled Bricrend*, he appears as a "frightful and terrifying" *bachlach* or herdsman challenging the Ulster heroes to face his axe-blows as part of the "beheading game".[145] The sound he makes in lifting his giantic axe to strike Cú Chulainn is described as "the loud noise of a tempest-tossed forest on a night of storm".[146] According to l. 6, "he held the tiller on the Southern Ocean" and several Irish sources refer to Cú Roí's voyages and adventures. In "Bricriu's Feat", Cú Roí lists his travels to "Europe, Africa, Asia, Greece, Scythia".[147] In *Mesca Ulad*, he is called the "man who traverses the streams of the ocean"[148] and in *Atbér Mór* he is described as "a blazing lion" who destroyed the south of the world.[149]

> *He plundered the south of the world,*
> *He smashed the army of the Dog-heads,*
> *Cú Roí over the Red Sea:*
> *Africa feasted*
> *Him out of fear.*[150]

---

136 Sims-Williams 2011, 52
137 Gantz 1981, 219–255; Koch 2003, 76–105
138 O'Rahilly 1967
139 Gantz 1981, 188–218; Koch 2003, 106–127
140 Thurneysen 1913, 193–196; Best 1905
141 Henry 1995
142 Meyer 1901b
143 Meyer 1901a
144 Sims-Wiliams 1982, 252–3
145 Gantz 1981, 251
146 Koch 2003, 105
147 Koch 2003, 103
148 Gantz 1981, 202; Koch 2003, 115
149 Rees and Rees 1961, 137; Meyer 1901a, 38
150 Sims-Williams 1982, 253

Lines 15–17 echoes the story in *Aided II* of Cú Roí's expedition with the men of Ulster to the Island of the Fir Fálgae, identified with the Isle of Man.[151] Initially, Cú Roí is denied his rightful share of the spoils and has to subdue and humiliate Cú Chulainn in order to gain his just reward – he is indeed a lord eager for his hoard! Eventually, he returns to his fortress at Sliabh Mis near Tralee with three magical speckled cows, the three otherworldly birds that sing to them to make them give milk and a huge cauldron that holds the milk of thirty cows. The greatest prize of all is his wife, Bláthnait.[152]

References in ll. 15 and 17 to Cú Roí's great wealth bring to mind *Amra Con Roí* where Cú Roí's poet, Ferchterne, sings his death-song and describes the many wondrous gifts bestowed upon him by his master while he lived:

> Cú Roí has given me ten farmlands,
> The son of Dáire (has given) ten bondwomen, ten golden bridles,
> Ten steeds with honour, ten fringed garments,
> Ten cauldrons, ten ivory-hilted swords ... [153]

Lines 5 and 12 ("Scarce have I heard of a man of greater misfortune") refer to the betrayal of Cú Roí by his wife Bláthnait and his murder by Cú Chulainn in both versions of *Aided Con Roí*.[154] In *Aided II*, Ferchterne the poet avenges his master by grasping Bláthnait and leaping over a cliff, taking her with him to their deaths. Their graves, says the tale are still there on the estuary of the river Shannon.[155]

Perhaps the most telling reference in *Marwnat Corroi* is that in l. 20 to Cú Roí's clashes with Cú Chulainn, the greatest of the legendary heroes of Ireland. As we have seen, the two heroes are bitter enemies in both versions of *Aided Con Roí*. Cú Roí defeats and humiliates Cú Chulainn in order to gain his share of the spoils of the Isle of Man and Cú Chulainn responds by seducing his wife and murdering him whilst he is unarmed.[156]

In the epic tale *Táin Bó Cúailnge* ("The Cattle-Raid of Cooley"), Cú Roí and Cu Chulainn are on opposite sides in the titanic struggle between the kingdoms of Connacht and Ulster. At one point, Cú Roí arrives to challenge Cú Chulainn to single combat, only to find him badly injured after a brutal encounter with another hero, Ferdiad. Unwilling to fight an injured man, Cú Roí takes on the magician-poet Amairgin in a battle where they hurl huge rocks at each other.[157] It has been argued that the mention in lines 20–21 of *Marwnat Corroi* of "frequent clashes"

---

151 Sims-Williams 1982, 251
152 Best 1905, 21–22
153 Henry 1995, 190–191
154 Best 1905, 23–27; Thurneysen 1913, 195–196
155 Best 1905, 31; Thurneyson 1913, 196
156 For a detailed discussion of their enmity, see Gray 2005
157 O'Rahilly 1967, 244–45

between Cú Roí and Cú Chulainn "for their borderlands" suggests that the Welsh poet was unfamiliar with Irish literature and geography because the two heroes "are never regarded as heroes of contiguous kingdoms".[158] However, in *Mesca Ulad* ("The Intoxication of the Ulstermen"), Cú Chulainn leads the army of Ulster into Cú Roí's kingdom of Munster and attacks and eventually destroys his fortress at Temuir Lúachra, which since then, says the tale, "has not been inhabited".[159] It seems clear to me that the author of *Marwnat Corroi* was familiar not only with some version of *Aided Con Roí* but also with *Mesca Ulad* and, possibly, other tales regarding the long-standing enmity between Cú Roí and Cú Chulainn.

This translation is based on Haycock with alternative readings and notes by Sims-Williams.[160]

From the fountain of wide ocean flows the tide,
it flows in, it ebbs, it smashes, it surges.
The death-song of Cú Roí has stirred me to grief;
sad the silencing of a man fierce by nature.
Scarce have I heard of a man of greater misfortune.   5
The son of Dáiri held the tiller on the Southern Ocean;
unsullied was his fame before his burial.

From the fountain of wide ocean, currents flow,
it flows in, it ebbs, it surges, it smashes.
The death-song of Cú Roí I sing: 10
sad the silencing of a man fierce by nature.
Scarce have I heard of a man of greater misfortune.

From the fountain of wide ocean, a deluge flows,
destructive currents charge and strike the shore.
The all-conquering one, great his wealth,   15
and after the Isle of Man, approaching homesteads,
do the monks know the eager hoard-lord?
Whilst he still lived, the swift, victorious one, fierce in morning battle,
(truly, tales from throughout the whole world are known to me)
there was conflict between Cú Roí and Cúchulainn   20
and frequent clashes for their borderlands;
the chief spearman of a suffering people broke.
The Lord has a fortress that shall neither fall nor quake:
blessed the soul who attains it.

---

158 Sims-Williams 1982, 251
159 Gantz 1981, 216–217; Koch 2003, 126
160 Haycock 2015, 467–477; Sims-Williams 1982, 248–50

40. Marwnat Dylan eil Ton ("The Death-Song of Dylan son of Wave")
(BT 67.8–17)

This poem deals with the death of Dylan eil Ton ("Sea son of Wave"), the son of Arianrhod and the twin brother of Lleu Llaw Gyffes in the Fourth Branch of the *Mabinogi*. Dylan was killed by his uncle Gofannon, the divine blacksmith of the family of Dôn, and his death-blow is named as one of the "Three Unfortunate Blows" of the Island of Britain.[161] This implies an underlying triad behind the story, but no such triad has survived.[162] The 9th–10th century *Stanzas of the Graves* tell us that Dylan's grave is at Llanfeuno, i.e. Clynnog Fawr on the Llŷn Peninsula and there is a huge rock on the shore nearby called *Maen Dylan* ("Dylan's Rock").[163]

The poem seems to describe Gofannon's trial by ordeal for the murder of his nephew by holding a bar of hot iron. The "ostler" awaiting the outcome so eagerly may be a mocking nickname for the divine smith.[164] This poem is almost certainly the work of Llywarch ap Llywelyn – the verb-forms *delis* and *swynas* in l. 2 ("upheld" and "conjured") are only found in his poems.[165] Llywarch also composed another poem describing his own trial by ordeal by iron bar for murder in Gwent or the Marches in about 1190.[166] (See Appendix I for a translation.)

> The one God, most exalted, the wisest wizard, greatest of rulers:
> What did the primordial metal uphold? who conjured it as trial by ordeal for the hand?
> Before him, who imposed peace as binding as a vice?
> The ostler awaits the outcome intently – he caused bitterness, an act of violence:
> stabbing Dylan, on a fatal shore, violence in the flowing waters.   5
> The wave of Ireland, and the wave of Man, and the wave of the Old North,
> and the wave of Britain, of splendid hosts, is fourth.
> I beseech the Father, God, the lord of the country that withholds nothing,
> Heavenly Creator, who will receive us in mercy.

41. Mydwyf Taliessin/Cunedaf ("I am Taliesin"/ "Cunedda")
(BT 69.9–70.16)

This poem is based on an oral composition describing events of c.AD 383–490, and so cannot be the work of the historical Taliesin but became attached to

---
161 Williams 1930, 77–78; Davies 2007, 54
162 Bromwich 2014, lxxii
163 Jarman 1982, 36; Bollard and Griffiths 2015, 16–7, 61–2
164 Haycock 2015, 486
165 Haycock 2015, 484
166 Jones and Jones 1991, poem 15, pp. 146–52; Jones 1992, 70; Andrews 2007, 35

the persona of the bard later in its transmission.[167] The date of the poem is still controversial – whilst John Koch regards it as a genuinely early piece, first written down in the period around AD 650, Marged Haycock assigns it to the 12th or 13th century.[168]

According to the *Historia Brittonum*, Cunedda was a 5th century chieftain who came from the Old North to Wales and won fame by driving Irish settlers out of north-west Wales.[169] He came to be viewed as the founder of the first royal dynasty of Gwynedd. His descendant, Cadwallon of Gwynedd, briefly conquered and ruled Northumbria in the years AD 633–5 and this may have been the impetus for recording the poem in manuscript.

> I am ardent Taliesin,
> I endow the world with song:
> praise-songs to the abundant wonders of the world
> between the high places, salt-sea and fresh water.
> Because of Cunedda's decline, there is fear and trembling 5
> in Caer Wair and Carlisle.
> Many will fear the attack,
> the wave-surge of fire, waves swamping the seas.
> Brave men will muster their comrades.
> Since he went to his sojourn in Heaven, 10
> the wind sighs among the ash-trees.
> His hounds [i.e. his warrriors] revelled in his presence,
> they kept the truce with the descendants of Coel,
> they give fine attire to poets skilled in bardic craft.
> It is Cunedda's death that I lament, that was lamented: 15
> there is lamentation for the stout defender, the staunch ally,
> invincible, noble in concerted battle,
> bound now in the deep, gaping grave.
> Question – where is the hard, bare grave
> of the man harder than bone to his foes? 20
> Lofty Cunedda, before the earth devoured him,
> his honour was maintained.
> A hundred times before the death of our guardian,
> they would bear away the men of Brynaich in battle.
> There would be a wailing for the fear and terror of him; 25
> a cold, sad journey to lay him in earth, his dire death.

---

167 Koch 2013a, 22, 32
168 Koch 2005, 7; Haycock 2015, 490
169 Morris 1980, 37

Like a swarm around the thicket's wattled barricade,
sheathing sword is cowardice worse than death.
I lament the sad sleep of death,
I lament for Cunedda's court, his shroud,   30
for the great sea-loch, for the swift current of ocean,
for herd and oven that I now lack.
Song-poets who disparage, I despise,
and others who sing praises I esteem.
A wonder in the fray with nine hundred steeds   35
before Cunedda's last Communion.
He gave me milch-cows in summer,
he gave me horses in winter;
he gave me sparkling wine and oil,
he gave me a troop of slaves against ill-luck.   40
He was tenacious, voracious in attack,
keen-eyed, a lion of a leader.
His enemy's land was left in ashes before Edern's son,
before the sore affliction of his death.
He was fierce, invincible, unyielding,   45
a surging wave of cruel death.
He bore his shield in the vanguard,
valiant men were his chieftains.
I am woken by lamentation and my wine-debt to the man of splendid deeds,
by the destruction of this descendant of Coel.   50

42. Marwnat Vthyr Pen[dragon] ("The Death-Song of Uthr Pendragon") (BT 71.6–72.8)

Another puzzling poem! Although the medieval title of the poem is quite clear, Uthr is not actually mentioned in it and any real connection with him seems somewhat tenuous. The poem divides into two distinct sections, possibly originally two separate poems. In the first half (ll. 1–24), a great warrior (presumably Uthr himself) boasts of his past prowess and victories. The emphasis on "It is I", "I am" certainly gives these lines a self-contained structure.[170] The second half (from l. 25 onwards) seems to be another of Taliesin's boastful poems, glorying in his poetic skills and his virtuosity as a harpist, piper and player of the ancient Welsh stringed instrument, the *crwth*.

---

170 Jones 2019, 136

In the 12th century, the traditional Welsh figure of *Uthr Pendragon* ("Chief of Dragons") became more widely known thanks to the major role given to him by Geoffrey of Monmouth in his *Historia Regum Britanniae* ("History of the Kings of Britain") published in 1136. Uthr was obviously an important character prior to Geoffrey of Monmouth and is mentioned in the early Arthurian poem *Pa Gur yv y Porthaur* ("What Man is the Gatekeeper")[171] which has been dated to the 10th or 11th century or, more precisely, to the period around 1100.[172] In Triad 28, Uthr is named as one of those involved in the "Three Great Enchantments" of the Island of Britain and this may refer to his famous shape-shifting in order to make love to Ygerna and so beget Arthur.[173]

> It is I who leads many hosts in battle:
> I would not yield between two war-bands without bloodletting.
> I am called "armed-in-blue":
> my ferocity was hostile to my foe.
> It is I who is a leader in the dark: 5
> may the guiding light transform me in the breach.
> I am a second Sawyl in the dreadful gloom:
> I would not yield without bloodletting between two war-bands.
> It is I who defended my stronghold
> to the death against the kinsmen of Casnur.   10
> I shed blood standing with Gwythur,
> with vigorous sword-strokes against the sons of Cawrnur.
> I have shared my stronghold:
> only a ninth part of my courage has Arthur.
> I have stormed a hundred fortresses,   15
> I have killed a hundred stewards,
> I have shared out a hundred mantles,
> I have cut off a hundred heads,
> I gave to Henben
> swords of great talismanic power.   20
> I made a truce,
> an iron door, a fire-break atop a mountain.
> In my bereavement, in my distress, once strong-thewed,
> I could not live but for my descendants.
>
> I am a poet, my skill is worthy of praise,   25
> may it be with the ravens and eagles and birds of prey;

---
171 Jarman 1982, 66; Roberts 1978, 296–309
172 Bromwich 2014, 513; Sims-Williams 1991b, 39
173 Bromwich 2014, 61

Afagddu – to him came just as much –
since fine men support themselves between two branches [or poles].
My desire was to ascend to the heavens,
far beyond the eagle, far beyond the fear of harm. 30
I am a poet, I am a harpist,
I am a piper, I am a *crwth*-player.
Seven score musicians
only equal the superb artistry of a single poet.
I was the destroyer with a shattered, lime-washed shield, 35
a bird swift on the wing.
To the Son, a poet-song,
to Mary, o Magician-Father,
my tongue to declaim my death-song.
The rampart of the world is rock, 40
when it is Britain's time – my sublime thoughts –
Ruler of Heaven, do not refuse my entreaties.

43. Kanu y Byt Mawr ("The Greater Song of the World")
(BT 79.8–80.6)

This poem forms a pair with *Kanu y Byt Bychan* (BT 80). It outlines an essentially Christian understanding of the cosmos, but partly drawing on ancient Roman and Greek sources. It may also betray some influence from Geoffrey of Monmouth's *Vita Merlini* ("Life of Merlin"), which dates to 1148–51.[174] There are some similarities between the esoteric knowledge claimed by Taliesin in our poem and that demonstrated by Telgesinus in the *Vita*.[175] At any rate, the poem offers the legendary Taliesin another opportunity to display the extent and depth of his learning!

I praise my Father,
my God, my sustainer,
who set spirit, through my head,
into my thoughts and mind.
He made for me, gladly, 5
my seven constituent elements:
from fire and earth,
and water and air,
and mist and flowers,
and the south wind. 10

---
174 Padel 2006, 38
175 Haycock 2015, 520–22; Walker 2011, 88–90

Secondly, the system of my senses
my Father designed for me:
one is that I breathe out,
two is that I draw breath,
three, that I cry out,
and four, that I taste,
and five, that I see,
and six, that I hear,
and seven, that I smell,
by all of which I shall come to the confining grave.
Seven heavens are there
above the wise man:
and three divisions in the oceans –
how restless they are!
How great a wonder it is
that the world is not uniform.

On high, God made
fine planets:
he made the sun,
he made the moon,
he made Mars,
and Mercury;
he made Venus,
he made the evening star,
he made the forbidding planet
and, seventh, Saturn.

The good God made
the five belts of the Earth –
as long as it will last.
One is freezing cold,
and two is cold,
and three has a heat
that breeds sickness;
four, Paradise,
welcomes people;
the fifth is temperate,
and feeds the world.

The earth was divided into three
according to another design:
first is Asia,   50
second is Africa,
third is Europe,
the realm of Christendom:
it will last until Judgment
when everything shall be judged.   55

He made my awen
that I might praise my king.
I am Taliesin
with the flowing eloquence of a wizard:
it will last until the end of time,   60
my praise for Elffin.

44. Kanu y Byt Bychan ("The Lesser Song of the World")
(BT 80.6–16)

Another essentially theological poem pondering the nature of the world but couched in a classic Taliesin-style challenge to the "poets of the world" to tell him (and us) how the cosmos is sustained. Taliesin provides his own answer – the world is sustained by the authors of the four Gospels and by the grace of the Holy Spirit. A great deal of academic ink has been spilled tracing the detailed philosophical and biblical background to the twenty-two lines of the poem.[176]

Skilfully have I sung, I shall sing
until the Day of Judgment.
I consider many things
which disquiet me.
I challenge the poets of the world –   5
since you will not tell me –
what sustains the world
so that it falls not into oblivion?
The world, if it fell,
onto what would it fall?   10
Who would support it?
The world, how vain it is

---

176 Haycock 2015, 526–535

if it falls into annihilation.
Yet, in truth,
how strange the world is,
that is falls not in that way.
The world, how singular it is,
how greatly does it shine!
John, Matthew,
Luke and Mark:
it is they that sustain the world
through the grace of the spirit.

PROPHETIC POEMS

Apart from *Armes Prydein Vawr* (s. 45) all the following translations of the prophetic poems in the Book of Taliesin (ss. 46–55) are based on the edited texts and translations of Marged Haycock.[1]

45. Armes Prydein Vawr ("The Greater Prophecy of Britain")
(Book of Taliesin 13.1–18.25)

The "Great Prophecy of Britain" is one of the longest poems in the Book of Taliesin and perhaps one of the most historically significant. It prophesies the coming of a great Pan-Celtic army and their allies to drive the Anglo-Saxons back into the sea and restore Welsh sovereignty over the Island of Britain. It is likely that the poem was composed c.AD 939–42 by a poet from Gwynedd inspired by the anti-English Viking leader Olaf Guthfrithsson of Dublin.[2] *Armes Prydein* is very much the product of the political situation at the time of its composition. It calls for resistance to English overlords and the heavy taxes imposed on the Welsh people by Athelstan, the first king of all the English. It is a rejection of the pro-English policies of Welsh princes such as Hywel Dda (who died in AD 950). *Armes Prydein* is the first in a long line of rallying cries by Welsh poets for their compatriots to throw off English oppression![3]

The poet rails against the English "tyrant" (i.e., Athelstan) and his stewards and tax-collectors. The Britons will be saved by the return of the great heroes of the past – Cynan Meiriadog, the legendary founder of Brittany, and of Cadwaladr of Gwynedd (ruled AD 655–664). These "sons of prophecy" appear in many of the other prophetic poems in the Book of Taliesin and figure in the prophecies of the bards throughout the medieval period. Their army will gather under the banner of Dewi Sant (St. David) and final victory will be ensured by his prayers and those of the saints.

Aber Peryddon (ll. 18, 71) was in Rockfield, a small village near Monmouth in south-east Wales, where the stewards of Cirencester would have had to cross the river Wye to gather their taxes in south Wales.[4] *Glywysing* (l. 99) is an ancient name for Glamorgan in south Wales and sometimes included Gwent.[5] *Gelli Gaer* (l. 197), also in Glamorgan, is the site of a sequence of Roman forts. *Manaw* (l. 172) was the old Welsh name for the area around Edinburgh on the south bank of the Firth of Forth.[6] The *Lego* and *Ailego* referred to in ll. 149 and 106 were once thought to

---

1 Haycock 2013
2 Charles-Edwards 2013, 533
3 Fulton 2019, 37
4 Williams 1955, xxx–xxxiv
5 Charles-Edwards 2013, 14
6 Charles-Edwards 2013, 5–6

be near Leicester but recent research favours Chester or Caerleon (both former Roman legionary fortresses and both called *Cair Legion* in Old Welsh).[7] The "river of Ailego" (l. 106) could therefore be either the Dee or the Usk.

The translation is based on the text edited by Ifor Williams and the rendering into modern Welsh by Gwyn Thomas with reference to the translation by Breeze.[8]

1

Awen foretells that they will hurry,
we will have riches and property and peace
and a far-reaching realm and generous lords
and after conflict, settlement in every place.
Fierce men, staunch in wrathful, vicious battle,   5
swift in attack, stubborn in defence!
Warriors will scatter the foreigners as far as Durham,
they will make merry after despoiling.
There will be a covenant between the Welsh and the Norse of Dublin,
the Irish of Ireland, Man and Pictland.   10
The men of Cornwall and Strathclyde will be welcomed by us.
When the Britons triumph, only the dregs will remain.
Long foretold is the time of the coming
of kings and their rightful possession of this island.
The men of the North will have the place of honour around them,   15
in the centre of the army they will charge in the front rank.
Myrddin foretells that they will strike
in Aber Peryddon the stewards of the tyrant:
and although their customs differ, they will lament death!
Of one mind and will shall they attack.   20
The stewards may gather their taxes,
but in the armies of the Welsh, none would pay
(a noble man is he who utters this)
none would come, none would pay under such duress.

2

Son of Mary, powerful of word, why did the Welsh not burst out   25
against the overlordship of the English and their overweening pride?
Begone you scavengers of Vortigern of Gwynedd!
The foreigners will be driven into exile,
none will take them in, they will have no toe-hold,
they will wonder why they wander at every river's mouth.   30

---

7 Breeze 1997, 15–17; Charles-Edwards 2013, 531
8 Williams 1955; Thomas 1970, 143–151; Breeze 1997, 210–15

When they bought Thanet through lying deception
with Horsa and Hengist, scarce was their nobility!
Ignoble was their gain at our expense
and after treacherous slaughter, churls now wear a crown!
Drinking of much mead means drunkenness,   35
the death of many means want,
wounds mean tears for women,
harsh lordship means heartbreak,
a world turned upside-down means grief
when the scavengers of Thanet are our kings.   40
May the Trinity shield us from the intended blow –
namely the destruction of the Britons and the settling of Saxons.
Better that the English retreat into exile
than that the Welsh should be landless.

3

Son of Mary, powerful of word, why do they not burst out,   45
the Welsh, against the infamy of nobles and lords?
Retinue warriors, patrons, they complain as one,
they are of one song, of one counsel, of one mind.
It is not from pride that they do not speak:
but, for fear of shame, they will reject every compromise.   50
To God and to Dewi they dedicate themselves –
may the deceit of the foreigners be revenged upon them,
they who commit atrocities for want of a home.
The Welsh and the English will meet in battle,
on every hand they will deal out destruction and strife,   55
great armies will test each other's mettle.
And on the hillside, blades and battle-cry and strength.
And on both banks of Wye, shout for shout around the gleaming pool
and a banner abandoned and a fierce onslaught.
And as food for wolves will the English fall.   60
The retinue warriors of the Welsh will form ranks as one man.
Spearpoints at the backsides of the palefaces, it will go ill with them!
Stewards, as payment for their deception, will wallow in blood,
their army will stand in a quagmire of blood around them.
Others will flee on foot through the woods,   65
through the fortress ramparts, like foxes they will flee
from war, never to return to the land of Britain.
They will slip away in sadness like the sea.

4

The stewards of Cirencester, bitterly they will lament,
some in the valley, some on the hill, this they cannot deny –   70
their coming to Aber Peryddon was not propitious.
Instead of taxes, they collected wounds.
With eighteen thousand men they attack:
(what a mockery!) except for four, none will return!
To their wives they will tell tales of war   75
and they their wives will wash their blood-soaked tunics.
The retinue warriors of the Welsh, reckless of their lives,
the men of south Wales will safeguard their taxes.
With sharp, well-honed blades they will cut them down;
No doctor will benefit from their actions.   80
The armies of Cadwaladr will come in power and splendour;
may the Welsh arise, they will make war.
To inescapable death have the stewards come;
at the end of their taxes, they will know death.
Others they stabbed cruelly,   85
Never will their tribute of cattle ever see a paddock.

5

In wood, in field, in vale, on hill,
a "candle in the darkness" [i.e., a hero] will walk with us –
in every attack, Cynan will be in the van,
("Woe is us", will cry the English before the Britons).   90
Cadwaladr will be a spear among his lords,
by cunning strategy will he harry them.
When his troops fall on them across the border,
there will be agony and red blood on the cheeks of the foreigners.
After every challenge – fierce despoiling.   95
The English flee to Winchester, faster and faster they retreat.
Happy are the Welsh when they say:
"The Trinity has delivered us from our former torment."
Let neither Dyfed nor Glywysing tremble,
no further tribute will be paid to the stewards of the tyrant,   100
nor to the champions of the English, be they ever so fierce!
They will have no joy from drunkenness at our expense
without paying dearly (a bitter fate!) for all they get
with orphaned sons and helpless ones.
By the intercession of Dewi and the British saints,   105
to the river of Ailego the foreigners will flee.

6

Awen foretells that the day will come
when the men of Wessex will come to one council,
one opinion, one purpose with the flame-bearing men of Mercia
hoping to dishonour our splendid hosts, 110
[line missing here ......]
the foreigners will wander aimlessly and flee all day:
he will not know where he goes, where, where he may stay.
The Britons will hasten to attack like a mountain bear
to avenge the blood of kinsmen.
A ceaseless flood of spear-thrusts will there be, 115
no man will spare the body of his opponent,
a head split in two, the brains spilled;
there will be widowed women and riderless horses,
there will be frightful wailing before the onslaught of warriors
and many a mangled hand before the armies part. 120
The heralds of Death will meet
when corpses stand up in the press of battle.
The taxes and daily tribute will be avenged
on the many envoys and their treacherous troops.
The Welsh will prevail in battle, 125
well-prepared, of one voice, united, of one faith.

7

The Welsh will prevail to rekindle battle
and peoples of many countries will gather
and will raise the sacred banner of Dewi
to lead the Irish under the linen flag. 130
And with us the Norse of Dublin will stand;
when they come to battle, they will not break their word.
They will ask the English what they sought,
how much land they held by right,
where are their lands from which they set forth, 135
where are their kin, from which region have they come?
Since the time of Vortigern they have trampled us.
They will not gain the inheritance of our kinsmen by right
nor by the privilege of our saints – why do they trample them?
nor by the commandments of Dewi – why did they break them? 140
The Welsh will withstand them when they face them,
no foreigner will stir from where they stand

until they have paid seven-fold for what they have done.
And death, doubtless, will be the price of their wrong-doing
and paid through the power of the kinsmen of Garmon [the Irish]   145
for four years and four hundred.

8

Fierce, long-haired men, masters of weapon blows,
will come from Ireland to harry the English.
An eager fleet will come from Lego
that will wreak destruction, tear armies apart.   150
From Dumbarton will come brave, staunch men
to harry them from Britain of the splendid hosts.
From Brittany will come handsome allies,
warriors on war-horses, without respect for their enemies.
Dishonour will come to the English from every quarter,   155
their age is past, they will have no homeland.
Death will come to the black hordes,
a deadly flux and sore wounds.
After gold and silver and precious things,
may the bushes be their refuge for their bad faith,   160
may the sea, may an anchor be their counsellors,
may blood, may death be their companions.
Cynan and Cadwaladr, powerful in our armies,
will be honoured until Doomsday – good fortune to them!
Two powerful lords of wise counsel [Cynan and Cadwaladr],   165
two of the Lord's elect trampling the English,
two generous ones, two gift-givers, cattle-raiders,
two fearless ones, eager, united in destiny, of one creed,
two defenders of Britain of the splendid hosts,
two bears, no dishonour will ever befall them in daily strife.   170

9

Druids foretell all that will come to pass.
All lands from Manaw to Brittany will be in their hands,
all from Dyfed to Thanet will belong to them;
from the Roman wall to the Forth and its estuaries;
their lordship will extend over Erechwydd.   175
For the English there will be no return.
The Irish will return to their kinsfolk.
May the Welsh arise, strong their armies –

hosts gathered around ale and revelry of warriors
and God's own kings, who kept the faith. 180
The men of Wessex will take to ships: the tumult will cease
and there will be reconciliation between Cynan and his kinsman [Cadwaladr].
The English will not be called warriors
but the beggars and hucksters of Cadwaladr.
Every Welshman's son will be merry and eloquent 185
because the tormentors of the island will die in swarms;
because their corpses will stand upright in the press of battle
all the way to Sandwich, a blessed thing!
The foreigners go into exile
returning to their compatriots one after the other. 190
The English ride at anchor on the sea every day:
the praiseworthy Welsh will triumph until Doomsday.
They will seek no sorcerers nor grasping poets;
there will be no other prophecy for this island but this.
Let us beseech God who created heaven and earth: 195
"May Dewi be a leader to our warriors
in the affliction of Gelli Gaer." He who stands for the God
who perishes not, flees not, retreats not,
withers not, fails not, turns not aside, wavers not.

46. Daronwy

(BT 28.22–29.20)

This poem is initially concerned with the protective power of two trees – *Daronwy* ("the oak tree of Goronwy"?) and the magic staff of Mathonwy, which is evidently now planted and flowering on the banks of the Gwyllionwy ("the wild water"). Goronwy is too common a name to be certain who is meant, but the magic staff of Mathonwy immediately brings to mind the staff of Math son of Mathonwy used in the Fourth Branch of the *Mabinogi* to transform Gwydion and Gilfaethwy into wild animals and to test the virginity of Arianrhod.[9] As a personal name, Daronwy appears in the triads as one of three oppressions that afflicted Anglesey and it has also been suggested that there may be a connection with a possible oak-goddess, *Daron*, and the Gaulish oak-goddesses called the *Dervonnae*.[10]

The promised redeemers here are Cynan and Rhun son of Maelgwn. The "four chief ruling powers and a fifth no worse" in ll. 20–1 probably refer to the Romans,

---

9 Haycock 2013, 24; Williams 1930, 74–7
10 Bromwich 2014, 52; Williams 1945, 36; Beck 2009, 479–80

Irish, English, Vikings and, finally, the Normans.[11] *Dineidyn* (l. 50) and *Caer Rhian* (l. 49) refer respectively to Edinburgh and Llanrhian in Pembrokeshire. *Caer Rhywg* is a legendary name, part of a submerged kingdom between St David's and Ireland, and *Dineidwg* seems to have been created to provide a suitable rhyme.[12] The poem probably dates to the 12th or early 13th century.

God saved Noah
from the Flood, its far-flung radiance,
swiftly it spread,
attacking beyond the billowing ocean.
What tree could be greater   5
than Daronwy?
He will give succour to those
around Noah's Ark.

There is a secret greater still –
the radiance of the men of Goronwy,   10
few know it.
The magic staff of Mathonwy,
as it grows in the wood,
bears abundant fruit
on the banks of the Gwyllionwy.   15
Cynan will secure them
when he assumes rightful power.
They will come once more
over ebb and shore –
four chief ruling powers   20
and a fifth no worse:
many strong men
bent on Britain.
Women shall speak boldly,
freemen will be enslaved;   25
an upsurge of longing
for mead and horsemanship.

Two haughty stubborn ones shall come:
a widow and a slender wife
with their iron wing   30
loudly reproaching men.

---
11 Haycock 2013, 35
12 Haycock 2013, 39–40

Champions will come
from the region around Rome.
Fitting will be the poem to them,
the poem in their praise will shoot forth leaves   35
like oaks and thorns –
it will be fitting in song.

A hound to sniff, a stallion to snort,
a bullock to gore, a hog to root.
And fifth, a blessed young animal that Jesus made   40
like Adam [...]
Wild woodland creatures, fine to behold,
whilst they lived, whilst he lived.
When the Welsh seek a hiding place
in a foreign region, who will love them now?   45

I leapt a leap by manifest fate –
who has had good fortune will not have bad.
The battle-fog of Rhun – it will threaten attack
between Caer Rhian and Caer Rhywg,
between Dineidyn and Dineidwg.   50
Sight sees a clear end in view:
when fire spreads swiftly, smoke rises
and our lord God shall defend us.

47. Glaswawt Taliessin ("The Verdant Song of Taliesin")
(BT 30.24–31.20)

This poem is concerned with Gwynedd and prophesises a great battle on the banks of the river Conwy where "vengeance shall be wrought" (l. 8). It may contain references to an actual battle fought on the Conwy in AD 881 to avenge the killing of Rhodri Mawr by the English in AD 878. It also refers in l. 26 to the "lineage of Anarawd". Anarawd son of Rhodri Mawr died in AD 916 and this has led some scholars to date the poem to the period AD 916–46 or to AD 940 or very shortly after.[13] Others are less certain.[14]

The poem has also been seen as an early reference to the battle of Brunanburh (l. 28) fought in AD 937 between Athelstan of England and an alliance of Dublin

---
13 Williams 1957, 23; Breeze 1999, 79
14 Haycock 2013, 43

Vikings, Scots and Strathclyde Britons.[15] On balance, the line in question probably does refer to Brunanburh.[16] How soon after any of these events the poem was composed is very much an open question.

> Mounted envoys have come to me, how noble they are!
> It causes me pain, the whole of my mind.
> Usual, an oar in salt-sea – Beli's drink –
> usual, a light shield in dead of night,
> usual, wrath and destruction from a feasting fortress   5
> and nine hundred stewards shall die.
> In May on Menai, there shall be a scene of carnage,
> there shall be worse on the river Conwy, vengeance shall be wrought.
> Cold the death brought about (a ready reward)
> by fierce iron, a shattering blow.   10
> Three fair, invincible ones – plunging, laden heavy with hosts –
> three fleets on the sea-flood, an omen before Judgment,
> three evening battles for three rightful rulers of their lands:
> death will necessitate a tomb
> (all three, three by three, three sins)   15
> and will judge the uplands of Eryri.
> A host of English, a second of Vikings, a third one grievous:
> in Wales, wives await widowhood.
> Before the roar of Cynan, fire will erupt.
> Cadwaladr will cause them grief;   20
> he will trample hill and sedge,
> thatch and roof, he will put houses to the torch.
> A strange thing shall come about:
> a man coupling with his brother's daughter.
> They [the Welsh] shall summon a man hard as steel   25
> from the lineage of Anarawd:
> from him shall spring
> the bloodstained warrior of the battle of Brunanburgh
> who will spare neither kin,
> nor cousin nor brother.   30
> At the blast of the warrior's horn
> nine hundred shall grieve,
> because of the powerful, cruel man
> (declaimed by the greenness of the verdant song)
> he will swoop on those who anger him.   35

---

15 Haycock 2013, 13
16 Haycock 2013, 57

48. Kychwedyl a'm Dodyw ("News has come to me")
(BT 38.11–40.3)

This poem is truly a puzzle! It seems at first glance to be a song in praise of Mabon and Owain ab Urien, but scholars disagree on the interpretation. Marged Haycock sees Mabon as a historical character – Mabon ab Idno, a first cousin of the Urien Rheged of the historical Taliesin poems – and interprets the poem as a form of propaganda using figures from the Old North.[17] John Koch sees these references as being to the Romano-British god Maponos and suggests that the Coeling dynasty of Rheged (Urien, Owain etc.) had an ancestral devotion to the deity.[18] Rheged, either side of the Solway Firth is well-attested archaeologically as the centre of the Romano-British cult of Maponos.[19] Jenny Rowland sees Owain ab Urien in the poem as the physical incarnation of the god Maponos and cites the late story of his being the son of the daughter of the king of Annwfn who seduces his father Urien in the guise of the washer at the ford.[20] It seems possible that traditionally the eldest son of the Coeling dynasty in Rheged was regarded in some way as the embodiment or incarnation of the god Maponos.

Calchfynydd (l. 1, lit. "chalk mountain") may possibly refer to Wessex. *Roda* (l. 21) may be the river Roden in Shropshire and *Rhun* (l. 46) may refer to Gwynedd. All the other place-names are obscure, though *cyfylchi* (in Pengyfylchi) means a round fort or hill-fort.

> News has come to me from Calchfynydd:
> of disgrace in the Southland, praiseworthy plunder.
> He gives wealth to brave men, cruelty to the world:
> populous is the floor of his valley, joyful possession,
> generous to hordes of people, generous to strange lands,   5
> battle-oppressor, the wrath of his realm.
> Rare is the Welshman who would say:
> "May the men of Dyfed raid the cattle of the son of Idno"
> and nothing ventured where he comes,
> despite payment of a hundred cows for a single calf.   10
> Your foes avoid the marches of your land;
> like burning fire, haze is found where he may be.
> When we sought safe passage across the land of Gwyddno,
> a slender, white corpse was there between the shingle and gravel.
> When the waters ebbed from the land of the Strathclyde men,   15

---

17 Haycock 2013, 3, 61
18 Koch 2003, 368–9
19 Ross 1967, 363–4; Rivet and Smith 1979, 395–6
20 Rowland 1990, 233–4

no cow lowed for her calf.
Mabon stood out – he from another realm –
when Owain defended his region's cattle.
Battle at Dumbarton ford, battle at Ywen,
battle at Gosulwyd and they wailed loudly; 20
battle before the men of Roda, white as snow,
black, gleaming spears [...].
Battle at a lightsome place, battle-leader sprung from battle-lineage,
shields in hand, a battle-enclosure in the attack.
Whoever saw Mabon on a light-maned, fierce steed 25
as they mingled before the cattle of Rheged –
unless they flew on wings
from Mabon, they could not escape without leaving corpses.
Hawk-stoop to the fray and battle-giving,
the irresistible destroyer came from Mabon's land; 30
when Owain attacked for his father's cattle,
lime and wax of shields splintered.
No spoils for anyone plundering the hillside cattle
[...] for fear of stubborn, bloody men,
for fear of the fiery, powerful warrior, 35
for fear of the resolute rising to battle,
for fear of gore on flesh,
for fear of widespread grief.

News has come to me from the cleared lands of the South,
the king well-spoken of, the best of generous men, 40
no plaintiffs need beseech you.
Around the border-ford, around the alder-marsh, his warbands:
when war was incited, dragon-lord king,
uneasy but not panicked were the cattle before Mabon.
By dint of the clash of a pack of warriors, 45
there were maggoty corpses, plunder in Rhun,
there was joy for ravens;
loud the stories of men after the sufferings of battle
that the shield of Owain was not unharmed:
dented was the shield of the resister [Owain] in the battle-tumult. 50
He would drive no cattle without causing a bloody face
on the blood-soaked men of the cattle-track, with great cruelty:
blood washed over their heads
and spattered their ashen faces.

Bloodstained was the golden saddle of he who mustered the host; 55
the herd requested by the men of Gwent was scattered.
A herd before fierce battle and fierce strangers,
the herd of Pengyfylchi, spear on shields,
the mighty, fearless ones, blades brandished overhead.
A battle before Owain the great, great his cruelty, 60
at mid-day men fell defending the land.
When Owain attacked for the blessed land of Erechwydd,
his reward from his father was carousel.

49. Dygogan Awen ("The Awen Foretells")
(BT 70.16–71.6)

Another poem foretelling the coming of a saviour, this time *Llyminawc* ("The Leaper", l. 15). Ifor Williams believed that this was a reference to Gruffudd ap Cynan, one of the most famous of the princes of Gwynedd, who died in 1137.[21] However, more recent opinion is divided and there can be no certainty on the matter. As a result, Ifor Williams's dating of the poem to c.1075–1100 is also uncertain.[22] Haycock makes a strong case for assigning the poem to Llywarch ap Llywelyn in the late 12th or early 13th century.[23]

Beli (l. 6) refers to the legendary figure Beli Mawr ap Mynogan, from whom, according to medieval tradition, the Romans conquered Britain.[24] Some scholars identify him with the Gaulish god *Belenos* or *Belinos*; others trace his origin to *Belgios* claimed by the Iron Age tribe of the Belgae as their divine ancestor.[25] The name Caswallon is derived from *Cassivellaunos*, an actual Iron Age king who led an alliance of Celtic tribes against Julius Caesar in 54 BC. His exploits left their mark on later Welsh legend where he is credited with driving Caesar out of Britain.[26] The *Iago* mentioned in l. 6 may be the 6th century Iago son of Beli, father of Cadwallon of Gwynedd or Iago son of Idwal Foel who ruled Gwynedd from c.AD 950 to AD 979.[27] The promontory of *Blathaon* (l. 8) is either John O' Groats or Duncansby Head in Caithness.[28]

---

21 Williams 1955, xxxvii
22 Haycock 2013, 84
23 Haycock 2013, 18, 92
24 Bromwich 2014, 288–9
25 Bromwich 2014 loc. cit.; Koch 1990
26 Bromwich 2014, 305–6
27 Haycock 2013, 92–3
28 Bromwich 2014, 251

The awen foretells that they will hasten;
we shall have wealth and riches and peace
and wide dominion and eloquent, ardent leaders;
and, after conflict, settlement in every place.

Beli's seven sons had arisen: 5
like the flooding tide, Caswallon and Lludd would envelop them;
the final blow was the loss of Iago from Pictland:
it will become a land seething with tumult to the ends of Blathaon,
weary their horses,
their reins hang loose,   10
the country despoiled by mongrel borderers.

The Welsh shall all lose the means of generosity
by their allegiance to the rule of vassals.

A Leaper shall come,
a man eager   15
for the conquest of Anglesey
and the ruination of Gwynedd –
from hinterland to heartland,
from beginning to end,
and the seizure of her hostages.   20

He whose honour is steadfast
bows to none –
neither the Welsh nor Saxons.

A Man from Hiding shall come
who will wreak bloody havoc   25
and battle on the foreigners.

Another shall come –
far-ranging his hosts,
a joy to the Britons!

50. Kein Gyfedwch ("A Fine Carousal")
(BT 72.9–22)

This is one of the strongest candidates among the prophetic poems as the work of Llywarch ap Llywelyn.[29] Normandy is named (l. 16) as is a succession of eight Norman kings of England, including Richard I, and culminating in the Lynx, which is certainly a reference to Henry III, crowned in 2016. Marged Haycock suggests that this poem may date to the 1220s and that the hero of the "wall-girt fortress" in l. 2 is Llywelyn the Great who built Dolbadarn Castle in a spectacular location on a neck of land between Llyn Peris and Llyn Padarn in Snowdonia.[30]

> A fine carousal around two lakes, a lake of drink around the company,
> a wall-girt fortress[31], a fortress free from challenge (so it was written),
> a splendid retreat before him – he of the well-built stronghold reinforced in stone.
> Dragon-like above the places of drinking vessels,
> strong drink in golden horns, golden horns in hands, hands awash with foam. 5
> The lord, the champion, I entreat you now, victorious Beli,
> son of King Manogan,
> who will defend his rights.
> The Honey-Isle of Beli:
> he would be her rightful ruler. 10
> Five leaders will come –
> of the Irish-Picts,
> of the warlike sinners,
> of a race of scum.
> Five others will come 15
> from Normandy.
> Sixth, a king will hold sway
> from seed-time to harvest.[32]
> Her seventh –
> whose grave is overseas. 20
> Eighth, a Lynx shall come:
> he will not protect the old.[33]
> By the loud cries of the people
> shall Eryri be summoned;

---

29 (Haycock 2013, 18)
30 (Haycock 2013, 98–107)
31 Dolbadarn Castle?
32 Richard I?
33 Henry III?

he [the Lynx] will not come easily. 25
Let us entreat the Hebrew God³⁴
that there shall be for us with the Lord
a home in Heaven to come.

51. Rydyrchafwy Duw ("May God raise")
(BT 72.23–73.19)

This poem foretells of an alliance between the men of the northern kingdoms of Gwynedd and Powys with Ceredigion against some un-named enemy in the far west of Wales and may preserve a memory of some previous alliance recycled for propaganda purposes.³⁵ The Cadwallon who returns across the sea and sets up his headquarters in the "uplands of Nefon" (l. 18) is a reference to Cadwallon son of Cadfan, the king of Gwynedd who in alliance with Penda of Mercia invaded and conquered the kingdom of Northumbria in AD 633.³⁶ In the *Triads of the Island of Britain*, his warriors are named as one of the "Three Faithful Warbands" who were with him seven years in exile in Ireland.³⁷ Idwal in l. 21 is Idwal Foel, another king of Gwynedd, killed by the English in AD 942.³⁸

Glyn Aeron (l. 10) is near Aberaeron in Ceredigion and *Llys Llonion* (l. 12) refers to the modern Llanion near Pembroke Dock, where according to Triad 26, the great white Otherwordly sow, Henwen, gave birth to a grain of barley and a bee "And therefore Llonion is the best place for barley".³⁹ *Din Clud* in l. 15 is Dumbarton Rock in Strathclyde. *Din Maerud*, *Din Daryfon*, *Din Rhieddon* and "the uplands of Nefon" (l. 18) are otherwise unknown and may be the creation of the poet.⁴⁰ The "ford on the *Taradr*" refers to somewhere between the source of the river Worm in Herefordshire and its confluence with the Wye and *Porth Wygyr* is Cemaes Bay in Anglesey.⁴¹

Ifor Williams dated this poem to the period AD 942–50, but others extend the possible date-range to the 960s.⁴²

May God raise over the Britons
the emblem of joy of the hosts of Anglesey.

---
34 "Eloi" in the text.
35 Haycock 2013, 13
36 Charles-Edwards 2013, 389–90
37 Bromwich 2014, 62
38 Haycock 2013, 110
39 Bromwich 2014, 50
40 Haycock 2013, 118–19
41 Coe 2001, 800–1; Haycock 2013, 122
42 Williams 1967, xxvi–vii; Charles-Edwards 2013, 661

The battle of the men of Gwynedd, swift war-bands
of shining fame, hostages taken in every skirmish.
The men of Powys shall come, praised in song as eager warriors, 5
fierce men who shall overcome false laws.
In two hosts shall they advance, they shall be as one,
united in instinct as in word, orderly and worthy.
The men of Ceredigion will do their fair share in battle.
When you see hardened men about the Vale of Aeron, 10
when Tywi and Teifi run sluggish in their grief,
they shall make battle in haste for the court of Llonion.
Those who stood firm went silent to their death in droves.
Fortresses are no protection from their swift warriors:
neither Din Clud, Din Maerud, Din Daryfon, 15
nor Din Rhieddon would be wholly unassailable.
When Cadwallon came across the Irish Sea,
he re-founded a court in the uplands of Nefon [or "of the Lord"].
The poets, I shall soon hear of their woes:
how eager the body of cavalry around Chester 20
and Idwal's vengeance on the Palefaces,
and playing ball with Saxon heads.
May he wreak havoc on the Speckled Cat and her foreign allies,
from the ford on the Taradr to Porth Wygyr in Anglesey,
the gentle young man, the refuge of his people. 25
When honey and clover are seized,
they will leave off their uproar and contention:
it is no unhappy thing to incite wrath against the foe.
May God raise over the Britons
the emblem of joy of the hosts of Anglesey. 30

52. Gwawt Lud y Mawr ("The Greater Song of Praise to Lludd")
(BT 74.12–76.14)

A long and difficult poem, which, despite its title, makes no reference at all to Lludd. The poem again foretells the return of the great redeemers Cadwaladr and Cynan (l. 29). The central tranche (ll. 45–103) describes the sufferings the Welsh will endure before their promised redemption.[43] The mention of *Seithennin* in l. 86, though based on an amendment of the original manuscript reading, refers to the story of the drowning of Cantre'r Gwaelod, also called Maes Gwyddno, the

---

43 Haycock 3013, 123–4

legendary lost kingdom submerged beneath Cardigan Bay.[44] In the earliest version of the story preserved in poem 39 in the 13th century Black Book of Carmarthen, it seems that the disaster is somehow the fault of the maiden Mererid.[45] Later versions blame the drunkenness of Seithennin for the deluge that drowned the kingdom. There is no mention of Cristin in the story and this and other references in the poem to people and places remain obscure, though Creuddyn (l. 77) is on the river Conwy.[46]

The Speckled Cow of l. 49 may be connected with *Yr Ych Brych* ("The Brindled Ox") that appears in *Preideu Annnwfyn* (s. 36, l. 39) as *yr ych brych, bras y penrwy* ("the Brindled Ox with his stout collar").

Although the influence of Llywarch ap Llywelyn has been discerned in the language of this poem, it also contains linguistic features that may suggest a pre-1100 date.[47] Could it be that the poem was adapted, rather than composed by the court poet?

1

The best song has praised
the eight hosts who give succour.
Monday, they shall come,
ravaging shall they go.
Tuesday, they will deal out   5
suffering to our enemies.
Wednesday, they shall possess
coveted splendour.
Thursday, they will let out
eager songs of praise.   10
Friday, day of triumph,
they will wallow in men's blood.
Saturday …
Sunday, in truth
and without doubt, they shall come.   15
Five ships and five hundred
(as poets will recount)
of Picts in turmoil,
without number.
Britons in turmoil,   20
thirst for gold-gifting,

---

44 Haycock 2013, 145
45 Jarman 1982, 80–1
46 Haycock 2013, 145
47 Haycock 2013, 15

like worthy trees
cruel enemies will come;
everyone shall come to the Lord
who redeems the apple trees [of Eden?].   25

2

A prophecy has come to pass,
a long cry in the face of arrogant bravado:
the long-standing, renowned, consistent prophecy
concerning Cadwaladr and Cynan.
The world is of little worth   30
when the sun's warmth has been destroyed.

3

The druid foretells
what has been and will be of value.
The cloud that crosses the uplands
(it is the poet who perceives its meaning)   35
will weep like a torrent
on the bellies of the hills.
Strong-voiced is the marten, well-fed the stag,
Britons act on counsel.
To the Britons shall come   40
blood from splendid, fierce fighting;
after gold and golden jewels,
Anglesey and Llŷn are laid waste
and refuge is taken in Eryri.

4

A perfect seer foretells   45
a refuge laid waste.
The Welsh of perfect language
will alter their speech.
The Speckled Cow shall come into being
who will wreak vengeance.   50
At mid-day, it will bellow,
at mid-night, it will incite turmoil,
ploughland shall be in ferment,
our sacred places will be destroyed.
A song of grief will be sung   55

around the boundaries of Britain.
They shall come of one mind
to throw back the foreign sea-raiders.
Let there be true joy
in this lamentable world. 60
A snare ...
to Dolaethwy he went.
The leader makes ample demands –
horse-herding without foaling,
no rustling of calving cows, 65
a world without succour.
A world that shall be laid waste and wretched,
the fate of cuckoos is sealed –
opulence is taken for ascetic purity –
puny men with deceitful hearts. 70
The cantering leader of hosts,
horse-breaker, pathfinder.
Knives cannot pierce
the swords of cowards.
I would not have wished on them 75
the one greedy for the wealth of the homestead,
nor on men the wrong-doing at Creuddyn.
Welsh, Angles, Irish, Picts,
the Welsh as swift as loss.
Wooden horses [ships] shall set forth on the sea: 80
the men of the North, killers, raiders,
of wrathful lineage on the cruel sea,
sprung from the stock of Adam.
A starling will be brought forth to arouse
a murder of ravens from a sacred retinue. 85
Slow to move is the war-band of Seithennin
anchored at sea against Cristin.
An attack by sea, an attack from the mountain,
an attack by sea, the wastelands in ferment,
wood, plain, hollow and hill. 90
Every entreaty goes utterly unheeded
by the lord of every place.
There will be turmoil and tumult
and widespread suffering:
vengeful acts mixed with constant, fine promises. 95

By angering the powerful Creator, holy God,
a long time before Judgment Day,
the day shall come
when a resurgence will be proclaimed
and an end to the fine land of Ireland.   100
To Britain shall come resurrection:
a Briton of noble Roman stock.
I shall be judged because of a troubled day.

5

The poet-seers foretell
in the land of the lost;   105
the druids foretell
that while there is sea, while there are Britons,
summer shall have no fine weather;
the lords shall be enfeebled
who, by deceiving the weak, come to them   110
from overseas …
A host of a thousand at the Judgment of sacred Britain,
and in the borderlands of the furnace.
Let me not fall into the forbidding swamp
of the inhabitants of the furthest depths of Hell,   115
the flaming lineage of Cain set trembling
by the Lord of the eternal realm.

53. Yn wir dymbi Romani kar ("Truly shall the kinsman of the Romans come") (BT 76.15–78.18)

Another poem that foretells the return of the hero Cadwaladr to free his people from their subservience to their enemies and to drive the Angles back across the sea. The "Thursday Battle" (l. 25) to be fought at a place called *Cyminawd* (possibly near Montgomery in mid-Wales) is a recurrent theme in bardic prophecies throughout the Middle Ages. The rivers Tern and Trannon are near Shrewsbury and Caersws (Powys) respectively.[48] The Battle of Winwæd refers to the defeat of Penda of Mercia near Leeds in AD 655. *Elfed* was the Welsh kingdom to the east of Leeds, the modern Elmet.

The figure of Hiriell as a promised saviour of the Welsh (l. 63) was well-known to the court poets of the 12th and 13th centuries. The Britons are often portrayed

---

48 Haycock 2013, 165–7

in the prophetic poems as the inheritors of the Roman mantle, especially in terms of their Christianity. The reference in line 42 to *kessarogyon* ("people of Caesar") may mean Romans or Britons.[49]

The language of the poem bears similarities with that of *Armes Prydein*, dated c.AD 939–42.[50]

1

Truly shall the kinsman of the Romans come,
unique among the sons of men, his nature Other.
Before him shall be heard great wailing
and an army and a bloodbath for his foes,
the blare of horns and commotion of a host   5
who'd pierce all they charged in sword-fight –
ravens and eagles craving blood.
His pathway like a ferocious bear, invincible in attack,
Cadwaladr in splendour, dazzling and bright,
the defender of armies in desolate lands.   10

2

Truly shall come from beyond the waves
the promised one, foretold from the beginning of time:
the victorious years of pomp, privileges due to majesty.
A winter coalition, on a grim passage he will steer ships,
the true, splendid leader of bondmen, his largesse like the flooding sea. 15
At high tide on the crest of waves,
he will bring swan-like steeds from the decks of ships.
A Bear and a worthy Lion, from glinting pools
their fierce warriors will strike with bloody javelins.
Suffering shall seek them out, a warning against wrong-doing,   20
before his fury and his overwhelming power.
Though the boar-like warriors may fall, they will fell hosts on the ramparts;
in battle, Cadwaladr is radiant, bright of fame.
May a Dragon arise in the southland
with a youth who battled by day on a Thursday.   25

3

Truly shall come a generous man of courage,
he of great glory shall have resounding praise,

---

49 Haycock 2013, 10–12
50 Haycock 2013, 16, 164

far-ranging, with many hosts, his dominion broad,
until seven nations serve the king of Gwynedd,
until all uproar shall pass away and cease. 30
A kindly king set over peoples united –
the scourge of Angles on their way from exile,
their descendants shall slink back across the sea.

4

Truly shall come the rightful heir to Anglesey,
a renowned Dragon, deliverer of the Britons, 35
a leader of hosts, commanding armoured warriors.
Profound is the prophecy of the sage's wizards
that they shall pitch their tents on Tern and Trannon,
that they shall harbour a desire to seize Anglesey,
until that long passage made from Ireland 40
by a fair and famous man, liberating the successors of Caesar.

5

The shaper of this prophecy foretells the horror of war
(I know the cause of battle on the Winwæd),
a Bear of south Wales threatening Gwynedd,
fighting for the glory of luxurious wealth: 45
the gracious drinking of liquor, the generous provision
for gift-giving at Winter Calends in the cleared lands.
May they lock their shields in battle, in sword-strife,
in Cadwaladr's contention against the lord of Gwynedd.

6

Truly this will come about, will come to pass: 50
The English all in chaos, their possessions ours,
seeing their pale, freckled men in flight
between arrow shafts and pale iron.
They will be summoned back to sea, expelled at spear-point,
they will quiver on the ocean, over the wide waters, 55
salt-seas and islands shall be their only refuge.

7

Truly shall come from beyond the Severn
the long-awaited one of Britain, the longed-for king,
a generous leader of armies drawn from many lineages,

the one worthy of a kingdom, cool in the face of hostility. 60
The people of the world shall indeed be joyful,
a dynasty of splendid men shall own dominions.
Hiriell will blaze in the land above the Severn.
The gathering of the Welsh shall be splendid, fearless;
may they go joyful into battle for Cadwaladr, 65
to the loud acclamation of poets, a battle of rare renown.

8

Truly shall be brought
both his army and his ships,
his driving back of shields,
exchanging blows with spears. 70
And, after gallant battle,
his will shall be done.
May he make his circuit around Britain,
may he blaze, the one famous in battle,
a Dragon who will not hide, 75
whatever may befall him.
No light ambition
is the conquest of Dyfed.
He will carry tribulation
beyond the Solway Firth; 80
a lord, a giver of gifts,
shall rule in Elfed;
a generous one of cunning strategy,
his struggles titanic.
I will praise him to the skies, 85
Cadwaladr, vigorous in strife.

54. Ymarwar Lludd Bychan ("The Short Poem on the Discussion of Lludd") (BT 78.18–79.8)

The legendary background to this poem is to be found in *Cyfranc Lludd a Llefelys* ("The Tale of Lludd and Llefelys"), the shortest of the four native tales in the *Mabinogion*. It tells of Three Oppressions (*gormesoedd*) afflicting Britain – the *Coraniaid*, foreign invaders who can hear anything spoken in the open air; a dreadful, supernatural scream every May Eve that renders people, beasts and the land barren and the mysterious disappearance of all food supplies. Lludd, the king of Britain, takes the advice of his brother Llefelys, king of France, and rids the island of the Oppressions.[51] It seems that the story in its current form dates to about 1200.[52] It also appears in the Triad 36 and in 13th century Welsh translations of Geoffrey of Monmouth's *Historia Regum Britanniae* ("History of the Kings of Britain").[53]

Based on the references to Arabs and Saracens in l. 9, the poem has been dated to the 11th century against the background of the First Crusade (1096–9).[54] However, the use of the phrase *Ymarwar Llut a Lleuelys* in a poem of c.1216 by Llywelyn Fardd II makes it clear that the story was known by this same name at that time.[55] The references to Arabs and Saracens could as well date to the time of the Third Crusade (1189–92) as the First and brings us nearer to the fixed point of c.1216. On balance, the poem probably dates to the late-12th or early-13th century. The name for Albion used in the poem (*y Wen Ynys*, l. 12) is only found elsewhere in Welsh translations of Geoffrey on Monmouth's *Historia Regum Britanniae* ("The History of the Kings of Britain"), the earliest of which dates to the mid-13th century.[56]

In the name of the Trinity, wise in charity,
a host of multitudes, cruel and horrific,
shall conquer Britain, the most exalted of islands;
men from Asia and the land of Cafis,
a people of wicked intention, from an unknown land.   5
A nation who couch their lances, marauders from the sea,
with trailing surcoats – who compares to them,
intent, though lordless, on a hostile deed?
To Europeans, Arabs, Saracens,
to all in bondage, Christ brought sure and steadfast deliverance   10
even before the discussion of Lludd and Llefelys.
The ruler of Albion shall tremble
before a Roman lord, beautiful and terrible.
Not fine nor wise is a king of overbearing speech,
who often saw, as I saw, strange-tongued foreigners.   15
The swamp of hell shall be prepared for them, a lantern-path,
before the stout warrior, roaring like wildfire.
May I deserve the Son of Grace, of fluent speech.
The Welsh shall gnash their teeth, wage war on slaves;

---

51 Roberts 1975; Davies 2007, 111–15
52 Stephens 1998, 131
53 Bromwich 2014, 90
54 Griffiths 1937, 125–8; Haycock 2013, 177
55 Randell 2009, 277
56 Haycock 2013, 177; Randell 2009, 272

I worry, and I wonder what their fate shall be, 20
those Britons who rose up in Wessex.

55. Darogan Kadwaladyr ("The Prophecy of Cadwaladr")
(BT 80.17–27)

The title of this poem speaks for itself! It is incomplete and fills the final, rather worn and grubby page of the manuscript. Cadwaladr, when he comes, will not need to lurk in the mountains of Eryri (Snowdonia); he will pitch his camp in the lowlands of Britain (ll. 5–6). The poem displays some of the word-use associated with Llywarch ap Llywelyn and may therefore date to the late-12th or early-13th century.[57]

A swift, clamorous horseman
on both wings of battle,
spreading terror, dealing death to unworthy men
and withdrawing to his fastness in Eryri.
But when Cadwaladr comes, he will pitch 5
his headquarters in Britain's lowland meadows.
... [MS illegible]
and I myself shall be joyful.
The Saxon will come to demand consumption
of the heroes' portion by voracious marauders. 10
A wife shall be yoked by her manservant,
old enmity will not sit well with me ...
the heroes' portion [eaten] by marauders ...
Have you seen my cousin with my brother?
I saw a slender corpse and ravens on flesh 15
and another soaked in blood, felled by wrongful sword-stroke
on the banks of ...

---
57 Haycock 2013, 188

MEDIEVAL PROSE TALES

56. Culhwch ac Olwen ("Culhwch and Olwen")
MS: White Book of Rhydderch (Peniarth 4), cols. 459–62

Culhwch ac Olwen is the oldest Arthurian prose tale. It concerns the quest of the hero, Culhwch, to marry Olwen ("White Track") the daughter of Ysbaddaden Chief of Giants. Ysbaddaden sets Culhwch a plethora of dangerous tasks to perform if he is to win the hand of his daughter. To complete the tasks, the hero enlists the help of his cousin Arthur and his men. In this scene, Culhwch has arrived at Arthur's court in Celliwig in Cornwall and seeks recognition of their blood relationship by requesting that Arthur cut his hair – an ancient ritual of bonding. Culhwch then asks for help in his quest in the name of all of Arthur's warriors and all the ladies of the court. The very long list includes Taliesin, who presumably acts as court-bard.

The date of *Culhwch ac Olwen* has long been a matter of debate among scholars. Whilst the original editors dated the tale to *c.*1100, others have suggested the period before *c.*1134 or even as late as 1155–1197.[1] The most recent reconsideration of the evidence places *Culhwch ac Olwen* firmly in the 1090s.[2]

This translation is based on the Welsh edition and notes by Bromwich and Evans with amendments from Davies.[3]

"Culhwch names his Boon"
"Name what you will."
"I shall. I would have my hair cut."
"You shall have that."
Arthur took a golden comb and shears with silver loops and combed his hair. And he asked who he was. Arthur said "My heart warms to you. I know you are descended of my blood. Tell me who you are." "I shall. Culhwch son of Cilydd son of the Cyleddon Wledig by Goleuddydd daughter of Anlawdd Wledig, my mother." Arthur said "That is true. You are a cousin to me. Name what you will, and you shall have it, whatever your mouth and tongue may name."
"By God's truth and by the truth of your kingdom?"
"You shall have it gladly."
"I call on you to obtain for me Olwen daughter of Ysbaddaden Chief of Giants; and I make this binding on all your warriors."

---
1 Bromwich and Evans 1997, xxvii, lxxxvii; Charles-Edwards 2010, 49; Rodway 2005, 43
2 Breeze 2018, 49
3 Bromwich and Evans 1997, 6–8; Davies 2007, 183–189

And he made his boon binding on Cai and Bedwyr, and Greidol Gallddofydd, and Gwythyr son of Greidol … and Gwyn son of Nudd … And Samson Dry-lip and Taliesin Chief of Bards, and Manawydan son of Llŷr … And on Gwenhwyfar, Chief Queen of this Island … and Creiddylad daughter of Lludd of the Silver Hand, the most majestic maiden who ever lived in the Three Islands of Britain – and for her Gwythyr son of Greidol and Gwyn son of Nudd fight every Mayday for ever until Judgment Day … And by all these Culhwch son of Cilydd claimed his boon."

57. Branwen Uerch Lyr ("Branwen daughter of Llŷr: The Second Branch of the Mabinogi")
(White Book of Rhydderch (Peniarth 4), cols. 56–60)

The Second Branch of the *Mabinogi* is the story of Branwen, sister of Brân the Blessed, king of Britain. She is married to the Irish king, Matholwch, and whilst in Ireland is badly treated and abused. She teaches a starling to speak, who carries the news to Brân and a terrible war ensues in Ireland at the end of which on the British side only Branwen, Brân and seven of his warriors survive. Here, the survivors return to the "Island of the Mighty". The episode of the eighty-year feast in Gwales is also referred to in *Golychaf-i Gulwyd/Kadeir Taliessin* (s.26) lines 3–4, where Taliesin sings "in a feast over sad drink … before the sons of Llŷr at Aber Henfelen". The "Three Fortunate Concealments" and the "Three Unfortunate Disclosures" also appear in Triad 37.[4]

The date of the Four Branches has long been an open question.[5] In his original edition, Ifor Williams assigned the tales to the period around 1060; others have placed them in the period between about 1050 and 1120.[6] The most recent analysis dates them to the 1120s or early 1130s.[7]

This translation is based on the edition by Ifor Williams with amendments from Sioned Davies.[8]

"The men who set out from Ireland"
"And through that, such victory as there was came to the men of the Island of the Mighty. And there was no victory through that, except the escape of seven men and Brân the Blessed wounded in the foot with a poisoned spear. The names of the seven who escaped: Pryderi, Manawydan, Glifiau son of Taran, Taliesin, and Ynog, Griddieu son of Muriel, and Heilyn son of Gwyn the Old."

---

4 Bromwich 2014, 94.
5 Sims-Williams 1991a, 61.
6 Williams 1930, xli; Charles-Edwards 1971, 298
7 Breeze 2018, 58
8 Williams 1930, 44–7; Davies 2007, 32–4

"And then Brân the Blessed caused his head to be cut off "And take the head," he said, "and carry it to the White Hill in London and bury it with its face towards France. And you will be a long time on the road: in Harlech you shall be seven years at feasting with the Birds of Rhiannon to sing to you. And the head shall be as good company to you as ever it was when it was on me. And in Gwales in Penfro you will stay eighty years. And as long as you do not open the door towards Aber Henfelen, towards Cornwall, you may stay there and the head along with you and incorrupt. And from the time you open that door, you cannot remain there. Make for London to bury the head. And so set out, over to the other side." And then his head was severed, and they set out with the head, those seven men, and Branwen as the eighth. And at Aber Alaw in Talebolion they made land. And then they sat and rested. She looked at Ireland and at the Island of the Mighty, what she could see of them. "Oh, by the son of God," she said, "alas that I was ever born. Two good islands have been devastated because of me." And she gave a great sigh and thereupon her heart broke. And a square grave was made for her, and she was buried there on the banks of the Alaw."

"And at that, the seven men walked towards Harlech and the head with them . . . And then they reached Harlech and began to sit and take their fill of food and drink. And as they began to eat and drink, three birds came and began singing to them such a song that every song they had ever heard was unlovely compared to it. And they had to peer far out to sea to see them. And yet the song was clear to them as if they were there alongside them. And at that feast they stayed seven years."

"And at the end of the seventh year, they set out for Gwales in Penfro. And there they had a fair, kingly place above the sea and there was a large hall and to the hall they went. Two doors they saw wide open; the third door was shut, the one that faced Cornwall. "See there," said Manawydan, "the door we must not open." And that night they stayed there lacking nothing and well content. And despite what they had seen of grief in their presence, and what they had suffered themselves, no memory came to them, neither of that nor of any grief in the world. And there they spent the eighty years so that they did not know that they had ever spent a happier or more lovely time than that. They were no less at ease than when they had come there and none of them could tell my looking at each other how long they had been there. And the presence of the head there was no more irksome to them than when Brân the Blessed had been alive among them. And from those eighty years, this was named the Assembly of the Noble Head. (The Assembly of Branwen and Matholwch was that which went to Ireland)."

"This is what Heilyn son of Gwyn did one day. "A curse upon my beard," he said, "if I do not open the door to see whether what is said of it is true." He opened the door and looked at Cornwall, and at Aber Henfelen. And as he looked, they were aware of all the losses they had ever suffered and all the kinsmen and companions they had lost and every evil that had befallen them as if it had befallen them then and there; and most of all for their lord. And from that moment on, they could not rest but set out for London with the head. However long they were on the road, they came to London and buried the head on the White Hill."

"And that was one of the Three Fortunate Concealments when it was concealed and one of the Three Unfortunate Disclosures when it was revealed; for no oppression would ever come across the sea to this island whilst the head lay in that hiding place. And that is what this tale tells of their adventure, and it is called "The men who set out from Ireland.""

EARLY MODERN PROSE TALES

58. Ystoria Taliesin by Elis Gruffydd
NLW 5276 (c.1529–1552)

Elis Gruffydd (c.1490–c.552), also known as the "Soldier of Calais", was a Tudor soldier, courtier, copyist, chronicler and translator. He was born at Llanasa in Flintshire in north-east Wales and was present at the Field of the Cloth of Gold, the famous meeting between Henry VIII of England and Francis I of France near Calais, in 1520. He returned to Calais as a soldier in 1529 and lived there for the rest of his life.

The "Story of Taliesin" originally formed one small episode in Elis Gruffydd's *Cronicl o Wech Oesoedd* ("Chronicle of Six Ages") a history of the world in Welsh from the Creation to his own day, the bulk of which remains unpublished. He tells us that the story was widespread in oral tradition throughout Wales in his own day and he makes clear reference to earlier written versions of the tale which, unfortunately, have not survived.[1]

This translation is based on Patrick Ford's edited Welsh text and notes.[2] The figures in square brackets refer to the line numbers in the original manuscript.

[1] Hereafter follows the tale of Gwion Bach, which is widespread in Wales.

[3] At the time of the beginning of [the reign of] Arthur, a noble man lived in the land called Penllyn, who was called Tegid Foel, whose patrimony as the story tells was the body of water today called Llyn Tegid. And this tale tells that he had a wife called Ceridwen who, so it is written, was skilled and learned in the triple arts, namely: magic, witchcraft and sorcery. Also, the writings reveal that Tegid and Ceridwen had a male heir who was exceedingly ugly of countenance and looks and in behaviour, called Morfran and, in the end, so dark was his complexion that he was named Afagddu.

[15] And on account of his wretched complexion, his mother took into herself great sadness, for she could clearly see that by no means or measure could her son be made acceptable among noble men unless he be possessed of qualities other than his looks. And to bring this matter about, she turned all her thought to the study of her arts to discover the best way that she could make him full of the spirit of prophecy and a great storyteller of the world to come hereafter. And after long labour in her

---
1 Ford 1992, 58; Williams 1957, 10.
2 Ford 1992

arts, she discovered that there was a way to achieve that very knowledge by virtue of the herbs of the earth and the effort and cunning of man; namely – to declare and name the same – by selecting and gathering a great amount of certain herbs of the earth at certain days and times and putting them all into a great cauldron with water and then set the cauldron on a fire, which had to be kindled constantly to boil the cauldron night and day for a year and day, by when, as she clearly perceived, three drops of all the virtues of the numerous herbs would leap out; and whichever person the three drops should land on, she perceived, would be extremely learned in various arts and full of the spirit of prophecy. And she also saw that the rest of the juice of these herbs – apart from the aforementioned three drops – would be the mightiest of all the mighty poisons of the world, which would shatter the cauldrons to pieces and pour the poison out onto the earth.

[40] And truly this story is irrational and contrary to faith and holiness. But, as before, the body of this tale clearly tells that she gathered great store of the herbs of the earth, which she put into the cauldron with water and set it on the fire. And the story tells that she took an old, blind man to stir and refine the cauldron. But the story tells us nothing of the name of this man anymore than it reveals who was the author of this tale. However, the tale does name the boy who acted as a guide for this man, Gwion Bach, whom Ceridwen set to kindle the fire beneath the cauldron. And in this manner, they all fulfilled their office, both in kindling the fire and in refining and stirring the cauldron with Ceridwen keeping it full of water and herbs for a year and a day.

[54] At the time appointed, Ceridwen took Morfran and set him close to the cauldron to receive the drops when the hour came for them to leap from the cauldron. Then Ceridwen set her buttocks down to rest and it came to pass that she fell asleep at the very time the three beneficial drops leapt from the cauldron, which fell on Gwion Bach, who had shoved Morfran from his place. And at that, the cauldron gave a piercing cry and burst with the power of the poison. And at that, Ceridwen awoke from her sleep like a person in a frenzy, which Gwion perceived, being so full of knowledge, and saw plainly that so venomous was her nature that she would execute him as soon as she learned the manner in which he had deprived her son of the beneficial drops. Accordingly, he took to his heels and fled. However, as soon as Ceridwen recovered from her frenzy, she questioned her son who revealed to her (by a long and tedious tale) the means by which Gwion had pushed him from the place where his mother had set him. On account of that, she ran from her house like a person in a frenzy in pursuit of Gwion Bach, who, as the narrative tells, saw her and fled away swiftly in the form of a hare. Consequently, she assumed the form of a black greyhound bitch and pursued it from place to place. And finally, after long

pursuit in various forms, so persistent was she [in her pursuit] of him that he was forced to flee into a barn in which was a large heap of winnowed wheat, and he immediately assumed the form of one of the ears among the grain. What Ceridwen did was assume the form of a tail-less black hen, so the story says, in which form she swallowed Gwion into her womb, where she carried him for nine months until she gave birth to him.

[83] But when she looked at him, having come into the world, she could not find it in her heart either to do him bodily harm by her own hand or to suffer anyone else to do so in her sight. And finally, she caused him to be placed in a coracle or skin bag which she caused to be made as snug and watertight [as possible] both above and below. In this she had the royal child ["edling"] placed and then thrown into the lake, as some books show, but others say that he was thrown into a river and [yet] others say that she had him thrown into the sea, from which place he was a long time afterwards retrieved, as this work will show in due course.

The story of the finding of Taliesin

[95] At the time that Maelgwn Gwynedd held his court at Degannwy Castle, the holy man called Cybi lived on Anglesey. And also at that time a wealthy squire lived near the fortress of Degannwy who, as the story tells, was called Gwyddno Garanhir, who had, the writings show, a fish weir on the banks of the river Conwy near the sea in which was caught every Nos Calan Gaeaf as much as ten pounds' worth of salmon. And the story tells how Gwyddno had a son named Elffin ap Gwyddno who was in service at the court of King Maelgwn. And the writings reveal that he was a gentlemanly, generous man and much loved among his companions, but the writings [also] show him to have been an extravagantly prodigal man, as are most courtiers. But whilst Gwyddno had the means, Elffin did not want for money to spend among his companions. And as Gwyddno's wealth began to diminish, he stopped supplying Elffin with money, who complained to his companions that he could no longer keep company and fellowship with them henceforth, due to his father having fallen into poverty.

[117] But, as before, he desired certain men of the court to go and ask for the fish from the weir as a gift to him against Nos Calan Gaeaf thereafter, which they did; to whom Gwyddno granted their request. And therefore when the day and time came, Elffin took certain of his servants with him and came to arrange and keep watch at the weir, which he kept from before flood-tide until lowest ebb. When Elffin and his people entered the arms of the weir, they could not see there head nor tail of a single young salmon, whose walls were customarily full on that night. But the story has it that he could see nothing then except some black shape in the bow-net.

[130] On account of this, he bowed his head and began to bewail his misfortune, saying as he turned his face towards home that his was the greatest misfortune and adversity of any man in the whole world. Then his thoughts turned to returning to see what was in the bow-net. There he found a coracle or skin bag covered above and below. Then he took his knife and cut the skin to reveal the forehead of a human being. As a soon as Elffin saw the forehead, he exclaimed "See, such a "tâl iesin"!" That is a "radiant brow". At these words, the royal child ["edling"] answered from the coracle "Taliesin! So be it!"

[142] Which, in the opinion of these people, was the spirit of Gwion Bach, who had been in the belly of Ceridwen, who having given birth had caused him to be thrown into the water or the sea as this work has shown previously, where he had been in the bag tossed on the ocean from the beginning of [the reign of] Arthur until about the beginning of [the reign of] Maelgwn, which was about forty years.

[149] This is truly far-removed from reason and good sense, but, as before I will follow the story that tells that Elffin took the bag and threw it across the back of one of his horses in a basket. From where Taliesin sang the stanzas called "Elffin's Solace". Then he spoke thus:

> Fair Elffin, cease your weeping;
> False hope never benefitted anyone;
> Never was caught in Gwyddno's weir
> As fair a catch as tonight's.[3]

[159] with various other stanzas that he sang to console Elffin on the way from there home. Thereafter, Elffin delivered his catch to his wife, who reared him dearly and with love.

[163] And from then on, Gwyddno's wealth multiplied better and better every day and day after day, as did his love and acceptance from the king, who a certain time after was keeping open court at Degannwy Castle at Christmas-tide with all the multitude of his lords of both degrees, spiritual and temporal, with a great and numerous abundance of knights and squires, among whom rose a conversation enquiring and speaking thus:

[171] "Is there in the whole world a king as wealthy as Maelgwn, to whom the heavenly Father has given as much as God has given to him of spiritual gifts, and primarily of good looks and fair countenance and gentility and strength, besides

---
3 Ford gives more verses from NLW 6209 in Notes, pp. 101–2.

all of the powers of his soul?" And with these gifts, they said that the Father had granted him a superior gift, which however surpassed all the other gifts, namely: the countenance and beauty, deportment and wisdom and chastity of his queen, in which virtues she surpassed all the ladies and noblewomen of the whole kingdom.

[181] And besides this, they asked themselves, who had braver men? faster horses? Who had lovelier and swifter horses and greyhounds? Who had more learned and wiser poets than those of Maelgwn, who at that time enjoyed great repute among the eminent men of the kingdom? And at that time, no-one fulfilled the office of those who are today called heralds, except men learned not only in the service of kings and princes, but also well-versed and proficient in genealogy and arms and the deeds of kings and princes, as well as of foreign kingdoms as of the ancestors of this kingdom, especially in the histories of the most exalted peers. Also, every one of them was required to be ready in their responses in various languages such as Latin, French, Welsh and English and in addition to this great storytellers and sound historians and skilled in poetry in order to be able to compose stanzas in verse in every one of these languages. And of these at this feast in Maelgwn's court were as many as twenty-four, and the chiefest of them was he they called Heinin Fardd.

[202] Therefore, when all had praised the king and his talents, it happened that Elffin spoke thus: "Truly, none can compete with a king but a king. But in truth, if he were not a king, I would say that I have a wife as chaste of body as any lady throughout the kingdom. And also I have a poet more learned than all the poets of the king."

[209] To whom, with a long tale, some of his companions revealed all of Elffin's boast, whom the king commanded to be put into a strong prison until he [the king] gain true knowledge of the chastity of his wife and the learning of his poet. And then Elffin was put into a tower of the castle with great shackles about his feet; and some people say that a silver shackle was placed on him, on account of his descent from the king's blood, who, the story tells, sent Rhun his son to test the chastity of Elffin's wife. And as the author reveals, Rhun was one of the most wanton men in the world. And the story tells moreover that no woman or maiden could escape without reproach if he once secured a moment to converse with her.

[222] And as Rhun hastened to Elffin's palace with his whole mind bent on defiling his wife, Taliesin warned his mistress (by a long narrative) of how the king had had his master imprisoned and how Rhun was hastening with the intention of violating her chastity. On this account, he caused his mistress to dress one of her kitchen

maids in her own clothing, which the noble lady did happily and without stinting, and covered her hands with the best rings she had received from her husband. And in this manner Taliesin caused his mistress to set her maid to sit at the table in the chamber ready for her supper, whom Taliesin transformed into the likeness of his mistress, and his mistress into that of the maid.

[235] And as they sat most beautifully at their supper in the aforementioned manner, Rhun suddenly appeared at Elffin's palace; who was taken in gladly, for all the servants knew him well. And hurriedly they ushered him into the chamber to their mistress, in whose likeness the maid arose from her supper and welcomed him gladly. And then she sat down again to supper and Rhun alongside her, who began bandying adulterous words with the maid, who kept the semblance of her mistress.

[245] And truly the tale tells how the maid became so drunk that she fell asleep, for the story has it that Rhun put a powder into her drink, which made her sleep so soundly (if the story can be believed) that she did not feel him cut her little finger from her hand, on which was Elffin's signet ring which he had sent as a sign to his wife a little before. And in this way, he did as he pleased with the girl and then took the finger with the ring on it as a gift to the king, to whom he demonstrated that he had violated her chastity by telling how he had cut off her finger as he left without waking her from her slumber.

[258] At these tidings the king took great delight. On that account, he sent for his council, to whom he related the whole tale from beginning to end, causing Elffin to be brought from the prison to be rebuked for his boast. And, at that, he said to Elffin thus: "Elffin, let it be known to you as a certainty that it is folly for any man in the world to give credence to his wife regarding the chastity of her body any further than he can see her. And so that you may be certain that your wife broke her marriage vows last night, see here her finger as a sign to you and your signet ring upon it, that he that lay with your wife cut from her hand as she slept, so that there is no means by which you can deny that your wife has broken her chastity.

[270] At this, Elffin said thus: "With your permission, honourable King, truly I cannot in any way deny my ring, for numerous people recognise it. But, truly, I will deny strenuously that the finger that has my ring around it was ever attached to my wife's hand, for certainly there are three remarkable things about it, none of which was ever on any of the fingers of my wife's hands. And the first of the three is surely, with your grace's permission, wherever my wife is now whether sitting, standing or lying down, that this ring would not fit her finger. And you can clearly see how difficult it is to push this ring over the tip of the little finger that was on the hand

from which this finger was cut. And the second thing is that truly my wife has never passed a Saturday since I have known her that she has not pared her nails before retiring to bed. And you can clearly see that the nail of this finger has not been cut for a month. And the third thing is truly that the hand from which this finger was cut has kneaded rye dough within three days of this finger being cut from its hand and I can truly affirm to your goodness that my wife has never kneaded rye dough since she has been my wife.

[292] And the story has it that the king took still greater umbrage with Elffin for resisting him so strongly regarding his wife's chastity. Consequently, the king ordered him to prison again saying that he would not be released from there until he truly proved the validity of his boast, as much regarding the skill of his poet as the chastity of his wife. They, all this time, were in Elffin's palace making merry until Taliesin revealed to his mistress how Elffin was in prison on their account. However, he urged her to be glad as he explained to her how he would go to Maelgwn's court to free his master. And she then asked him how he would set his master free. He replied thus:

[305] I shall travel on foot
and to the gate shall I come,
I shall make for the hall
and my poem shall I sing,
and my song of praise shall I declaim
and poets of the barons shall I check
before the chiefest,
I shall demand [justice]
and I shall defeat them.

And when poetic contention arises
in the presence of the lords
and a summons to musicians
for precise, harmonious poetry,
in the court of noblemen's sons,
carousing with Gwion,
some there are who will grow pale
from grief of great pain.

Their churlish words shall be silenced,
whatever may befall of ill, it shall be like Arthur (most generous of men)
with his long blades red

with the blood of noble men,
the work of a king on his enemies:
from noble men blood shall run
due to battle at wood's edge
brought from the distant North.

Let there be no grace nor good appearance
on Maelgwn Gwynedd,
and may his injustice
and his violence and arrogance be avenged at last;
for the actions of Rhun his heir,
may his lands be barren,
may his life be short;
may vengeance be long
on Maelgwn Gwynedd.

[339] And thereafter he took his leave of his mistress and came at last to Maelgwn's court, who in royal state was entering his hall to sit down to dinner, as was the wont of kings and princes at that time. And as soon as Taliesin entered the hall, he perceived a place he might sit in an out of the way corner beside the place where the poets and minstrels would have to pass to do their service and duty to the king (as is still customary in the courts) by proclaiming largesse on high feast and holidays, except that nowadays they proclaim in French.

[350] And so the time came for the poets or heralds to enter and proclaim the largesse and power and strength of the king. In they came, past the place where Taliesin crouched in the corner; who thrust out his lip at them and with his finger played "blerwm blerwm" on his lip. They paid little attention to him in passing by, but walked on until they came before the king, to whom they made their customary bow as was proper for them to do, uttering not a word but [instead] thrust out their lips and mocked the king by playing "blerwm blerwm" with their fingers on their lips just as they could see a young lad doing at them.

[362] The sight of this caused the king great amazement and surprise, thinking to himself that they were drunk on an excess of strong drink. As a result, he ordered one of the lords waiting at his table to approach them and demand that they call to mind and contemplation where they were and consider what they *should* do and what they *were* doing. Which the lord did gladly, but no faster did they desist in their inanity. Consequently, he sent a second time and a third to require them to leave the hall. And, at last, the king ordered one of his squires to strike the chiefest

of them a blow, namely Heinin Fardd. And the squire took up a platter and struck him on the head so that he collapsed onto his backside, from where he rose to his knees and begged for mercy of the king and his permission to explain that this defect had not come on them either through lack of learning nor drunkenness, but by virtue of some spirit in the hall. And then Heinin said "O honoured King, may your Grace know that it is not by the ardour of a concoction of excess of strong drink that we are mute and unable to talk (like drunken men) but by virtue of a spirit that sits in yonder corner in the form of a small man."

[386] From where the king ordered a squire to bring him, who went to the little nook where Taliesin sat and brought him before the king, who asked him what he was and where he had come from. He answered the king in verse, saying thus:

> I am general chief bard
> to Elffin,
> and my native land
> is the country of the cherubim.

[395] And then the king asked him what people called him; and he answered the king by saying:

> John the Divine
> called me Myrddin;
> now all kings
> call me Taliesin.

[403] And then the king asked him where he had been; and thereafter he recounted his history to the king, as follows hereafter in this work:

> I was with my Lord
> in highest heaven
> when Lucifer fell
> into deepest hell.
> I bore the banner
> before Alexander;
> I know the names of the stars
> from north to south.
> I was in the fortress of Gwydion
> in Tetragrammaton;
> I was in Canaan

when Absalom was slain;
I bore seeds
down the Vale of Hebron;
I was in the court of Deon[4]
before the birth of Gwydion;
I was a prophet
to Elijah and Enoch,
I was chief supervisor
of the work of the tower of Nimrod;
I was on the cross
with the son of merciful God;
I spent three sojourns
in the prison of Arianrhod;
I was in the ark
with Noah and Alpha;
I saw the destruction
of Sodom and Gomorra;
I was in Africa
before Rome was built;
I came here
to the survivors of Troy;
And I was with my Lord
in the manger of ox and ass;
And I gave strength to Moses
through the waters of Jordan;
I was in the sky
with Mary Madlen;
I received awen
from the cauldron of Ceridwen;
I was harper-bard
to Lleon of Llychlyn;[5]
I was on the White Hill
in the court of Cynfelyn,[6]
in stocks and shackles
for a year and a day;
I was enfolded
in the land of the Trinity;

---

4 or "the court of lords" or "of Dôn"
5 or "to the legions of Llychlyn"
6 Cunobelinos

I was learned
in all medical lore;
And I shall be until Judgement Day
on the face of the earth;
No-one knows what my flesh is –
whether meat or fish;
And I was indeed nine months
in the womb of Ceridwen the witch;
I was formerly Gwion Bach,
but now I am Taliesin.

[462] And the story goes that the king and his retinue wondered greatly at this poetry. And he sang then this poem to reveal to the king and his people the cause of his coming there and what he sought, as this poem reveals in this work hereafter:

Narrow-minded poets, I engage now in bardic contest,
I could never hide my bardic feats;
I would prophecy
to those who would listen;
I seek earnestly
to restore my loss,
to recue Elffin from his punishment,
[to release him] from the fortress of Degannwy.

My ruler shall tear from himself
the chains and shackles
of the chair of the fortress of Degannwy;
my pride is all-powerful,
worth three hundred songs and more
is the poem that I would sing;
the poet who does not know it
shall have neither spear,
nor stone, nor ring
nor a place in my bardic circle.

Elffin son of Gwyddno,
on account of his indiscreet remark,
is bound by thirteen locks
for praising his bardic teacher.
I, however, am Taliesin,

chief of the poets of the West,
and I shall release Elffin
from his golden shackles.

[493] The, as the writings show, he sang a supporting poem; when, it is said, such a tempest of wind arose that the king and his people thought that the castle would fall in on them. And on that account, the king caused Elffin to be escorted urgently from his prison and set before Taliesin. On that very spot, it is said, he sang a poem that opened the shackles about his feet. To my mind, only with the greatest difficulty could anyone believe this story to be true. Despite that, I shall follow the story and those of his poems that I have seen written down. Then he sang an ode called "Gorchestion y Beirdd" ("The Contentions of the Bards") which follows hereafter:

Who was the first man
that Alpha made?
What fair language
did the Lord make most lovely?

What food, what drink?
Who brought his raiment?
Who would deny
the cunning of a [whole] country?

Why is stone hard?
Why is the thorn sharp?
Who is as hard as rock
and as salty as salt?

Why is a nose ridged?
Why is a wheel round?
Why does the tongue declare
more than any [other] member?

[521] And then he composed this poem called "Cystwy y Beirdd" (The Chastisement of the Bards), which begins thus:

If you are a fierce poet
of contentious awen,
be not contentious
in the court of your king,

unless you know the name of *rimin*
and the name of *ramin*,
and the name of *rimiad*,
and the name of *ramiad*,
and the name of your forefather
before his baptism.

And the name of the barm [of poetry],
and the name of the elements,
and the name of your nation,
and the name of the province.
Retinue-poets above,
retinue-poets below;
my beloved is below
in the fetters of Arianrhod;
you, it is certain, can comprehend
nothing that my lips sing,
nor, doubtless, [tell] the difference
between truth and falsehood.
Petty poets of your own land,
why do you not flee?
No poet may silence me,
no respite shall he have
until he goes into the hiding place of the grave
under gravel and shale;
and he that listens to me,
may God give ear to him.

[553] And then follows the series of stanzas called "Bustl y Beirdd" (The Galling Diatribe against the Poets):

The common rhymesters, from corrupt habit,
use godless doggerel as their praise,
their custom is to lie;
they deride the innocent,
they violate married women,
they defile the sacred virgins of Mary;
their life and times they waste in vanity;
they carouse by night, they sleep by day,
the church they hate, the tavern they frequent;

they wander every village, every town, every land;
they give neither hospitality nor charity;
psalms and prayers they never recite;
they do not worship on the sabbath or holy days;
they do not fast for vigils or ember days.
Birds fly,
fish swim,
bees make honey,
insects crawl;
every living thing wanders
to seek its food,
except lazy rhymesters and thieves
and worthless Jews.
I do not revile your wandering minstrelsy,
(for God instituted it against wicked blasphemy)
but those who, leading it in corruption,
revile Jesus and his ministry.

[580] And once Taliesin had set his master free from his prison and vindicated the chastity of his mistress and silenced the poets (so that none of them could utter a single word), he asked Elffin to make a wager with the king that he had a horse swifter and fleeter of foot than all the horses of the king, which Elffin did. And on the day, time and place appointed, to the spot now called Morfa Rhianedd came the king and the people and twenty-four of the swiftest horses in his possession. Presently, after some deliberation, the course was set out and the horses set to run. To that spot came Taliesin with twenty-four rods of holly charred black, which he caused the boy riding his master's horse to thrust into his belt, commanding him to let all of the king's horses pull ahead of him and, as he overtook each horse in turn, to take one of the rods and strike each horse across its hind-quarters and then drop the rod on the ground and then to take another rod and do the same to each of the horses as he overtook them. He also gave the rider strict orders to be on the look-out without fail for the place where his horse should stumble and to throw his cap down on that spot.

[602] All of which the boy fulfilled, as well in giving each of the king's horses a rod-blow as in throwing his cap down where his own horse stumbled. To which place Taliesin brought his master after his horse had won the race. On that very spot, he caused Elffin to set men to dig a pit where, once they had dug into the earth to a certain depth, they found a large cauldron full of gold. At that moment, Taliesin said "Elffin, see, here is payment and reward for taking me out of the weir and

raising me from that day to this." In that very place stands a pool of water which, from that day to this, is called "Y Pyllbair" (Cauldron Pool).

[613] And after that, the king caused Taliesin to be brought before him and from him sought an account of the origins of human kind. Whereupon he composed the series of stanzas which follows hereafter, which is today called one of the Four Pillars of Poetry and which begins thus:

> Pantion created
> on the ground of the Vale of Hebron,
> with his blessed hands,
> I know, the image of Adam.

> He created beautifully
> in the court of Paradise,
> from a left rib he made
> the radiant female.

> Seven hours
> they kept the orchard
> before the importuning of Satan,
> the most ardent of suitors.

> From there were they driven,
> through ice and cold,
> to pass their lives
> in this world.

> To bear in anguish
> sons and daughters,
> to gain sovereignty
> over the land of Asia.

> One hundred and eighty
> in great anguish
> she bore, a mixed brood
> of males and females.

> And then without concealment
> she bore Abel
> and inconsolable Cain,
> the most irredeemable of men.

To Adam and his spouse
were given shovel and spade
to dig the earth
to win their bread.

And pure white wheat
to sow in ploughland,
to feed every mouth
until the final day.

Angelic permission
from our exalted Father
brought the seed of growth
to Eve.

She, however, hid
a tenth part of the gift
so that she did not sow completely
the entire garden.

The black rye was got
instead of good wheat
to show the waste
brought about by theft.

For this false turn,[7]
says Saturnus, all must
give their tithe
to God most high.

The cinnabar-red wine
was planted in broad daylight;
on a night of waxing moon
was planted white wine.

From the truly privileged wheat,
from the generous red wine
is made the delicate body
of Christ son of Alpha.

---

7 or "false handful" – a pun on "twrn" and "dwrn"!

The wafer-host is the flesh,
the wine the flowing blood,
and the words of the Trinity
consecrate it.

Every mystical book
of the work of Emmanuel
was brought by Raphael
to give to Adam

when he stood in foam
up to his neck[8]
in the waters of Jordan,
fasting his penitential fast.

Moses received
in the waters of Jordan
strength by virtue of the three
most remarkable rods.

Samson was given
in the tower of Babylon
all the arts
of the land of Asia.

I, however, received
in my bardic poetry
all the arts
of Europe and Africa.

And I know their journey,
their home and their licence,
the tribute owed to them, their fate
until the Final Day.

Oh, God! how wretchedly
with great lamentation
will the prophecy befall
the progeny of Troy!

---

8 lit. "over his jaws"

A coiled female serpent,[9]
proud and merciless,
golden her wings,
[shall come] from Germania.

She shall conquer
England and Pictland
from the shores of Scandinavia
to the Severn.

Then shall the Britons be
like captives
with the status of foreigners
in Saxony.

Their Lord they shall praise,
their language they shall keep,
their land they shall lose,
except wild Wales.

Until the day shall come,
after long penance,
when the two arrogant ones
shall be equally matched.

Then the Britons shall regain
their land and crown,
and the foreigners
shall vanish.

And then the words of the angel,
in peace and war,
shall make secure
Britannia.

[738] And after that, he recounted in verse various prophecies to the king regarding the world to come, of which there follow hereafter as many of them as I have seen in writing.[10]

---
9 or "armoured"
10 A list is given at Ford 1992, 131–32.

59. Hanes Taliesin by John Jones, Gellilyfdy
NLW Peniarth 111 (c.1607)

John Jones (c.1585–1657/58) of Gellilyfdy in Flintshire in north-east Wales was a life-long copyist and collector of ancient Welsh manuscripts. He travelled around Wales to copy manuscripts but much of his work was done whilst in the debtors' prisons at the Fleet in London and in Ludlow in the Welsh borders, then the administrative capital of Wales and the Marches. When he died in the Fleet Prison, there were several ancient manuscripts in his cell, but, thankfully, these were rescued by Robert Vaughan of Hengwrt near Dolgellau, the one-time owner of the Book of Taliesin itself. Jones's text dates to c.1607[11].

This translation is based on Patrick Ford's edited Welsh text and notes.[12] The figures in square brackets refer to the line numbers in the original manuscript.

[1] There was once a man in Penllyn called Tegid Foel and his ancestral home was in the middle of Llyn Tegid and his lawfully wedded wife was called Ceridwen. And of that wife was born a son called Morfran ap Tegid and a daughter called Creirfyw and she was the fairest maiden in all the world. And they had a brother who was the ugliest man in all the world, called Fagddu. And then Ceridwen thought that he was unlikely to gain acceptance among gentlemen by reason of his ugliness, unless he were possessed of some distinguished skills or knowledge – for this was at the beginning of [the reign of] Arthur and the Round Table.

[11] And then, by the arts of the books of Fferyllt, she ordained that a cauldron be boiled for her son [full] of awen and knowledge that his reputation might be enhanced by his knowledge and learning concerning the world to come.

[15] Then she began to boil the cauldron, which having once begun to boil, the boiling could not stop for a year and a day and until three blessed drops be obtained through the blessing of the Holy Spirit. And Gwion Bach, the son of a yeoman from Llanfair in Caereinion in Powys, she set to tend the cauldron and a blind man called Morda to kindle the fire under the cauldron and commanded him that he should not let the boiling cease until a year and a day had passed. And, from books of astronomers and by the hours of the planets, she [gathered] every day all manner of various virtuous herbs. And as Ceridwen gathered herbs one day, drawing towards the end of the year, it happened by accident that three drops fell from the virtuous water of the cauldron onto the finger of Gwion Bach and, due to their heat, he thrust his finger into his mouth. And so soon as he put those valuable

---
11 Ford 1992, 133
12 Ford 1992, 133–44

drops into his mouth, he knew beforehand all things that would come to pass. And he perceived clearly that his greatest care should be against the wiles of Ceridwen, for great was her knowledge: and from great fear he fled towards his own country. And the cauldron broke in two, for all the water was poisonous except for those three drops; so that it poisoned the horses of Gwyddno Garanhir who drank the water from the confluence to which the water from the cauldron ran. And, because of that, the confluence has ever since been called "Gwenwynfeirch Gwyddno" (The Poisoned Horses of Gwyddno).

[36] And, at that, Ceridwen came in and saw all her labour for a whole year lost and snatched up a wooden ladle and struck the blind man Morda on his head so that one of his eyes came out upon his cheek. He said: "Wickedly have you disfigured me and I innocent. You have not suffered loss on my account." "You have spoken truly," said Ceridwen "Gwion Bach it was who despoiled me." And she went running after him and he saw her and assumed the form of a hare and fled. She turned herself into a greyhound bitch and she turned him and drove him towards the river Aerwen. He then leapt into the river and turned himself into a fish and she in the form of a she-otter contended with him underwater until he was forced to turn into a bird and took to the air. And she turned into a hawk to pursue him and gave him no peace in the air. And, as she was closing in on him, he saw a heap of winnowed wheat on the floor of a barn and descended to the wheat and turned himself into one of the grains. And she then assumed the form of a crested black hen and went to the wheat and scratched him up with her feet and recognised him and swallowed him. And, as the story has it, she was nine months pregnant with him and, having given birth, she could not in her heart kill him because he was so fair, but instead enclosed him in a skin bag and threw him at the mercy of God into the sea on the twenty-ninth day of April.

[57] And at that time, Gwyddno's weir stood on the beach between Dyfi and Aberystwyth near his own castle. In that weir could be found a hundred pounds' worth [of fish] every May Eve. And at that time, Gwyddno had an only son called Elffin – one of the most graceless and profligate of young people and an oppression to his father, who thought him born at an evil hour. And by the urging of his counsellors, his farther gifted him that year's catch from the weir to see whether grace would come to him and establish harmony between them. And the next day, Elffin looked and there was nothing in it: but, as he left, he caught sight of a skin bag on the pole of the weir. And then one of the weir-keepers said to Elffin "You never were unhappy until tonight, for you have broken the innate virtue of the weir in which could be found a hundred pounds' worth every May Eve. And tonight, there was nothing but this scrap of skin." "What now?" said Elffin "perhaps

there is a hundred pounds' worth of goods in it." And the bag was opened and he who opened it saw the forehead of a boy-child and exclaimed to Elffin "Here is a radiant brow!" "Taliesin let him be," said Elffin and picked the boy up in his hands, bewailing his misfortune, and carried him crestfallen across his shoulder. And that very hour, he caused the horse to amble, which beforehand had cantered and led him as if he sat in the most comfortable chair in all the world. And soon after, the boy-child composed a poem of consolation and praise for Elffin and prophesied great honour for Elffin. And the consolation was as you see.

Elffin's Consolation

Elffin, cease your weeping,
let none revile his own,
false hope never benefitted anyone,
a man cannot see what feeds him,
the prayers of Cynllo shall not be in vain,
God will not break his promise;
never was caught in Gwyddno's weir
as fair a catch as tonight.

Elffin of remarkable qualities,
be not angry at your find;
although I am small in my cot,
my tongue has power.
Recalling the name of the Trinity,
you need not fear;
whilst I am here to protect you,
nothing may oppress you.

Fair Elffin, dry your cheeks,
there is no comfort in dejection;
although you thought you had no profit,
too much grief does no-one any good;
do not doubt the miracles of God,
although I am small, I am skilled.[13]
From the sea and the rivers
God sends good things to fortunate men.

---

13 "celfydd" can also mean "a magician" or "enchanter"

Elffin of agreeable nature,
do not lament so loudly,
better God than evil prophecy.
Although I am small and frail,
due to the seething ocean,
I shall ease your grief
better than sixty young salmons.
      Taliesin sang it.

[115] And this was the first song that Taliesin sang, to console Elffin in his sadness at losing the weir's catch and his belief that his was the greatest grievance and misfortune in all the world. And then Gwyddno Garanhir asked what he was, a man or spirit? And then he sang this narrative and spoke thus:

Hanes Taliesin

I am general chief bard to Elffin
and my native place is the land of cherubim,
the prophet John called me Myrddin,
now every king calls me Taliesin.

I was with my Lord in highest heaven,
when Lucifer fell into deepest hell.
I was in a banner before Alexander,
I know the names of the stars from North to South.

I was in the fortress of Gwydion with Tetragrammaton,
I brought seeds to the earth of the Vale of Hebron,
I was in Canaan when Absalom was slain,
I was in the court of Dôn before the birth of Gwydion.

I was a prophet to Elijah and Enoch,
I was on the wood of the cross with the son of merciful God,
I spent three sojourns in the prison of Arianrhod,
I was chief supervisor of the work of Nimrod's tower.

I was in the Ark with Noah and Alpha,
I saw the destruction of Sodom and Gomorra,
I was in Africa when Rome was built,
I came here to the survivors of Troy.

> I was with my Lord in the manger of the ox,
> I gave strength to Moses in the waters of Jordan,
> I was in the sky with Mary Magdalen,
> I received awen from the cauldron of Ceridwen.
>
> I was harper-bard to Lleon of Llychlyn,[14]
> I was on the White Hill with Cynfelyn,[15]
> I suffered starvation for the son of the virgin
> in stocks and shackles for year and a day.
>
> I had my rightful place in the land of the Trinity,
> no-one knows what my flesh is, meat or fish.
> I was teacher to the whole universe,
> I shall be on the face of the earth until Domesday.
>
> I was indeed nine months
> in the belly of Ceridwen the witch,
> I was formerly Gwion Bach;
> from now on, I shall be Taliesin.
>   Taliesin sang it.

[159] (John Jones' note: "Here are the stanzas that should be placed immediately after the Consolation of Elffin, in my opinion.")

[161] Here are the stanzas that Taliesin sang when he was found in the weir. Then Elffin brought Taliesin to the house of Gwyddno, his father. And Gwyddno asked him "Was the catch in the weir good?" He, for his part, told him that he had found a thing better than fish. "What was it?" said Gwyddno. "A poet," said Elffin. And then Gwyddno said "Alas, pitiful boy! What good will that do you?" Then Taliesin himself answered, saying "It will do him more good than the weir ever did you." Then Gwyddno asked him "Can you speak, small as you are?" Then Taliesin, for his part, answered, saying "I can speak of more than you can ask me." "Let me hear what you can say," said Gwyddno.

> Water is blessed a hundred-fold,
> man has true understanding,
> fitting it is to pray to God earnestly,
> for his blessings are unstinted.

---
14 Llychlyn – Scandinavia
15 Cunobelinos

> Three times was I born, I studied diligently,
> pitiful would it be for a man to seek
> all the arts of the world marshalled in my womb,
> because he who was, shall be again.
>
> I beseech my Lord for protection,
> I hail Him that skill may come from Him;
> for a relic of Mary's son, great is my longing,
> for the world every hour cleaves to him.
>
> God taught me to expect
> a true creature of heaven to be my protection.
> Skilful are the daily prayers of the saints,
> for the Lord God draws all to Himself.
> Taliesin sang it.

[190] Thus answered Taliesin the above questions.[16]

[The continuation of *Hanes Taliesin* beginning on p. 366 of the MS]

[192] And there Taliesin stayed until he was thirteen years old. And then Elffin ap Gwyddno was invited to the court of Maelgwn Gwynedd (for he was his uncle) and went. And there he praised Taliesin at the court of Maelgwn and then he was imprisoned until Taliesin came to set him free with his own poetry. There Taliesin composed a series of poetic stanzas before the twenty-three poets. From then on, he was called Taliesin Ben Beirdd (Taliesin Chief of Poets) and therefore called that poem "Bustl y Beirdd" (The Gall of the Poets), which follows hereafter:

> The common rhymesters, from corrupt habit,
> use immoral ditties as their praise;
> vain, fleeting poems do they declaim,
> their custom is to lie;
> the commandments and laws of God they break,
> they defile lawfully wedded wives,
> they satirize the innocent,
> their life and times they waste in vanity;
> they carouse by night, they sleep by day,
> idly and without labour they become fat,

---

16 Here, John Jones inserts a series of four poems from *Llyfr Taliesin*. The prose tale is taken up again on p. 366 of the MS.

the church they hate, the tavern they seek out,
they do not use a psalter or recite a pater,
hospitality and charity they give to none,
they disseminate all senseless speech,
every mortal sin they praise,
every village, every town, every land they wander,
in every sin of pride they lead the way;
the commandments of the Trinity they despise,
they do not worship on the sabbath or the holy days;
they do not concern themselves with preparing for death;
excess of foods they guzzle,
they pay neither tithes nor offerings to God,
the commandments of God they do not fulfil,
saints' days and ember days they do not heed,
those who keep the commandments they deride;
Birds fly,
fish swim,
bees make honey,
insects crawl;
every living thing wanders to seek its food,
except lazy rhymesters, fools and worthless thieves.
I do not revile your wandering minstrelsy,
(for God instituted it against blasphemy)
except for those who revel in corruption,
mocking Jesus and his ministry.

[237] John Jones' note: "The name of Taliesin begins the line that followed that which came before: and that which comes after followed the name of Taliesin with no difference in the world between what went before and that which follows, so that that which follows brought to an end part of that which went before: therefore, I will begin that which follows with a special letter in case they be separate things."[17]

Be silent, you false, boastful, bungling bards!
You do not know truth from lies;
I am a seer
and a general chief poet
who knows every horseblock[18]
at the borders of the West.

---
17 No, I don't understand it, either!
18 Or "whoreson"

If I release Elffin
from the depths of the stone tower,
I shall disclose to the king
all its secrets.
A strange creature shall come
to Morfa Rhianedd,
its fur shall be golden,
golden its eyes and teeth,
and he shall make an end
of Maelgwn Gwynedd.

I was first made in the image of fair man
in the court of Ceridwen among the ears of corn;
although I was small, once seen I was taken in gently,
I was large on the floor of the place to which I was led;
precious was my lodging, the sweet-voiced awen caused it.
A lawless one, bereft of kindred, tormented me –
an old, unhappy witch; when she grew furious,
terrible was her intent as she attacked.

I fled with all my might,
I fled as a frog,
I fled as a crow,
barely resting;
I fled fiercely,
I fled as a chain,
I fled as a young roe-buck
that hid in a thicket;
I fled as wolf-cub
of wolves in wilderness;
I fled as a mistle-thrush
who consulted omens;
I fled as a fox,
a swift shape-shifting!
I fled as a marten,
little did it avail!
I fled as a squirrel,
a vain concealment!
I fled as a stag's antler
that leapt freely.

I fled as iron thrust into fire,
I fled as a spearhead, the bane of him who chose it!
I fled as a bull who fought ardently,
I fled as a bristling boar that held a dyke,
I fled as a white grain of fine wheat;
at the edge of the winnowing sheet, she ensnared me.
She seemed as big as a brood-mare in foal
that swells like a splendid ship.
Into a dark bag she set me,
into the ocean that carried me away;
a fine thing it was when I was praised,
[when] the Lord God set me free.
      Taliesin sang it.

[302] Pantion created
on the ground of the Vale of Hebron,
with his blessed hands,
the handsome form of Adam.

Five centuries,
with little shelter,
he lay there,
before he was endowed with *anima*.

Elohys created,
in the court of Paradise,
from a left rib
the radiant female.

Seven hours
they kept the orchard,
before the importuning of Satan,
the most ardent of suitors.

From there were they driven,
by force and through cold,
to live out their lives
in this world.

To bear in anguish
sons and daughters,
to gain sovereignty
over the land of Asia.

Nine hundred and eight
she bore in great anguish,
she bore a mixed brood
of males and females.

And then without concealment …

[Here the page ends.]

60. A Fragment of the Hanes Taliesin by Llywelyn Siôn of Llangewydd
NLW MS 13075B (c.1590)

This fragment of the tale of Taliesin was recorded in about 1590 by Llywelyn Siôn (1540–1615?) a professional poet and scribe from Llangewydd near Bridgend in Glamorgan. Llywelyn is a natural storyteller and his style is more colourful and engaging than other versions of the tale and it is possible that he was drawing on an oral tradition as much as any written sources.[19] If so, this shows that in Elizabethan times the story of Taliesin was as well known in the far south of Wales as in other parts of the country.

This translation is based on Patrick Ford's edited Welsh text, translation and notes.[20] The figures in square brackets refer to the folio numbers in the original manuscript.

How Taliesin Came to be Found

Once, there was a nobleman called Tegid Foel, and his family seat was at Bala in Penllyn and the lake is called Llyn Tegid to this day. And by his wedded wife, Graidwen, a son was born to him who was called Morfran ap Tegid and a daughter called Crairw, who was the fairest maiden in the whole Island of Britain; and the son was the ugliest Christian in the world. And then Graidwen his mother began to think that he was unlikely to gain acceptance among honourable noblemen unless

---
19 Ford 1975, 453
20 Ford 1975

he possessed some useful skills or some exalted knowledge, for this was at the beginning of the reign of Arthur and the gathering of the Round Table. And then Graidwen his mother ordained by the arts of the books of Virgil that a cauldron of *awen* and knowledge should be boiled up for the boy, so that he might be better greeted and of better reputation for his arcane knowledge and learning. And then [52v] the boiling of the cauldron was commenced, and once the boiling has begun it could not be interrupted for a year and a day, until the knowledge be obtained.

And she set Gwion Bach, the son of a yeoman from Llanfair in Caereinion in Powys, to stir the cauldron, and Dallmor Dallme to kindle a fire under the cauldron. And she commanded them not to allow the boiling to be interrupted for a year and a day whilst she, by books of astronomy and hours and planets, foraged every day for all manner of various efficacious herbs. And one day, as she foraged, almost at the year's end, it chanced that three droplets of that bubbling potion splashed onto Gwion Bach's finger. And so hot was it that he thrust his finger in his mouth and no sooner had he sipped of those precious droplets than he knew beforehand all that should come to pass. And then he knew that his direst peril lay in the intentions and wiles of Graidwen, for great was her knowledge. And in sheer terror, he thought to flee to his own country. And so, the cauldron burst into fragments when the precious droplets left it, for all that potion was poisonous except those three droplets, so that it poisoned the horses of Gwyddno Garanir where the water ran into the stream below the house. And because of that, that very stream was called Gwenwynfairch from then on.

And at that, behold [53r], Graidwen came in and saw all her labour for a whole year lost, and she took the paddle and struck Dallmor Dallme on the head so that one of his eyes fell out onto his cheek. And he said, "An evil thing have you done to me, an innocent man, for you have not suffered any loss on my account." "You speak the truth," said she, "it is false Gwion who has robbed me." And out she went the same way as he had gone before, lifting up her petticoats and running. And so, she caught sight of him climbing the mountain about a mile and a half from her. And Gwion Bach saw her also. And then he turned himself into a hare and ran away. What she did then was turn herself into a greyhound bitch and set off in pursuit of him. And, finally, she headed him off downhill towards the river. What he did then was turn himself into a fish and leap into the river. What she did then was to turn herself into a she-otter and pursue him under the hollow riverbanks until he was forced to assume the form of a bird and take to the air. And she took the shape of a hawk, and so she gave him not one moment of peace in the air. And so, when he was utterly exhausted and in fear of his life, he spied a heap of winnowed wheat on the floor of a granary in the river valley. What he did was land and turn himself into an ear among the wheat. And she turned into a black, tailless hen and recognised him among the wheat and swallowed him.

And so, the story [53v] says that he was nine months in her belly, and that after she had given birth to him, she did not have the heart to kill him, but had him sewn into a skin bag and thrown into the sea at the mercy of God, on the twentieth of April.

And at that time, there was a fish-weir belonging to Gwyddno Garanir on the beach between the rivers Dyfi and Ystwyth, near a castle of his. And in that weir, a hundred pounds' worth [of fish] was caught every May Eve. And Gwyddno Garanir had a son called Elffin ap Gwyddno. And he was one of the most unlucky of young men, and most in need of means, for he was profligate. And it lay heavy on his father and his mother that he was so, thinking that he had been born at an evil and unhappy hour. And at the entreaty of his wife, his father gave Elffin whatever might be caught in the weir that year, to see whether God would ever send him any luck or good fortune. And on May Eve, they found nothing in the weir but that skin bag. And then the serving lad said to Elffin "If ever you lacked luck before, you are unluckier still tonight, for you have broken the innate virtue of your father's weir in which was always found on May Eve a hundred pounds' worth. And there is nothing here tonight but this piece of skin." "Well, man," said Elffin, "it may be worth a hundred pounds." And they opened the skin bag over the boy's face, and then Elffin said, "There is a lovely forehead!" "Let his name be Taliesin [54r] then," said the lad and set the boy up on the horse between Elffin and the pommel. And then Taliesin caused the horse, which had been trotting before, to amble as smoothly as if they were sitting in the most comfortable chair in the whole Island of Britain. And then Taliesin composed a praise-poem to cheer Elffin and to foretell great dignity for him, which is called Elffin's Consolation, and he began thus, in *englyn* metre:

> Elffin, cease your weeping,
> let none revile his own;
> despair brings no consolation,
> a man cannot see what sustains him;
> the prayers of Cynllo shall not be in vain,
> God will not break his promises;
> never was caught in Gwyddno's weir
> as fair a catch as tonight.
>
> Fair Elffin, dry your cheeks,
> you will find no comfort in blushing,
> although you thought you had no profit;
> too much desire does no-one any good
> lest we doubt the Lord's miracles;
> for from ocean and mountain

and from the depths of rivers,
God sends wealth to fortunate men.

Elffin of agreeable nature,
unsoldierly is your intention;
you need not lament so excessively,
better God than evil prophecy.
Although I am small and frail,
due to Dylan's seething ocean,
I will give you on the destined day
riches better than three hundred!

Elffin of remarkable qualities,
be not angry at your catch;
although I am weak in my skin bag,
there is power in my tongue.
You need not have excessive fear
whilst I am here to protect you;
by recalling the name of the Trinity,
no-one may oppress you.

        Taliesin sang it.

61. Triad 87: Tri Bardd Kaw ("Three Skilful Bards")
MS: Peniarth 252, p. 169

Trioedd Ynys Prydein ("The Triads of the Island of Britain") grouped ancient Welsh stories and characters into groups of three that were readily memorised. They evolved as part of the training given by medieval Welsh bards to their pupils. The students were required to learn the triads by heart, which in turn helped them to remember the huge repertoire of stories and characters that they were required to master as part of their bardic training.[21] The earliest written version of the triads dates to the period *c*.1250–75, but it is also clear that they were transmitted orally for centuries prior to that.[22] Having said that, Triad 87 occurs only in a late manuscript dating to the 17th century.[23] In placing Taliesin at the court of Arthur, it echoes the earlier description in *Culhwch ac Olwen* (see s. 56 above).

---

21 Bromwich 2014, lviii
22 Bromwich 2014, xvi, lxxxviii
23 Bromwich 2014, xxxi

The translation given here is that of Bromwich.[24]

Three Skilful Bards who were at Arthur's Court:

> Myrddin son of Morfryn,
> Myrddin Emrys,
> and Taliesin.

---

24 Bromwich 2014, 228–9

EARLY MODERN ORAL TRANSMISSION

62. William Aubrey by Siôn Dafydd Rhys
Cambrobrytannicae Cymraecaeve Linguae Institutiones et Rudimenta (1592)

In this excerpt from his grammar, Siôn Dafydd Rhys gives us a delightful picture of an evening spent with his friend and neighbour, William Aubrey, sitting by the fire and exchanging poems of Taliesin learned by heart.

Siôn Dafydd Rhys (1534–c.1619), also known as Dr. John Davies, was one of the foremost Renaissance scholars of his day. Born in Anglesey, he was educated at Oxford and the University of Siena and travelled widely across Europe. He returned to Wales in 1574 and later practised medicine from his home Clun Hir below Pen y Fan in the Brecon Beacons. His most important work is his grammar of the Welsh language published in Latin as *Cambrobrytannicae Cymraecaeve Linguae Institutiones et Rudimenta* in 1592. The book included a treatise on the rules of the traditional poetic metres and a selection of Welsh poetry.[1]

William Aubrey (c.1529–1595) was a distinguished civil lawyer and judge. He also served as MP for Carmarthen and Brecon and served as sheriff of Breconshire in 1545. His family seat was at Cantref near Brecon and he was a neighbour of Siôn Dafydd Rhys. Although living and working in London, he regularly returned to Brecon "to make merye with his frendes".[2] It may have been on such a visit that the events described here took place. At any rate, this episode shows that the Taliesin story and poems were still being transmitted orally in south Wales in the 1590s.

I am grateful to Prof. Ronald Hutton for his assistance in translating this excerpt from the original Latin. Any remaining errors are entirely my own.

> "Moreover, now, and because of their authority, and the fact that they belong here among other things, he [the author] will not hesitate to add some of the most ancient Cambro-British poems of Taliesin, stolen by me stealthily (which is my audacity) and without his knowledge [from William Aubrey], and committed [to paper] with a clatter of the pen, from his own mouth, [as he sat] by chance in the evening at his own fire, confident as usual in his chair, and this, together with other poems, memorized and (not without a certain delight) recited by that most decorated and learned man, Lord William Aubrey, a Cambro-Briton, a descendent of the family of the Aubreys, very skilled in the Cambro-British language, and a decoration and ornament to his excellent country;"[3]

---

1 Stephens 1998, 638–9
2 Lloyd and Jenkins 1959, 17
3 Rhys 1592, 182

APPENDIX I

FOUR POEMS BY LLYWARCH AP LLYWELYN

63. Mawl Gwenllïan ferch Hywel ab Iorwerth ("In Praise of Gwenllïan daughter of Hywel ab Iorwerth")
(Hendregadredd MS f. 113; Red Book of Hergest, col. 1424–5)

Gwenllïan was the daughter of Hywel ab Iorwerth the powerful ruler of Caerleon and Gwynllŵg in Gwent in south-east Wales. He, his father and brother had resisted the Norman attacks in the south-east for many years. The poem probably dates to the period around 1190 when Llywarch ap Llywelyn was court poet to Rhodri ab Owain Gwynedd, the uncle of Llywelyn the Great. Gwenllïan's mother, Gwerfyl, was related to Cynfelyn and Nest of Cyfeiliog in mid-Wales (ll. 9–12) and to the poet's patron. Llywarch has been sent from Gwynedd to Gwent with a string of fine horses as a wedding gift for Gwenllïan.[1]

Translation based on the edited text by Jones and Jones, the rendering into Modern Welsh in Jones and the Welsh text and English notes in Andrews.[2]

> This is Whit Sunday, warriors arise for battle,
> Take the warrior's path, a fine arising!
> Set off, white-cruppered stallion, with the most precious string of horses,
> Step lively, the sun rises splendidly,
> Go fearlessly straight to the destination,   5
> Foam-flecked, dignified steed, with easy gait,
> Past the territory of Tudyr, the land of Elise,
> Famous Cyfeiliog, of sad memory,
> Past the daughter of Cynfelyn, who makes nobles pale with love,
> Although she be a lady, she is aloof.   10
> (Nest told me: "Nothing will come of it;
> A man often prepares the warp he does not weave.")
> I am called Llywarch, he who follows armies,
> England's destruction, the mighty warrior who destroys strongholds,
> Familiar is my shield where the foe is scattered,   15
> Enemies are used to my spears in their hearts!
> Where I walk, the ravens croak boldly.
> A man furious on the battlefield,

---

1 Andrews 2007, 124–5
2 Jones and Jones 1991, poem 14; Jones 1992, 64–66; Andrews 2007, 30, 124–28

I raise many a sigh in my sore plight,
They rise, from my desire, higher than heaven.　　　　　　　　　20
Waters flow through their channels,
Past rose campion, slender shoots, flocks of birds,
Past the cuckoos' shelter, the woods teeming [with life],
But a girl has made me pale with love.
The river Usk has a hundred paths along her margins,　　　　　25
She bears away to the Meadows of Caerleon the leaves of many a hill;
But I lead large, splendid stallions, fierce and lustful,
To the one deserving of praise, like the sun in splendour,
To the strongholds of Gwenllïan scattered throughout Gwynllŵg,
To the beloved fair maiden, the radiant light of the border.　　30
As she will not come to me as I wish, I am ablaze
For the beauty of the gentle maiden who is as bright as dawn.
I feel my broken heart aflame for her,
Burning for her like a great, blazing bonfire.
Her form is faultless in her golden gown;　　　　　　　　　　35
Truly, a string of white-maned horses has been sent to her
To carry her due, to spread her praise
As far as the sun sets and rises.

64. Awdl yr Haearn Twym ("Ode to the Red-Hot Iron")
(Hendregadredd MS, f. 114; Red Book of Hergest, col. 1424)

This one of the most remarkable and original of the poems of the court poets and demonstrates the idiosyncrasy that Llywarch may have brought to the Taliesin persona. The poet has been accused of murder and is to undergo trial by ordeal in which he will have to carry a bar of red-hot iron in his hand for three steps. His burns would then have been bandaged for three days and, if found to be healing well, his innocence would have been proven. If the wound showed signs of infection, he was deemed guilty. Trial by ordeal was introduced to Wales by the Normans.[3] However, it was not recognised by native Welsh law and the action of the poem can only have taken place in the Marches, possibly in Gwent.[4] The procedure is mentioned in one of the documents of the Bishop of Llandaff in 1126 but was banned by the Pope in 1215.[5] The poem must therefore pre-date 1215. The Madog whom Prydydd y Moch is accused of murdering is otherwise unknown. What a drama must lie behind this short poem!

3　Jones and Jones 1991, 146–7
4　Jones 1992, 72
5　Jones and Jones 1991, 146; Andrews 2007, 137

Translation based on the edited text and rendering into Modern Welsh in Jones and the Welsh text and English notes in Andrews.[6]

> Creator of heaven, loyal to his servant,
> I would trust to this as to [the gospel of] St. John.
> The steely judge of the blessed law created by the Lord,
> I am obedient to you as my witness.
> May your justice glow white-hot,   5
> Your fiery zeal is no enemy to my purpose.
> Consider in your judgement the extent of my lineage;
> Creature that causes searing pain, consider what created you.
> I beseech Peter, the follower of Christ
> Who bore the cross with grace,   10
> By the fair intercession and entreaty of Thomas
> And Philip and Paul and Andrew.
> By the grip of my hand, blue-white blade,
> For acquittal of the blood-guilt of murder.
> Good iron, bear witness that when   15
> Madog was murdered, it was not by my hand,
> Any more than that Cain and his followers
> Shall attain any part of the nine kingdoms of heaven.
> And I seek good fellowship,
> God's goodwill towards me and deliverance from his wrath.   20

65. Y Canu Bychan a gant Prydydd y Moch i Lywelyn fab Iorferth
("The Short Song that Prydydd y Moch sang to Llywelyn son of Iorwerth")
(Hendregadredd MS f. 109; Red Book of Hergest, col. 1422–4)

This poem celebrates Llywelyn's victories in his campaigns in the Marches and southern Wales in 1217. His sweeping territorial gains, as well as his status as *de facto* Prince of Wales, were recognised by Henry III of England in the Treaty of Worcester in 1218. This the context for the composition of the poem.[7] It is almost certain that the legendary Taliesin poem *Teithi Edmygant* (s. 32) was composed by Llywarch on the same occasion, possibly for a feast or gathering of Llywelyn's allies in east or south-east Wales.[8] This is the first of two occasions where Prydydd y Moch composed his traditional court poetry to mark Llywelyn's political successes before adopting the *persona* of Taliesin for other purposes.

---

6 Jones and Jones 1991, poem 15; Jones 1992, 67–8; Andrews 2007, 35, 137–8
7 Jones and Jones 1991, 247
8 Haycock 2015, 371–2

Caerllïon (l. 18) may refer either to Chester or Caerleon in south-east Wales. *Rhuddlan Deifi* was a castle on the border between Ceredigion and Carmarthenshire in west Wales, whilst *Rhuddlan Degeingl* is in north-east Wales. The Owain referred to in l. 45 is Llywelyn's grandfather Owain Gwynedd (*c*.1100–1170), one of the greatest of the princes of Gwynedd. Rhodri in l. 48 refers to Rhodri Mawr (*c*.820–877) another of Llywelyn's illustrious ancestors. *Beli Hir* (l. 49) refers to Beli Mawr ap Mynogan who appears in the Four Branches as the grandfather of Brân the Blessed, Branwen and Manawydan and in the Triads as the father of the children of the goddess Dôn. In origin, he may be identified with the Gaulish god *Belenos*.[9]

This translation is based on the edited text and modern Welsh version of Jones and Jones.[10]

I entreat my Lord for *awen* of splendid greeting,
the very words of Ceridwen, lady of poetry,
in the manner of Taliesin in releasing Elffin,
in the style of poetic art hailed by poets with loud applause.
I praise my lord, ruler of the men of Wales,   5
the most able Welshman ever created by God,
mighty Llywelyn, no man challenges him,
the border of Wales is his only limit and his host defends it.
Eagle-lord of kings, I have drunk his mead,
in times of peace, in times of war, at the king's right hand;   10
I have drunk his wine from his magnificent drinking horn
and I have received his golden robes through his generosity.
In the court of Aberffraw sponsoring poetic learning,
in great Carmarthen raising armies,
in the fortress of Degannwy, in Swansea,   15
in the powerful march against Cydweli town,
in Caernarfon with a poem of praise,
(and in Caerllïon where my leader shall come!)
in Shrewsbury, in the lovely settlements of the lord,
in the fortresses of gentle Cardigan,   20
in the mighty fortress of Ellesmere, in renowned St Clears,
in courtly Brecon, her river flowing strong,
in Montgomery Castle, among the warbands of Ceri,
in the township of Haverford, dwelling-place of strife,

---

9   Bromwich 2014, 284, 288
10 Jones and Jones 1991, poem 25, 247–59

in Rhuddlan Deifi, a lovely place hated by the English, 25
in Rhuddlan Degeingl with her fine dwellings,
in the court of Mold with the men of England armed for battle,
many were our battles as our fury grew;
in the courts of the South, in the settlements of the English,
many a conspicuous tower is set ablaze, 30
in the vanguard of battle a mighty warrior directs the strife,
in the Island of Britain our lodging is well-provided.
Never a single inch did we gain but by assault, by battle,
of the borderland of Gwynedd in her service,
let alone in Powys with her rugged lands 35
and her merciless troops that could not defend her,
or the host of mighty England and her leader's venomous hatred
and her eager forces beyond the sea,
they received no quarter at our hands,
only dishonour and a total rout in battle. 40
Myrddin foretells that a king shall come
from among the Welsh through heroism;
the druids foretold the rebirth of generous lords
from the lineage of the eagle-lords of Eryri.
From among the grandsons of Owain, defender of Britain, 45
there is one of fine qualities whose rightful place is august London,
a lion-like hero who strikes down the English, Iorwerth is his forebear,
generous Llywelyn, descended from Rhodri.
I will not conceal him, I proclaim him Beli Hir,
neither his birthright nor his valour can be concealed 50
for the sake of every charge he led against armoured, bull-like warriors,
against every sullen churl to put him to shame;
for the sake of all the blood of wounded men about our feet,
for the sake of every wall so easily put to flame,
for the sake of all his feats, secret and open, 55
at the head of mighty armies subduing castles.
As you accept, God, the vain endeavours of man,
accept Llywelyn, the war-leader;
I beseech you, Lord of lords,
that this hero of fearless warriors may be reconciled with you. 60

66. Mawl Rhys Gryg o Ddeheubarth ("In Praise of Rhys Gryg of Deheubarth")
(Hendregadredd MS f. 111–13; Red Book of Hergest, col. 1442; Jones and Jones 1991, poem 26)

Rhys Gryg (*c.*1170?–1234) was the prince of large parts of south-west Wales and an ally of Llywarch's chief patron, Llywelyn the Great, from 1212 to 1234. This majestic and ambitious poem was composed to celebrate their victorious campaign in the summer and autumn of 1220 against the English occupation of south-west Wales. The poem was probably sung in the presence of Llywelyn the Great on a visit to the court of Rhys Gryg to celebrate their victory and seal a new alliance. This may be Llywarch's last recorded poem, composed in his seventies. If so, it shows no slackening in his skill or poetic power from his earlier works.[11]

It has been argued that the legendary poem *Aduwyneu Taliesin* (s. 21) was composed on the same occasion.[12] The celebration would have called for entertainment as well as praise-poetry and Llywarch may have been required to sing "official" verse in his own voice but then assume the *persona* of Taliesin to entertain the court.

The English settlements at Rhos, Pembroke, Haverford, Wiston and Arberth were captured or destroyed in 1220. Carmarthen, St Clears and Swansea had all been attacked in earlier campaigns. Derllys was an old name for the area around Carmarthen.[13]

In the triads, Nudd, Mordaf and Rhydderch are described as the "Three Generous Men of the Island of Britain" whilst Hercules, Hector and Samson are the "Three Men who received the might of Adam". Rhun (l. 49) probably refers to Rhun son of Maelgwn Gwynedd, described in the triads as "Rhun of Great Wealth".[14]

This translation is based on the edited text and modern Welsh version of Jones and Jones.[15]

> Christ the Creator, the Emperor who rules over us,
> Christ the Lord, pillar of peace,
> Christ son of Mary who gives me wisdom of pure lineage,
> Before awareness of sin;
> Dearest Jesus, my steadfast companion, 5
> Lord, you came into my life.
> I shall go first to the hall of Deheubarth,
> to the court of the true king of kings,

---

11 Jones and Jones 1991, xxiv, 275
12 Haycock 2015, 92–3
13 Jones and Jones 1991, 277
14 Bromwich 2014, 5, 129, 209
15 Jones and Jones 1991, 260–78

I will go to Rhys son of Rhys in my pomp,
to the battle-charger, descended from Cadell; 10
wandering bards flock to his court,
they flock to the champion for his generosity.
You carried destruction to sheltered Rhos
and to Pembroke with great rejoicing.
You breached the walls of Carmarthen with hosts and fell on the Normans 15
and many a Norman fled;
and Swansea, a scene of destruction,
her towers broken – there is peace there today!
and to St Clears with her fine, splendid lands;
not English are the men who rule her now; 20
in Swansea, key stronghold of the English,
all their wives are widows!
The eagle-lord of warriors loves no lounging, sleeping,
nor a retinue bereft of battle.
Customary is mounting a charger, shield on left arm, 25
the armour of him who is the breastplate of kings;
Customary are spears in fierce conflict
and penetrating spear-thrusts through men;
customary at his hand is bloody handiwork
driving foreigners into exile. 30
Customary for his hosts is cutting down men in slaughter
for the grey ones, the cubs of the woods.
Customary is the cruel eagle above roaring estuaries,
the leader of the wolf-pack at their feast,
and magnificent ravens feasting on flesh, 35
like butchers at their augury.
Thirdly, customary is a band of eager bards
around his delectable table;
and his spoils and his fine wine and feasting
and his vast, much-vaunted herds 40
and his red gold, his wealth, his property
and his swift, obedient, well-trained steeds;
and to myself, for my skills, he gives satisfaction,
wealth beyond measure comes to me
from the South, astounding in her generosity, 45
a region splendid for enriching bards.
Lordly by nature, it is not fitting that I stand in any need,
chief of riches, when I go to Gwynedd;

named like Rhun, small wonder
that I journey there to gain wealth. 50

Yours is the wealth of kings by dint of prowess
against mighty, splendid chieftains,
a hard attack you made against them,
a powerful charge, no diffident onslaught.
As numerous as the stars, your enemies fell 55
in their own blood, thanks to your tactics.
The men of Rhos are exiled, the people of Pembroke have lost their heads,
all Christian lands have heard tell of it;
the court of Haverford and her busy roads belong to you,
all her land burnt utterly, 60
all foiled, all cut down, all of it, utterly,
even the pigs in their sties;
swiftly you subdued Wiston
and Arberth, a notable sacking;
your unfettered power is death to your foes, 65
your retinue brought it all to pass.
They call you Little Rhys – a lie!
Great, proud Rhys in shield-wall, in battle;
Hoarse Rhys they call the pillar of his land:
Rhys is not hoarse doing harm to his enemies! 70
Rhys, neither two nor ten thousand can make him retreat,
when Rhys goes forth armed splendidly for battle!

An armed man slaying, may he slay his foes!
A long life is not their fate!
Soldiers fell like stars, so many fell 75
by his hand and bloody blade.
Hero of Dinefwr, as innocent as Adam!
I went and saw you,
a Welshman among Welshmen,
your lordship the most exalted in Christendom; 80
from every region comes tribute to our lord,
he who will not pay, let him beware!
His brindled horses are divided among petitioners
and his red gold, his wealth, his liberality,
and though I insisted on travelling for gifts, 85
my lord brings them to me himself.

I possess gold and silver – no deceit –
and swift-trotting, grain-fettled horses;
I have men and land, an extensive homestead,
and fearless kinsmen; 90
I have a renowned, unstinting lord,
liberal also in his understanding,
who has shown me respect with ostentation
and a golden clasp on three hundred mantles.
The greatest lord ever born 95
since Arthur, the generous leader of armies.
He pours gold into the laps of eager poets,
like the full, ripe fruits of the woods:
Llywelyn, lord of Christendom,
son of Iorwerth, my help, my shelter. 100
To you, Lord of Deheubarth, comes praise,
oh, generous man, because I have sought you out for patronage.
You need defer to none, wealthy, honourable man,
for your nature, your life of such liberality,
[not even] to Mordaf and Nudd when gold was shared out 105
[nor to] the largesse of Rhydderch;
by your courage, by your manly might,
you cause terror like Hercules
and Samson – warriors who fought for praise alone –
and Hector in his sore trial; 110
and the beauty I see here proves it is no lie
that Jesus has allowed no hardship to befall you,
considering the glory of the Trinity, the beauty of Adam,
I have come to you for patronage!
The equal of Rhun, respected by the Welsh, 115
fierce in his valour, the leader at the ford, open-handed,
Rhys son of Rhys, with rightful claim to Britain,
the object of the hopes and wishes of the bards;
Rhys of Derllys, we deserve his gift;
Rhys the lord, his by right is Dyfed. 120

Lord of Dyfed, your inflicting of wounds, your fame, your foes,
your martial prowess are far-renowned;
we have heard your sword ring out on many a shield
and your bloody spear in furious attack.
Your banner held high with pride and passion, 125

a sight to strike terror into any war-band,
our rallying-point against the oppression of enemies,
the men of England know it all too well!
Your shield has been smashed before you three hundred times
in a battle of three hundred charges; 130
and your inexhaustible red gold, abundant in your court,
and your eager stallions,
and your precious, lively herds,
and your booty and your prodigal gifts.
I see you for what you truly are, 135
I see nothing that exceeds your praise,
a man so mighty, he surpasses all others,
all the quarrelsome nations.
The goodwill of God, surely,
aids you in preparing for death. 140
As no promise vouchsafes our stay here long,
Dragon of Britain, look to your future!
When you leave this world, a lovely covenant,
Were I here still here, I would be speechless with the loss of you, 145
may your winter home and summer dwelling be in heaven, lord,
in the kingdom of God above!

APPENDIX II

REFERENCES TO CERIDWEN BY THE COURT POETS

The five dateable references to Ceridwen in the work of the court poets show that she was well-known and held in great regard by the poets of north and south Wales alike from at least the beginning of the 12th century. Her name is regularly coupled with *awen* ("muse, poetic inspiration") and *ogyrfen* ("inspiration") and she is regarded as the source of fine words and well-crafted poetic expression. Stories of her cauldron and her connection with the story of Taliesin's freeing of his patron Elffin were certainly current by the early 13th century.

The translation in section 1 from the poem to Cuhelyn Fardd is based on the rendering of the poem into modern Welsh by R. Geraint Gruffydd.[1] The translations of Cynddelw and Casnodyn are based on modern Welsh versions by Marged Haycock.[2] The excerpts from the work of Llywarch ap Llywelyn are based on modern Welsh versions by Elin M. Jones and Nerys Ann Jones.[3]

1, Anonymous

The first of the five datable references to Ceridwen by the court poets dates to c.1100–1130 and occurs in an anonymous poem in praise of Cuhelyn Fardd ("Cuhelyn the Poet") who was a powerful landowner in the Preseli hills in northern Pembrokeshire:

> Lord God, allow me *awen* (amen, so may it be),
> As eager praise, a powerful declamation and the boast of a multitude,
> According to the dignity of the song of Ceridwen of varied inspiration,
> Varied in its abundance, a ready speech for skilled reciters,
> For Cuhelyn the Poet, weaver of splendid Welsh,
> A gift of poetry, a fitting gift for those without enmity.[4]

2, Cynddelw Brydydd Mawr

Cynddelw Brydydd Mawr (fl. c.1155–c.1200) was the leading court poet of the 12th century and served the dynasty of Powys in north-east Wales. The reference to

---
1 Gruffydd et al. 1994, 33
2 Haycock 2003, 154–7
3 Jones and Jones 1991, 102; 255
4 Gruffydd et al. 1994, 2.1–6

Ceridwen is found in a death-song for two princes of Powys killed sometime in the 1160s:

> Such a master of poetry am I, but wounded nonetheless,
> Such a renowned poet among the inspired bards,
> But well-acquainted with grief, I am not joyful,
> How well-versed am I in the ways of the arts of Ceridwen;
> How bereft am I that they have been taken in their prime,
> The unyielding defenders whose career was fierce! [5]

Cynddelw also refers in the final section of the poem to Taliesin as the poet of the war-band of Urien Rheged. It is possible therefore that the connection between Taliesin and Ceridwen was current as early as the 1160s.

3, Llywarch ap Llywelyn, Prydydd y Moch

The first reference by Prydydd y Moch dates to the end of the 12th century (possibly the period 1194–1200) and occurs in *englynion* (short, four-line stanzas) to Gruffudd ap Cynan, grandson of Owain Gwynedd and uncle of Llywelyn the Great.[6] This is the earliest reference outside the Book of Taliesin to the cauldron of Ceridwen and its "lovely *awen*":

> The Lord God gives me the gift of lovely – awen
> As from the cauldron of Ceridwen,
> To entertain a lord wrathful but lenient,
> The fierce hero of the battle of Meigen.[7]

4, Llywarch ap Llywelyn, Prydydd y Moch

The second mention of Ceridwen is found at the beginning of the *Canu Bychan* ("short song") celebrating the victories of Llywelyn the Great in the Marches and south-west Wales in 1217:

> I entreat my Lord for *awen* of splendid greeting,
> The very words of Ceridwen, lady of poetry,
> In the manner of Taliesin in releasing Elffin,
> In the style of the poetic art hailed by poets with loud applause.[8]

---

5 Jones and Parry Owen 1991, 24.5–10
6 Jones and Jones 1991, xxix
7 Jones and Jones 1991, 10.1–4, p. 102
8 Jones and Jones 1991, 25.1–5

5, Casnodyn

The fifth reference to Ceridwen dates to after 1329 and occurs in a death-song by Casnodyn, a Glamorgan poet, to Madog Fychan of Tir Iarll near Margam in south Wales. The poet sings his lament:

> For Madog of great wealth, of profound awen,
> A blameless lord of inspiration like the cauldron of Ceridfen,[9]

---

[9] Daniel 1999, poem 2

Bibliography

Acken, J.T. 2006. *History and Terminology in Auraicept Na n-Éces* (unpublished PhD thesis, University of Toronto) available at: https://tspace.library.utoronto.ca/bitstream/1807/111717/3/NR21982_OCR.pdf

Andrews, Rh. M. 2007. *Welsh Court Poems* (Cardiff: University of Wales Press).

Beck, N. 2009. *Goddesses in Celtic Religion – Cult and Mythology: A Comparative Study of Ancient Ireland, Britain and Gaul* (PhD Thesis: Université Lumière Lyon 2/University College Dublin), published on-line at http://theses.univ-lyon2.fr/documents/lyon2/2009/beck_n#p=0&a=top

Best, R.I. 1905. "The Tragic Death of Cúrói Mac Dári", *Ériu* 2, 18–35.

Bollard, J.K. 1990. "Myrddin in Early Welsh Tradition", in Goodrich, P. (ed.) *The Romance of Merlin* (New York: Garland), 13–54.

Bollard, J.K. 2019. "The Earliest Myrddin Poems", in Lloyd-Morgan, C. and Poppe, E. (eds.) *Arthur in the Celtic Languages* (Cardiff: University of Wales Press), 35–50.

Bollard, J.K. and Griffiths, A. 2015. *Englynion y Beddau/The Stanzas of the Graves* (Llanrwst: Gwasg Carreg Gwalch).

Breatnach, L. 1981. "The Caldron of Poesy", *Ériu* 32, 45–93.

Breeze, A. 1997. "Armes Prydein, Hywel Dda, and the reign of Edmund of Wessex", *Études Celtiques* 33, 209–222.

Breeze, A. 1999. "The Battle of Brunanburh and Welsh Tradition", *Neophilologus* 83, 479–83.

Breeze, A. 2002. "The Kingdom and Name of Elmet", *Northern History* 39:2, 157–171.

Breeze, A. 2010. "Yrechwydd and the River Ribble", *Northern History* 47:2, 319–328.

Breeze, A. 2015. "Urien Rheged and the Battle at Gwen Ystrad", *Northern History* 52:1, 9–19.

Breeze, A. 2018. "The Dates of the Four Branches of the Mabinogi", *Studia Celtica Posnaniensia* 3 (1), 47–62.

Bromwich, R. (ed. and trans.) 2014. *Trioedd Ynys Prydein: The Triads of the Island of Britain* (4th ed.) (Cardiff: University of Wales Press, repr. 2017).

Bromwich, R. and Evans, D.S. (eds.) 1997. *Culhwch ac Olwen* (Cardiff: University of Wales Press, repr. 2012).

Bromwich, R., Jarman, A.O.H and Roberts, B.F. (eds.) 1991. *The Arthur of the Welsh* (Cardiff: University of Wales Press).

Charles-Edwards, T.M. 1971. "The Date of the Four Branches of the Mabinogi", *Transactions of the Honourable Society of Cymmrodorion: Session 1970*, 263–98.

Charles-Edwards, T.M. 2010. "The Date of Culhwch ac Olwen" in McLeod, W. *et al.* (eds.) *Bile ós Chrannaibh: A Festschrift for William Gillies* (Ceann Drochaid: Clann Tuirc), 45–56.

Charles-Edwards, T.M. 2013. *Wales and the Britons 350–1064* (Oxford: Oxford University Press, repr. 2014).

Clarke, B.F.L. (ed. and trans.) 1973. *Life of Merlin: Vita Merlini* (Cardiff: University of Wales Press).

Coe, J.B. 2001. *The Place-Names of the Book of Llandaf* (unpublished PhD thesis, University of Wales, Aberystwyth).

Coe, J. 2004. "Dating the boundary clauses in the Book of Llandaf", *Cambrian Medieval Celtic Studies* 48, 1–43.

Constantine, M-A. 2003. "The Battle for 'The Battle of the Trees'" in Firla, A. and Lindop, G (eds.) *Graves and the Goddess: Essays on Robert Graves and the White Goddess* (Selinsgrove: Susquehana University Press), 40–51.

Cross, T.P. and Slover, C.H. (eds.) 1936. *Ancient Irish Tales* (New York: Barnes and Noble, repr. 1996), 328–332.

Daniel, R.I. (ed.) 1999. *Gwaith Casnodyn* (Aberystwyth: Centre for Advanced Welsh and Celtic Studies).

Davies, S.M. (trans.) 2007. *The Mabinogion* (Oxford: Oxford University Press).

De Gray Birch, W. 1912. *Memorials of the See and Cathedral of Llandaff* (Neath: John E. Richards), 12–13.

Dumville, D.N. 1986. "The Historical Value of the *Historia Brittonum*", *Arthurian Literature VI*, 1–26.

Dumville, D.N. 1972–4. "Some aspects of the chronology of the *Historia Brittonum*", *Bulletin of the Board of Celtic Studies* 25, 439–445.

Ellis Evans, D. 1970. "Welsh Aladur", *Études Celtiques* 12/2, 509–11.

Evans, G. and Fulton H. (eds.) 2019. *The Cambridge History of Welsh Literature* (Cambridge: Cambridge University Press).

Evans, J. G. and Rhŷs, J. 1893. *The Book of Llan Dav: Liber Landavensis* (repr. 1979, Aberystwyth: National Library of Wales)

Falileyev, A. 2012. "Why Jews? Why *Caer Seon*? Towards interpretations of *Ymddiddan Taliesin ac Ugnach*", *Cambrian Medieval Celtic Studies* 64, 85–118.

Fleming, A. 1994. "Swadal, Swar (and Erechwydd?): early medieval polities in Upper Swaledale, *Landscape History* 16:1, 17–30.

Ford, P.K. 1975. "A fragment of the *Hanes Taliesin* by Llywelyn Siôn", *Études Celtiques* 14, 451–60.

Ford, P.K. 1983. "On the significance of some Arthurian names in Welsh", *Bulletin of the Board of Celtic Studies* 34, 41–50.

Ford, P.K. 1992. *Ystoria Taliesin* (Cardiff: University of Wales Press).

Foster, I. Ll. 1953. "Gwynn ap Nudd" in Murphy G. (ed.) *Duanaire Finn*, Part III (Dublin), 198–204.

Fulton, H. 2019. "Britons and Saxons: The Earliest Writing in Welsh", in Evans and Fulton 2019, 26–51.

Gantz, J. 1981. *Early Irish Myths and Sagas* (London: Penguin Books).

Goetinck, G.W. (ed.) 1976. *Historia Peredur vab Efrawc* (Cardiff: University of Wales Press).

Gray, E.A., 2005. "The warrior, the poet and the king: 'the three sins of the warrior' and Cú Roí" in Nagy, J. F. and Jones, L. E. (eds.) 2005. *Heroic Poets and Poetic Heroes in Celtic Tradition: a Festschrift for Patrick K. Ford* (Dublin: Four Courts Press), 74–90.

Green, T. 2007a. *Concepts of Arthur* (Stroud: Tempus).

Green, T. 2007b. "A note on Aladur, Alator and Arthur", *Studia Celtica* 41, 237–41.

Griffiths, M.E. 1937. *Early Vaticination in Welsh* (Cardiff: University of Wales Press).

Gruffydd, R.G. 1994. "In Search of Elmet", *Studia Celtica* 28, 63–79.

Gruffydd, R.G. *et al.* (eds.) 1994. *Gwaith Meilyr Brydydd a'i Ddisgynyddion, Cyfres Beirdd y Tywysogion I* (Cardiff: UWP).

Gruffydd, R.G. 1999. "A Welsh 'Dark Age' court poem" in Carey, J., John T. Koch, and Pierre-Yves Lambert (eds.), *Ildánach Ildírech. A Festschrift for Proinsias Mac Cana* (Andover and Aberystwyth: Celtic Studies Publications) 39–48.

Gruffydd, R.G. 2002. *'Edmyg Dinbych': Cerdd Lys Gynnar o Ddyfed* (Aberystwyth: University of Wales Centre for Advanced Welsh and Celtic Studies).

Haycock, M. 1983–4. "'Preiddeu Annwn' and the figure of Taliesin", *Studia Celtica* 18/19, 52–78.

Haycock, M. 1988. "Llyfr Taliesin", *Cylchgrawn Llyfrgell Genedlaethol Cymru* 25/4, 357–86.

Haycock, M. (ed.) 1994. *Blodeugerdd Barddas o Ganu Crefyddol Cynnar* (Cyhoeddiadau Barddas).

Haycock, M. 2003. "Cadair Ceridwen" yn Daniel, I. (*et al.*) (eds.) *Cyfoeth y Testun: Ysgrifau ar Lenyddiaeth Gymraeg yr Oesoedd Canol* (Cardiff: University of Wales Press), 148–75.

Haycock, M. 2006. *Taliesin a Brwydr y Coed* (Aberystwyth: University of Wales Centre for Advanced Welsh and Celtic Studies).

Haycock, M. (ed. and trans.) 2013. *Prophecies from the Book of Taliesin* (Aberystwyth: CMCS Publications).

Haycock, M. (ed. and trans.) 2015. *Legendary Poems from the Book of Taliesin* (2nd ed.) (Aberystwyth: CMCS Publications).

Henry, P.L. 1979/80. "The Caldron of Poesy", *Studia Celtica* 14/15, 114–28.

Henry, P.L. 1995. "Amra Con Roi (ACR): discusion, edition, translation", *Etudes Celtiques* 31, 179–194.

Historia Brittonum Digital text http://www.bl.uk/manuscripts/FullDisplay.aspx?ref=Harley_MS_3859

Howell, R. 2004. "From the fifth to the seventh century", in Griffiths, R.A. *et al.* (eds.) *The Gwent County History: Vol. I – Gwent in Prehistory and Early History* (Cardiff: University of Wales Press and the Gwent County History Association), 244–68.

Isaac, G.R. 1994. "Some Welsh etymologies", *Études Celtiques* 30, 229–231.

Isaac, G.R. 1998. "Gweith Gwen Ystrat and the Northern Heroic Age of the Sixth Century." *Cambrian Medieval Celtic Studies* 36, 61–70.

Isaac, G.R. 1999. "Trawsganu Kynan Garwyn mab Brochuael: a tenth-century political poem", *Zeitschrift für celtische Philologie* 51, 173–185.

Isaac, G.R. 2002a. "*Gwarchan Maeldderw*: a lost Welsh classic?", *Cambrian Medieval Celtic Studies* 44, 73–96.

Isaac, G.R. 2002b. "'Ymddiddan Taliesin ac Ugnach': Propaganda Cymreig yn Oes y Croesgadau?", *Llên Cymru* 25, 12–20.

Jarman, A.O.H. 1967. *Ymddiddan Myrddin a Thaliesin* (Cardiff: University of Wales Press).

Jarman, A.O.H. 1982. *Llyfr Du Caerfyrddin* (Cardiff: University of Wales Press).

Jarman, A.O.H. (ed.) 1988. *Y Gododdin: Britain's Oldest Heroic Poem* (Llandysul: Gomer).

Jones, E.M. and Jones N.A. (eds.) 1991. *Gwaith Llywarch ap Llywelyn Prydydd y Moch, Cyfres Beirdd y Tywysogion V* (Cardiff: University of Wales Press).

Jones, N.A. 1992. "Prydydd y Moch: Dwy Gerdd 'Wahanol'", *Ysgrifau Beirniadol* 18, 55–72

Jones, N.A. (ed.) 2019. *Arthur in Early Welsh Poetry* (Cambridge: Modern Humanities Research Association).

Jones, N.A. and Parry Owen, A. (eds.) 1991. *Gwaith Cynddelw Brydydd Mawr I, Cyfres Beirdd y Tywysogion III* (Cardiff: UWP).

Jones, T. 1967. "The Black Book of Carmarthen 'Stanzas of the Graves'", *Proceedings of the British Academy* 53, 97–137.

Kinsella, T. 1970. *The Táin* (Oxford: Oxford University Press, repr. 1990).

Koch, J.T. 1989. "Some suggestions and etymologies reflecting upon the mythology of the Four Branches", *Proceedings of the Harvard Celtic Colloquium* 9, 1–10.

Koch, J.T. 1990. "Brân, Brennos: an instance of early Gallo-Brittonic history and mythology", *Cambridge Medieval Celtic Studies* 20, 1–20.

Koch, J.T. 2003. *The Celtic Heroic Age* (Aberystwyth: Celtic Studies Publications).

Koch, J.T. 2005. "Why was Welsh literature first written down?" in Fulton, H. (ed.) *Medieval Celtic Literature and Society* (Dublin: Four Courts Press), 15–31. The pagination given here refers to the version downloaded from Koch's Academia page: https://www.academia.edu/7441412/Why_Was_Welsh_Literature_First_Written_Down (Accessed 25/03/2022)

Koch, J.T. (ed.) 2006. *Celtic Culture: A Historical Encyclopedia* (Santa Barbara: ABC-CLIO), 750–2.

Koch, J.T. 2013a. *Cunedda, Cynan, Cadwallon, Cynddylan: four Welsh poems and Britain 383–655* (Aberystwyth: University of Wales Centre for Advanced Welsh and Celtic Studies).

Koch, J.T. 2013b. "Waiting for Gododdin: thoughts on Taliesin and Iudic-Hael, Catraeth, and unripe time in Celtic Studies" in Woolf, A. (ed.) *Beyond the Gododdin: Dark Age Scotland in Medieval Wales* (St. Andrews: St. John's House), 177–204.

Lloyd, J.E. and Jenkins. R.T. (eds.) 1959. *The Dictionary of Welsh Biography* (London: Honourable Society of Cymmrodorion).

McManus, D. 1988. "Irish letter-names and their kennings", *Ériu* 39, 127–168.

McManus, D. 1991. *A Guide to Ogam* (Maynooth: An Sagart).

McManus, D. 2004. *The Ogam Stones at University College Cork* (Cork: Cork University Press, repr. 2018)

Meyer, K. (ed.) 1901a. "Gedicht auf Cúrói Mac Dári", *Zeitschrift für Celtische Philologie* 3, 37–39.

Meyer, K. (ed. and trans.) 1901b. "Brinne Ferchertne", *Zeitschrift für Celtische Philologie* 3, 40–46.

Meyer, K. (ed. and trans.) 1904. "The Boyish Exploits of Finn", *Ériu* 1, 180–90.

Morris, J. (ed. and trans.) 1980. *Nennius: British History and the Welsh Annals* (London & Chichester: Phillimore).

Nash, D.W. 1858. *Taliesin, or The Bards and Druids of Britain* (London: J.R. Smith).

O'Rahilly, C. (ed. and trans.) 1967. *Táin Bó Cúailnge, from the Book of Leinster* (Dublin: Institute for Advanced Studies).

Padel, O.J. 2006. "Geoffrey of Monmouth and the development of the Merlin legend", *Cambrian Medieval Celtic Studies* 51, 37–65.

Randell, K.A. 2009. "'And there was a fourth son': Narrative Variation in *Cyfranc Lludd a Llefelys*", *Proceedings of the Harvard Celtic Colloquium* 29, 288–281.

Rees, A. and Rees, B. 1961. *Celtic Heritage: Ancient Tradition in Ireland and Wales* (London: Thames and Hudson, repr. 1995).

Rhŷs, J. 1901. *Celtic Folklore: Welsh and Manx*, Vol. I (Oxford: Clarendon Press).

Rhys, Siôn Dafydd. 1592. *Cambrobrytannicae Cymraecaeve Linguae Institutiones et Rudimenta* (London: Thomas Orwin), 182.

RIB: Collingwood, R. & Wright, R. 1965. *Roman Inscriptions of Britain*, vol. 1, *Inscriptions on Stone* (Oxford, The Clarendon Press); now available on-line at https://romaninscriptionsofbritain.org/

Rivet, A.L.F. and Smith, C. 1979. *The Placenames of Roman Britain* (London: Batsford).

Roberts, B.F. (ed.) 1975. *Cyfranc Lludd a Llefelys* (Dublin: Dublin Institute for Advanced Studies).

Roberts, B.F. 1978. "Rhai o gerddi ymddiddan Llyfr Du Caerfyrddin" in Bromwich, R. & Jones, R.B. (eds.) *Astudiaethau ar yr Hengerdd* (Cardiff: University of Wales Press), 281–325.

Rodway, S. 2005. "The date and authorship of *Culhwch ac Olwen*: a reassessment", *Cambrian Medieval Celtic Studies* 49, 21–44.

Romer, F.E. (ed.) 1998. *Pomponius Mela's Description of the World* (Ann Arbor: University of Michigan Press).

Ross, A. 1967. *Pagan Celtic Britain* (London: Routledge Columbia, repr. 1968).

Rowland, J. 1990. *Early Welsh Saga Poetry* (Cambridge: DS Brewer).

Sims-Williams, P. 1982. "The evidence for vernacular Irish literary influence on early mediaeval Welsh literature" in Whitlock et al. 1982, 235–57.

Sims-Williams, P. 1991a. "The Submission of Irish Kings in Fact and Fiction: Henry II, Bendigeidfran, and the Dating of the *Four Branches of the Mabinogi*", *Cambrian Medieval Celtic Studies* 22, 31–61.

Sims-Williams, P. 1991b. "The early Welsh Arthurian Poems" in Bromwich, et al. 1991, 33–71.

Sims-Williams, P. 2011. *Irish Influence on Early Medieval Welsh Literature* (Oxford: Oxford University Press).

Sims-Williams, P. 2014. "Powys and Early Welsh Poetry", *Cambrian Medieval Celtic Studies* 67, 33–54.

Skene, W.F. 1868. *The Four Ancient Books of Wales: Containing The Cymric Poems attributed to the Bards of The Sixth Century* (Edinburgh: Edmonston and Douglas).

Stephens, M. (ed.) 1998. *The New Companion to the Literature of Wales* (Cardiff: University of Wales Press).

Stokes, W. 1905. "The Eulogy of Cúrói (Amra Conrói)", *Ériu* 2, 1–14.

Tatlock, J.S.P. 1950. *The Legendary History of Britain: Geoffrey of Monmouth's Historia Regum Britanniae and its Early Vernacular Versions* (Berkeley and Los Angeles: University of California Press).

Taylor, T. (trans.) 1925. *The Life of St. Samson of Dol* (London: Society for Promoting Christian Knowledge).

Thomas, G. (ed.) 1970. *Yr Aelwyd Hon: Diweddariadau o Hen Farddoniaeth Gymraeg* (Llandybie: Llyfrau'r Dryw).

Thomas, G. 2015. *Hen Englynion* (Cyhoeddiadau Barddas), 109–111.

Thurneysen, R. 1913. "Die Sage von CuRoi", *Zeitschrift für Celtische Philologie* 9, 189–234

Tymoczko, M. (ed. and trans.) 1981. *Two Death Tales from the Ulster Cycle : The Death of Cú Roí and The Death of Cú Chulainn* (Dublin: Dolmen Press).

Walker, M. 2011. *Geoffrey of Monmouth's Life of Merlin: A New Verse Translation* (Stroud: Amberley).

Whitlock, D., McKitterick, R. and Dumville, D. (eds.) 1982. *Ireland in Early Mediaeval Europe* (Cambridge: Cambridge University Press).

Williams, I. (ed.) 1930. *Pedeir Keinc y Mabinogi* (Cardiff: University of Wales Press, repr. 1978).

Williams, I. (ed.) 1938. *Canu Aneirin* (Cardiff: University of Wales Press, repr. 1989).

Williams, I. 1944. *Lectures in Early Welsh Poetry* (Dublin: Dublin Institute for Advanced Studies, repr. 1970).

Williams, I. 1945. *Enwau Lleoedd* (Liverpool: Gwasg y Brython).

Williams, I. (ed.) 1955. *Armes Prydein* (Cardiff: University of Wales Press)

Williams, I. 1957. *Chwedl Taliesin* (Cardiff: University of Wales Press)

Williams, I. (ed.) 1960. *Canu Taliesin* (Cardiff: University of Wales Press, repr. 1977).

Williams, I. 1980. "Two poems from the Book of Taliesin" in Bromwich, R. (ed.) *The Beginnings of Welsh Poetry* (Cardiff: University of Wales Press, repr. 1990), 155–172.

Williams, I. (ed.) and Williams, J.E.C. (trans.) 1968. *The Poems of Taliesin* (Dublin: Dublin Inst. for Advanced Studies, repr. 2010).

Winterbottom, M. (ed. and trans.) 1978. *Gildas: The Ruin of Britain and Other Works* (London and Chichester: Phillimore).

Index

Abbey Cwm Hir, 24
Aber Henfelen, 90, 159–161
Aber Peryddon, 132–133, 135
Aberconwy, 24
Aberffraw, 198
Aberystwyth, 23, 181
Adam, 60, 119, 140, 151, 176–178, 188, 200, 202–203
Aeddon, 14, 53–54
Aergol, 31
Aeron, 38, 40, 105, 147–148
Afagddu, 18, 67, 95–96, 128, 162, 180
Afaon, 108
Aladur, 92–93
Albion, 156
Alexander, 110–112, 170, 183
Amaethon, 54, 75
Anarawd, 140–141
Aneirin, 12–14, 23–24, 28–29, 48
Anglesey, 14, 28, 31, 45, 53–54, 91, 97, 101, 105, 107, 138, 145, 147–148, 150, 154, 164, 194
Annwfn. See also Otherworld, 9, 19, 57, 66, 69, 75–76, 83, 90, 112–117, 142
Annwfyn. See Annwfn
Arawn, 75
Arberth (Narberth), 200, 202
Arddunion, 44
Arfderydd, 55, 56, 107
Arfon, 53
Arianrhod, 95, 97, 124, 138, 171, 174, 183
Arkendale, 34

Arthur, 74, 76, 84, 92–93, 107–108, 112–115, 118, 120, 127, 158, 162, 165, 168, 180, 190, 192–193, 203
Arthur a'r Eryr ("Arthur and the Eagle"), 120
Athelstan, 132, 140
Aubrey, William, 194
Avalon, 114
awen, 10–12, 14, 17–19, 21–22, 29–30, 40, 66, 69, 71, 74, 85, 88, 90, 93–94, 130, 133, 136, 144–145, 171, 173, 180, 184, 187, 190, 198, 205–207
Awydd, 109
Ayr, 44

Bala Lake. See Llyn Tegid.
Bamburgh, 29
Bardsey Island, 90–91
Bathgate, 45
Battle of the Trees, 18, 74–84, 90–91
Bede, 97
Belenos, 144, 198
Beli Hir, 198–199
Beli Mawr, 144, 198
Black Book of Carmarthen, 15, 23–24, 55, 57, 115–116, 149
Blathaon, 144–145
Bláthnait, 122
Bleiddudd, 14, 50, 52
blerwm blerwm, 12, 169
Blodeuwedd, 75
Blwchfardd, 29

Book of Aneirin, 14, 23–24, 48
Book of Taliesin, 10, 12, 14, 16–17,
    19–24, 55, 59, 66, 74, 78, 85, 90,
    100, 110, 132, 180, 206
Brân the Blessed, 90–91, 93, 105, 113,
    159–160, 198
Branwen, 159–160, 198
Brechin, 45
Brecon, 194, 198
Breconshire, 107, 194
Brewyn, 38
Brindled Ox. See also Yr Ych Brych,
    116, 118, 149
Brittany, 15, 115, 132, 137
Brochfael of Powys, 30–31, 90
Brunanburh, 140–141
Brwyn of the Wily Breast, 109
Brychan Brycheiniog, 31, 107
Bustl y Beirdd, 22, 174, 185

Cadell, 30, 201
Cadfan, 55, 147
Cadwaladr, 20, 132, 135, 137–138,
    141, 148, 150, 152–155, 157
Cadwallon, 20, 125, 144, 147–148
Caer Caradoc, 45
Caer Nefenhyr, 74–75, 79
Caer Rhywg, 139–140
Caer Seon, 14–15, 53, 57–58, 97, 105
Caer Siddi, 90–91, 113, 116–117
Caerleon, 104, 133, 195–196, 198
Caerllïon, 198
Caernarfon, 198
Caersws, 152
Calais, 58
Calchfynydd (Wessex), 142
Caledfwlch, 114
Canaan, 110, 170, 183
Cantre'r Gwaelod, 148
Canu Bychan. See Y Canu Bychan

Canwelw, 50
Caradog, 47, 93, 107–108
Cardigan, 198
Cardigan Bay, 149
Carlisle, 31, 34, 125
Carmarthen, 15, 23–24, 55, 57, 64,
    115–116, 149, 194, 198, 200–201
Carmarthen Priory, 24
Casnodyn, 17, 205, 207
Caswallon, 144–145
Catraeth, 32, 40
Catterick, 13, 34
Caw, 37, 39
Cawrdaf, 93
Cawrnur, 93, 127
Cedfyw, 55
Cedig, 95
Ceidio, 107, 109
Celliwig, 158
Ceredigion, 25, 147–148, 198
Ceri, 198
Ceridwen, 11–12, 16–19, 67, 85,
    90–91, 95–97, 162–165, 171–172,
    180–181, 184, 187, 198, 205–207
Cernyw, 30–31
Chester, 30, 133, 148, 198
Christ, 11, 15, 54, 66, 76, 79, 80, 85,
    119, 156, 177, 197, 200
christianity, 12, 20, 22–24, 76, 97, 101,
    106, 107, 118, 128, 153, 189, 202
Cian, 28–29, 66–67
Cirencester, 132, 135
Clun Hir, 194
Clydwyn, 44
Clynnog Fawr, 124
Coed Celyddon, 55, 57
Coel, 37, 105, 125–126, 142
Constantine, 107
Conwy (river), 24, 53, 57, 97, 140,
    148–149, 164

Cornan ("the horned horse"), 108
Cornwall, 30, 93, 107, 133, 158, 160–161
court poets, 12, 14–15, 17–20, 92, 97, 100, 116–117, 119, 196, 205–207
Crairw, 189
Creiddylad, 107, 159
Creirfyw, 180
Cristin, 149, 151
Cú Chulainn, 114, 116, 121–123
Cú Roí, 116, 120–124
Cuhelyn Fardd, 17, 205
Culhwch, 158–159
Culhwch ac Olwen, 25, 92, 107, 113–114, 116, 158–159, 192
Cumbria, 13, 31, 44
Cunedda, 124–126
Cunin Cof, 107
Custennin, 107, 109
Cydweli, 198
Cyfeiliog, 195
Cynan, 17, 20, 49, 132, 135, 137–139, 141, 144, 148, 150, 206
Cynan Garwyn, 30–31
Cynddelw Brydydd Mawr, 17, 97, 205–206
Cyndur, 56
Cynfeirdd, 13
Cynfelyn, 57, 171, 184, 195
Cyngen, 31
Cynlas, 49

Dallmor Dallme, 190
Darius, 110
Defwy, 40, 116, 118
Degannwy, 17, 19, 53, 90–91, 100, 164–165, 172, 198
Deheubarth, 200–204
Derllys, 200, 203
Dervonnae, 138

Dewi Sant (St. David), 132, 134–136, 138
Dinas Dinlle, 57
Dinefwr, 202
Diwrnach the Irishman, 114
Dolbadarn Castle, 146
Don (river), 43
Dôn, 14, 15, 19– 21, 38, 59, 96, 124, 171, 183, 198
Dragon, 28, 39, 45, 49, 54, 89, 127, 143, 146, 153–155, 204
druidic, 22, 78
druids, 20, 76, 78, 84, 89, 137, 152, 199
Du Moroedd, 109
Dumbarton, 38, 47, 137, 143, 147
Dumfries, 47
Duncansby, 144
Dyfed, 31, 51, 55, 63, 92, 135, 137, 142, 155, 203
Dyfi (river), 181, 191
Dygen, 104–105
Dylan eil Ton, 19, 21, 75, 83, 86, 94, 124, 192
Dyrnwch the Giant, 114
Dywel, 56

Echdor, 119
Eden (Garden of), 150
Eden (river), 31
Edinburgh, 35, 44–45, 49, 132, 139
Edwin of Northumbria, 43
Einion ap Rhiwallon, 64–65
Elestron, 61, 91
Elfed, 43, 152, 155
Elffin, 14–15, 17, 19, 53, 55, 57, 68, 73, 90–91, 93, 95, 97, 100–101, 130, 162–179, 181–189, 191–192, 198, 205–206
Elgan, 56
Eliwlod, 120

Ellesmere, 198
Elmet, 43, 45–46, 152
Erbin, 50–51, 56
Ercwlff, 119
Erechwydd, 33–34, 37, 137, 144
Ergyng, 103
Errith, 56
Eryri (Snowdonia), 20, 141, 146, 150, 157, 199
Eufydd, 53–54, 61, 91
Euron, 75, 82–83, 96
Euronwy, 96
Eurwys, 75, 82
Eve, 177

Fagddu. See Afagddu
Ffaraon, 49
Fferyll(t). See Virgil
Fflamddwyn, 36, 42–43
Ffroenfoll, 109
Finn mac Cumhaill, 11
Firth of Forth, 35, 132
Flame-Bearer. See Fflamddwyn
folk-tale, 16, 23, 57, 67
Forest of Celyddon, 55, 57
Four Branches. See *Mabinogi*
Four Pillars of Poetry, 22, 120, 176
Francis I of France, 162

Galloway, 36, 45, 75
Gelli Gaer, 132, 138
Genethog, 108
Geoffrey of Monmouth, 15, 55, 114, 127, 128, 156
Geraint, 71
Gilfaethwy, 138
Glamorgan, 17, 107, 132, 189, 207
Glifiau, 159
Glywysing, 132, 135
Goddau, 36–37, 39, 74–75

Gododdin. See Y Gododdin
Gofannon, 61–62, 124
Gowrie, 45
Graidwen. See Ceridwen
Graves, Robert, 74, 76–77
Grei ("grey"), 108
Griddieu son of Muriel, 159
Gruffydd, Elis, 23, 25, 162
Gwair, 112–113, 117
Gwales, 159–160
Gwallawg, 13, 41, 43–47
Gwawrddur, 107–108
Gwen Ystrad, 31–32
Gwenddolau, 107
Gwenllïan (daughter of Hywel ab Iorwerth), 104, 195–196
Gwent, 30, 92, 103–105, 124, 132, 144, 195–197
Gwenwynfeirch Gwyddno, 181
Gwion Bach, 11, 16–17, 21, 23, 59, 62, 67, 88, 89, 162–179, 180–192
Gwrfoddw, 103, 105
Gwri, 92
Gwrion, 91
Gwrrith, 56
Gwyddawl, 44–45
Gwyddien, 38, 41
Gwyddno Garanhir, 116, 142, 148, 164–165, 172, 180–192
Gwydion, 15, 21, 37–38, 53–54, 57–60, 67, 72, 74–75, 79, 82, 90–91, 95–97, 138, 170–171, 183
Gwyllionwy, 138–139
Gwyn ap Nudd, 15, 57, 107, 116
Gwynedd, 12, 18–20, 28–29, 52–53, 55, 125, 132–133, 140, 142, 144–145, 147–148, 154, 195, 198–199, 201
Gwynllŵg, 195–196
Gwythur son of Greidawl, 107–108, 127

Haearddur, 45
Harddnenwys, 105
Hardenhuish, 104
Haverford, 198, 200, 202
Hebron, 171, 176, 183, 188
Hector, 119–200, 203
Heilyn son of Gwyn the Old, 93, 159, 161
Heinin Fardd, 166, 170
Hengwrt, 180
Henry III of England, 146, 197
Henry VIII of England, 162
Henwen, 147
Henwyn ("old white"), 109
Hercules, 110, 119–120, 200, 203
Herefordshire, 45, 103, 147
High Rochester, 44
Hiraddug, 109
Hiriell, 20, 152, 155
Horsa and Hengist, 134
Hyfaidd, 38–39, 45
Hywel ab Iorwerth of Caerleon, 104, 195
Hywel Dda, 132

Iago, 144–145
Ida of Northumbria, 28–29, 36
Iddon of Gwent, 103
Idwal Foel, 144, 147
imbas, 10–11
Ireland, 10, 15, 75, 90–91, 93, 101, 113–114, 116, 122, 124, 133, 137, 139, 147, 152, 154, 159–161
Irish, 10, 11, 50, 59–60, 62, 77, 91, 114, 116, 120–123, 125, 133, 136–137, 139, 146, 148, 151, 159–161
Irvine, 45
Isle of Man, 116, 122–124, 133
Iudic-hael, 15

John Davies. See Siôn Dafydd Rhys
John Jones, Gellilyfdy, 25, 180, 184–186
John O' Groats, 144
Jordan (river), 171, 178, 184

Kaer Sidi. See Caer Siddi
Kethin, 109
Kynan Garwyn. See Cynan Garwyn

Leeds, 43, 152
Lindisfarne, 13, 43
Llachar, 83
Llamrei ("grey leaper"), 109
Llanfair Caereinion, 180, 190
Llanfihangel Nant Teyrnon, 92
Llanion, 147
Llantarnam, 24, 92
Llech Faelwy, 52
Llefelys, 155–156
Lleminog, 112, 114
Lleon, 95, 171, 184
Lleu Llaw Gyffes, 21, 37–38, 57-60, 75, 90-91, 95–96, 107–108, 124
Lluagor, 107
Lludd, 145, 148–152, 155–157, 159
Llwyd, 109
Llwyfenydd, 34–35, 38, 40–41, 43
Llyminawc, 144
Llyn Tegid, 162, 180, 189
Llyn y Fan Fach, 64
Llŷr, 90, 113, 159
Llywarch ap Llywelyn (Prydydd y Moch), 17, 18–20, 59, 64, 78, 97, 103–104, 110, 119, 124, 144, 146, 149, 157, 195–204, 205–206
Llywelyn ab Iorwerth. See Llywelyn the Great
Llywelyn Fardd II, 156

Llywelyn Fawr. See Llywelyn the Great
Llywelyn Siôn, 189
Llywelyn the Great, 19–20, 64, 103–104, 146, 195, 197–199, 200, 203, 206
Llywy, 53–54
Loch Ryan, 91, 93
London, 160–161, 180, 194, 199
Ludlow, 180
Lyvennet (river), 34

Mabinogi (Four Branches), 74–75, 90, 92, 95, 113, 124, 138, 159
Mabon son of Modron, 21, 45, 113, 142–144
Macsen, 93
Madog, 120, 196–197, 207
Maeldderw, 14, 24, 48–50, 82
Maelgwn Gwynedd, 12, 17, 28–29, 45, 55–56, 90–91, 100–101, 105, 138, 164–169, 185, 187, 200
Maeog, 107, 108
Maes Gwyddno, 148
Manaw Gododdin, 35
Manawydan, 21, 159–160, 198
Manddwy (fort), 116, 118
Maponos, 21, 142–144
Mars Alator, 92–93
Mary Magdalen, 184
Math, 21, 53–54, 59, 61, 67, 74–75, 82, 138
Matholwch, 159–160
Mathonwy, 138–139
May Eve (Calan Mai), 92, 107, 155, 181, 191
Melyngan, 84
Menai (Strait), 31, 53, 141
Mererid, 149
Merlin. See also Myrddin, 15, 55–57, 107, 114, 128
Modron, 21, 75, 83, 96, 113

Môn. See Anglesey
monks, 14, 59, 85, 116–119, 123
Montgomery, 152, 198
Morda, 180, 181
Mordaf, 200, 203
Morfa Rhianedd, 175, 187
Morfran, 162–163, 180, 189
Morgant, 13
Moses, 171, 178, 184
mounds (fairy), 57, 116
Mount Sion, 60
Myddfai, 64
Myrddin, 15, 20, 24, 55–57, 75, 107, 133, 170, 183, 193, 199

Nant Ffrancon, 97
Narberth. See Arberth
Nennius, 12, 28
Nimrod, 171, 183
Nine Maidens, 114–115, 117
Nine Witches of Gloucester, 114–115
Noah, 139, 171, 183
Normandy, 146
Normans, 19–20, 139, 196, 201
Northumbria, 13, 28, 36, 43, 125, 147
Nwython of Strathclyde, 45, 107, 108

Ogham, 77
ogyrfen, 66, 205
Olaf Guthfrithsson, 132
Old North, 12, 24, 39, 75, 101, 124–125, 142
Olwen, 158
Otherworld, 15, 57, 64, 66, 74–75, 90, 112–113, 116
Owain Gwynedd, 104, 119, 195, 198–199, 206
Owain son of Urien, 13, 36–37, 42–43, 142–143
Oxford, 194

pagan, 22, 74, 76, 93
Pantion (Almighty God), 22, 176, 188
Pebyrllei ("lively-grey"), 108
Pembroke, 147, 200–202
Pembrokeshire, 50, 139, 205
Pen Coed, 44–45
Pen y Fan, 194
Penally, 50
Penda of Mercia, 147, 152
Pengyfylchi, 142, 144
Peredur son of Efrawg, 114
Pharaoh, 72
Phylip Brydydd, 17
Pictland, 44, 133, 145, 179
Picts, 31, 45, 51, 146, 149, 151
Poets of the Princes. See also court poets, 19, 119
Poisoned Horses of Gwyddno, 181, 190
Pomponius Mela, 115
Portskewett, 115
Powys, 30, 38, 90, 147–148, 152, 180, 190, 199, 205–206
Pryderi, 91–92, 112–113, 117, 159
Prydwen (Arthur's Ship), 112, 117–118
Prydydd y Moch. See Llywarch ap Llywelyn
Pwyll, 112–113, 117
Pyllbair, 176

radiant brow, 11, 165, 182
Red Book of Hergest, 23, 59, 195–197, 200
Red-Hot Iron, 104, 196–197
Rheged, 13, 32–34, 37–39, 43, 75, 142–143
Rhiannon, 92, 160
Rhodri ab Owain Gwynedd, 104, 195
Rhodri Mawr, 140, 198
Rhos, 200–202
Rhuddlan Degeingl, 198–199

Rhuddlan Deifi, 198–199
Rhun (river), 142–143
Rhun of Galloway, 45, 49
Rhun son of Maelgwn Gwynedd, 138, 140, 166–167, 169, 200, 202–203
Rhydderch Hael (R. the Generous), 107
Rhydderch Hen (R. the Old), 13
Rhys Gryg, 64, 110, 200–204
Richard I of England, 146
Rockfield, 132
Rome, 20, 89, 140, 171, 183
Rossington Moor, 45

Sadyrnin, 107, 109
salmon, 11, 73, 164, 183
Samson. See also St. Samson, 119, 178, 200, 203
Samson Dry-Lip, 159
Saracens, 95, 156
Saxons, 13, 20, 30, 59, 61, 103, 132, 134, 145,
Saxony, 179
Scáthach, 114
Segais (well of), 11
Sein (Isle de), 115
Seithennin, 148–149, 151
Selyf, 30
Senchán Torpeist, 11
Severn (river), 30, 59, 61, 90, 154–155, 179
Shrewsbury, 152, 198
Siena, 194
Siôn Cent, 11
Siôn Dafydd Rhys, 23, 194
Snowdonia. See Eryri
Sodom and Gomorra, 171, 183
Solway Firth, 13, 142, 155
Speckled Ox. See Yr Ych Brych
St. Clears, 198, 200–201
St. Samson, 114–115

St. David. See Dewi Sant
Strata Florida, 25
Strathclyde, 45, 107, 133, 141–142, 147
Swaledale, 33–34
Swansea, 198, 200–201

Talhaearn Tad Awen, 28, 29, 66, 69, 71
Tegid Foel, 162, 180, 189
Tenby, 14, 50–52, 112
Tetragrammaton (Jehova), 170, 183
Teyrnon Twrf Liant, 18, 92–95
Thanet, 134, 137
Theodric of Bernicia, 13, 36
Theomaca, 115
Thirteen Treasures of the Island of Britain, 114
Three Fortunate Concealments of the Island of Britain, 159, 161
Three Generous Men of the Island of Britain, 39, 200
Three Unfortunate Blows of the Island of Britain, 124
Three Unfortunate Disclosures of the Island of Britain, 159, 161
transmigration of souls, 78
tree alphabet, 77
Triads of the Horses, 106–107
Triads of the Island of Britain, 25, 39, 55, 74, 93, 103, 106–107, 113, 116, 119, 124, 127, 138, 147, 156, 159, 192, 198, 200
trial by ordeal, 104, 124, 196–197
Troy, 171, 178, 183
Tryffin, 104
Twrch Trwyth, 93

Uffin, 105
Ugnach, 15, 24, 53, 57–59, 97
Urien Rheged, 13, 18, 31–43, 75, 90, 105, 107, 142, 206
Usk (river), 133, 196
Uthr Pendragon, 19, 120, 126–128

Vaughan, Robert, 23, 180
Vikings, 20, 60, 139, 141
Virgil, 74, 76, 85, 180, 190

Welshpool, 104
Wessex, 105, 136, 138, 142, 157
Wharfe (river), 43
White Book of Rhydderch, 25, 158–159
White Goddess, The, 74, 76–77
White Hill, 160–161, 171, 184
wild Wales, 179
Winchester, 135
Winsterdale, 31, 44
Winwæd (battle of), 152, 154
Wiston, 200, 202
Wlff, 37–38
Worcester, 103, 105, 197
Wye (river), 30, 45, 132, 134, 147

Y Canu Bychan, 104, 197–199
Y Gododdin, 13, 24, 35, 38, 48, 75, 105, 107
Ynyr of Gwent, 103, 105–106
York, 33, 44
Yorkshire, 13, 33–34, 43
Yr Ych Brych, 149
Ysbaddaden Chief of Giants, 116, 158
Ysgwyddfrith, 109
Ystawingun, 115

www.ingramcontent.com/pod-product-compliance
Ingram Content Group UK Ltd.
Pitfield, Milton Keynes, MK11 3LW, UK
UKHW050254140126
466956UK00007B/125